"How many soldiers would you say are on this base? Including the ones down inside?"

"A couple of hundred, maybe," Danny said, looking over the edge.

"Five hundred and forty," Razor said. "There're also seventeen armored personnel carriers, twenty-four jeeps, eight choppers, and in about two weeks we'll be getting some big guns. There's no way on Earth anyone is going to get in here without ending up looking like Swiss cheese. Swiss cheese with a *lot* of ketchup."

Renata dropped back to the roof. "And it's all for our protection?"

"That's it," Razor said. "You superhumans don't really *need* protection, but the rest of us do."

"Then let's look at the facts. We're surrounded by hundreds of highly trained soldiers. There's a huge fence that even I'd have a tough time getting past. When the big guns arrive they'll be active at all times, right?"

"That's right," Razor said. "Much as I hate to admit it, this is going to be a very safe place."

"Then you're looking at it wrong, Razor. All that firepower will be great at keeping people out. But it'll be just as effective at keeping people *in*."

Danny swallowed. "I think you're right. Sakkara isn't a fortress. It's a prison."

OTHER BOOKS YOU MAY ENJOY

QUANTUM PROPHECY
BOOK 3

THE
RECKONING

MICHAEL CARROLL

03

PUFFIN BOOKS
An Imprint of Penguin Group (USA) Inc.

PUFFIN BOOKS
Published by the Penguin Group
Penguin Young Readers Group, 345 Hudson Street, New York, New York 10014, U.S.A.
Penguin Group (Canada), 90 Eglinton Avenue East, Suite 700, Toronto, Ontario, Canada M4P 2Y3
(a division of Pearson Penguin Canada Inc.)
Penguin Books Ltd, 80 Strand, London WC2R 0RL, England
Penguin Ireland, 25 St Stephen's Green, Dublin 2, Ireland (a division of Penguin Books Ltd)
Penguin Group (Australia), 250 Camberwell Road, Camberwell, Victoria 3124, Australia
(a division of Pearson Australia Group Pty Ltd)
Penguin Books India Pvt Ltd, 11 Community Centre, Panchsheel Park, New Delhi - 110 017, India
Penguin Group (NZ), 67 Apollo Drive, Rosedale, North Shore 0632, New Zealand
(a division of Pearson New Zealand Ltd.)
Penguin Books (South Africa) (Pty) Ltd, 24 Sturdee Avenue,
Rosebank, Johannesburg 2196, South Africa

Registered Offices: Penguin Books Ltd, 80 Strand, London WC2R 0RL, England

Published in Great Britain by HarperCollins Children's Books, London
First American Edition published by Philomel Books,
a division of Penguin Young Readers Group, 2009
Published by Puffin Books, a division of Penguin Young Readers Group, 2010

3 5 7 9 10 8 6 4

THE LIBRARY OF CONGRESS HAS CATALOGED THE PHILOMEL EDITION AS FOLLOWS:
Carroll, Michael Owen, 1966–
The reckoning / Michael Carroll.—1st American ed.
p. cm. — (Quantum prophecy bk. 3)
Summary: The conflict that has been simmering between the new superhumans and
the Trutopians begins to boil over, threatening the world with extinction.
ISBN 978-0-399-24727-9 (hc)
[1. Science fiction. 2. Heroes—Fiction. 3. Adventure and adventurers.] I. Title.
PZ7.C23497Re 2009 [Fic]—dc22 2008042013

Design by Marikka Tamura

Puffin Books ISBN 978-0-14-241570-2

Printed in the United States of America

This book is dedicated to a real hero:
Adam Dodson.
Find out more about Adam at
www.dodsonchallenges.co.uk.

THE
RECKONING

Her eyes streaming from the smoke that billowed from the burning battle-tank, Energy limped across the shrapnel-strewn battlefield to where Titan was sitting propped up against an overturned jeep. The hero was tearing his blue cape into strips—he'd already used several to bind a stick to his broken right leg.

He looked up as Energy approached. "Hey . . . You OK?"

"I'll live." Holding on to the jeep to steady herself, Energy carefully sat down next to him. "Just so you know, the medics are bringing their own bandages."

Titan forced a smile. "Had to keep busy. Didn't want to pass out."

"So, did we win or lose today?"

Titan dropped the shredded cape and took hold of her hand. "I don't think that's something we're going to know for a long time."

Energy nodded, then paused. "Diamond didn't make it. She was in her crystalline form when it happened. Without her powers, she wasn't able to change back."

"God . . . what was her name? Her *real* name?"

"She never told me. Max said he didn't know either."

"How are we going to find her family, tell them what happened?"

Energy didn't answer.

Titan leaned his head back against the jeep. "She was just a kid."

"I know."

A voice called, "So how are you guys doing?"

They looked up to see Paragon striding toward them.

"We're alive," Energy said. "Thanks to you."

"That's all part of the job description." Paragon unclipped his jetpack and checked a tiny readout on the back. "Damn. Left thruster's just about blown. Not that it's worth repairing now. If it's true that you superhumans have all lost your powers, then I'm going to quit the business too."

Titan began, "No, you should—"

Paragon raised his hand to his helmet. "Hold it. . . . Go ahead, Max. . . . Got it. I'm on the way." Slinging his jetpack back into place, he said to Energy and Titan, "He thinks they've just found Ragnarök's base."

He soared into the sky.

Energy activated her communicator. "Paragon, you're crazy! You can't go after him without your armor!"

His voice came back. "Dioxin destroyed most of it. But maybe he did me a favor; the armor slows me down. Without it, I can get there a lot faster."

"I'm on the way, Max," Paragon said. "Tell me everything."

"Ragnarök's battle-tank was built a hundred and fifty kilometers west of here, big warehouse outside Westmoreland. My people have been checking the satellite images and traffic records. Their analysis shows a large SUV making regular trips between the warehouse and Sherman's Bay, Chautauqua Lake. Same SUV came back today, arrived in the warehouse an hour before the battle-tank emerged."

Paragon said, "Max, that doesn't mean it was Ragnarök!"

"They also detected a vapor trail from Ragnarök's escape craft going in the same direction. They were able to pick it up by analyzing—"

"Skip the details," Paragon interrupted. "Just give me the exact location."

"I'm sending you the coordinates now."

Paragon glanced at the map that was projected on to the inside of his visor. "I see it."

"Checking it against the city's ordnance database. It's . . . Good Lord. . . . It's an apartment block. We've been searching for this maniac for *years* and he's been living in an ordinary apartment block!"

The army ambulance raced over the rough ground, hit a furrow and bounced. Inside, lying on the stretcher, Titan gasped as the pain in his right leg flared up again.

"Take it easy up there!" Energy called to the driver. She turned back to Titan and checked the temporary splint on his leg. "You OK?"

Titan gritted his teeth. "Not really."

The truck bounced again and Energy grabbed a handrail to steady herself. "You're going to be off your feet for the next few months."

"I know." He nodded. "Look, if our powers never come back—"

"We'll survive."

"Yeah, but—"

The ambulance swerved sharply to the left.

"Hey!" Energy shouted. "Watch where you're going!"

"That wasn't me!" the driver called back. "Something hit—"

Titan was thrown from the stretcher as an explosion ripped through the side of the ambulance.

"Paragon, this is General Piers. Backup is about ten minutes behind you."

"I'm not waiting," Paragon said. The visor's readouts showed that the jetpack's shuddering was being caused by the left thruster. *Just hope I can get there before this thing shuts down completely.*

He dropped down to fifty meters—high enough to avoid the power lines, but not as low as he'd have preferred to fly with a malfunctioning jetpack. He knew that even if he'd still had his armor, hitting the ground from this height would be fatal.

OK. There it is. The visor's map showed the apartment block less than a kilometer ahead.

The homes and gardens of Sherman's Bay streamed by below him as Paragon steered himself toward the building.

"General, I can't see the craft. . . . Either he's already gone or—" Paragon's jetpack suddenly sputtered, lurching him to the left. "Hell. Jetpack's on the way out!"

"Pull out, Paragon!"

"No, it can run on only two thrusters . . ." The apartment block loomed up ahead. "Just not very well." Paragon angled upward, slowing as he neared the roof, and switched his helmet to infrared. "I'm getting two heat patterns in there. Neither of them big enough to be Ragnarök. Could be pets. General, better get your people to widen the search radius. Ragnarök's long gone." He touched down on the building's flat roof. "What's the intel on this place?"

"He's been living in the penthouse apartment for six years," Piers replied. "Seems that the building manager thought he was a European rock star living in tax exile. Paid a lot of money to leave him alone."

Paragon stopped in front of the door to the stairway and pulled a small device from a pouch on his belt. "Scanning . . . I'm picking up a lot of sensors on the door. Could be booby-trapped. I'll check the windows." He walked to the edge of the roof and stepped off, activating his jetpack at the same time.

He hovered in front of one of the large windows. "Sensors on the window too. . . . The infrared shows—"

The general's voice interrupted, "Paragon. We've just heard that the ambulance carrying Titan and Energy has been hit. It must be Ragnarök!"

"All right, I'll . . . Oh my God. . . . That can't be right!"

"What is it?"

Paragon didn't reply. He aimed his armor's grappling gun and fired it directly at the window. The small but heavy hook plowed through the thick glass, showering the room inside with crystal fragments.

He kicked out at the window, widening the hole, then pulled himself through.

Ahead of him, six large glass canisters were mounted on a workbench. Cables ran from the canisters to a small monitoring computer.

Paragon swallowed. "General . . . better get your people in here. Right now."

"Talk to me, Paragon! What is it?"

"I . . . I don't . . . four of them are empty. But the other two . . ."

"For God's sake, man! Just *tell* me!"

"They look like they're about three years old. They're suspended in some sort of fluid. . . . There's . . ." Paragon walked around the canisters, staring at them. *How could he have done something like this?*

Floating inside the nearest canister, the black-haired baby girl reached out and placed her hand against the glass.

Paragon stared at her.

She stared back.

And smiled.

A ripple of pain tore through Titan's body, bringing him back to consciousness. He opened his blood-caked eyes to see a shadowy figure standing over him.

"You're awake. Good." Ragnarök leaned close, baring his teeth. "I didn't want you to die without knowing who'd killed you."

Titan looked around wildly. The ambulance was more than twenty meters away, burning. "Energy . . ."

"She's unconscious, but alive. For the moment." Ragnarök locked his massive fists around Titan's neck and lifted him off the ground. "You ruined *everything*. I spent over a year working on that machine. I would have been the only superhuman left."

Gasping, struggling for breath, Titan slammed his left fist into Ragnarök's stomach.

The villain staggered. "You destroyed my force field! Now *my* powers have been stripped too! You realize what that means?"

"You're . . . gonna have to . . . get a real job?"

Ragnarök let go and stepped back.

Titan collapsed to the ground, landing heavily on his broken leg.

Ragnarök lashed out with his foot, catching Titan in the ribs. "Without your powers, you're no stronger than the average man, are you? Me, I work out." He grabbed hold of Titan's arm, and began to drag him along the ground. "There's enough space in my flyer for the two of us. I'm going to take you somewhere they'll never find you." Ragnarök paused, then he reached out and tore the mask from Titan's face. "Huh. So that's what you look like. . . . You got a family, Titan? A wife? A couple of kids, maybe? I'll find them."

Titan scrambled around with his free hand, trying to find something—anything—he could use as a weapon.

Then he spotted something in the distance, racing toward them through the sky. "One question. Allow me that."

"What?" Ragnarök said, turning to him.

"I just want to know . . . why? What made you like this?"

"You want the whole sob story? How society treated me badly, so I turned to a life of crime?" Ragnarök rolled his eyes. "You think I can't tell when someone is stalling?"

Then Paragon was on them, roaring out of the sky, slamming into Ragnarök's back.

Paragon took a moment to check that Titan was still alive, then looked back to where Ragnarök was getting to his feet.

The large man balled his fists and launched himself at Paragon.

He's fast! Paragon dodged to the left just as Ragnarök reached him, and lashed out with a punch that caught Ragnarök in the chin and sent him staggering backward.

Ragnarök recovered almost instantly, dropping to the ground and sweeping his right leg to crash into Paragon's.

Paragon toppled backward, then whipped out with his left hand, grabbing Ragnarök's ankle. He activated his jetpack.

He shot backward along the ground, dragging Ragnarök behind him.

With his free foot, Ragnarök kicked at Paragon's hand, forcing him to break his grip. "Give it up!" Ragnarök roared, rolling on to his feet once more. "I'm stronger and faster than you are!"

Paragon spun about, raced toward Ragnarök and flipped over at the last second, aiming his heavy boots at Ragnarök's head.

But Ragnarök suddenly ducked, locked his hands around Paragon's belt as he passed overhead and used the hero's own momentum to slam him face-first into the ground.

He tore Paragon's helmet from his head, then unclipped the jetpack's shoulder straps and threw it aside.

He locked his hands around Paragon's neck and began to squeeze. "You're just as bad as your friends there, Paragon. No, you're *worse*! You're not even one of us. You're an ordinary man *pretending* to be a superhuman."

Paragon struggled to breathe. "We found your apartment . . . those kids . . . You'll pay for what you did to them!"

"What I *did* to them? You know nothing, Paragon." Ragnarök smashed his knee into the small of Paragon's back. "I'm gonna get my girls back, and then I'm gonna kill every single one of you people."

Then the pressure on Paragon's back was suddenly gone, the hands whipped away from his neck.

Gasping, Paragon rolled on to his back and looked around wildly. Ragnarök was nowhere to be seen.

Nor was Titan.

Then he heard a scream coming from above.

Paragon looked up and saw Titan soaring into the air, his arms locked around Ragnarök's chest.

He can fly again! His powers are back!

Paragon squinted, tried to focus.

No. . . . He's not flying on his own.

"Put me down!" Ragnarök roared. "Put me down or I swear to God, Titan, you and everyone you ever met will regret it!"

Titan felt the straps of Paragon's jetpack cutting into his shoulders, but he didn't care. Compared to the pain in his shattered leg, it was nothing. "Shut up, Ragnarök. It's over. You're not getting out of this."

"You don't even know how to fly that thing!"

"I'm learning as I go. Now stop struggling. You wouldn't survive the drop."

"I'll make a deal with you, Titan. I know everything about the powers. I can tell you where they come from."

"Shut up. You're going to jail."

"No. . . . You don't know what they do with people like me. I'm *not* going to end up in that godforsaken hole!"

"You don't have any choice, Ragnarök. You're a mass-murderer."

The jetpack's left thruster sputtered and died, lurching them to the left. They began to lose altitude. *Aw hell,* Titan thought. *Can't set him down: He's more than a match for me on the ground.*

"That thing can't carry both of us, Titan." Ragnarök was silent for a moment, then said, "Let go."

"What?"

"Let go."

"You'll die!"

"That's the point."

"You really think I'll just let you fall to your death and deprive the world of the trial of the century?"

"How's that broken leg of yours?"

Titan glanced down at the top of Ragnarök's head. "What do you think? Hurts like hell."

"Good."

Before Titan could react, Ragnarök jabbed backward with his right elbow, slamming it into Titan's leg.

Titan screamed.

Then Ragnarök reached up, grabbed Titan's hands, broke his grip.

And fell.

White-faced and shaking, Titan drifted back to the crashed ambulance, where he found Paragon tending to Energy.

"She'll be OK, I think," Paragon said.

Titan touched down, keeping his weight on his good leg.

Paragon stepped up to him, tucked his shoulder under Titan's left arm and lowered him to a sitting position. "What happened?"

"He . . . he let go. He forced me to . . ." Titan gasped, and shuddered. "He killed himself. My fault. I shouldn't have flown so high. I should have stayed only a few meters up."

For a moment, Paragon was silent. Then he crouched down next to Titan. "It's *not* your fault." He forced a smile. "Look at you! He had you beaten to a pulp, you've got a broken leg, no superpowers and you still managed to save my life." He slapped Titan on the shoulder. "It's not powers that make a hero—"

Titan finished the sentence for him. "It's courage."

In the distance, they could hear a helicopter approaching.

"If we can't get our powers back, then this is the end of the superhumans," Titan said.

"Hey, I was never a superhuman to begin with." Paragon grinned. "When you get that leg mended, you come have dinner with me and my wife. She's always saying she wants to meet the people I work with."

"You're married too, huh?"

"Yeah. Five years now. We've got twin girls. Cute as buttons and already smarter than their old man. You?"

Titan nodded. "A son. He's three. Just about." Titan smiled. "But you already know his mother." He nodded toward Energy.

"Yeah, I figured that one out a long time ago."

"Seriously? I thought we were being so careful about it!" Titan held out his hand. "My name's Warren. Warren Wagner."

Paragon shook it. "Good to know you, Warren. And I want you to know *this*. You've saved my life before—heck, we've all saved each other's lives dozens of times—but today was different. You ever need anything—anything at all—you come and see me. My name is Solomon Cord."

1

COLIN WAGNER SAT UP SUDDENLY, A gunshot still echoing through his ears. He was on his feet in an instant, looking around wildly for the source of the sound.

His shoulders sagged. *Just the dream again . . .*

He rubbed his eyes. *Where am I?* The smell of dry hay and damp cow manure reached his nostrils. *Oh. Right.* He remembered sneaking across the farmyard a few hours earlier. Almost overcome with exhaustion, he'd crept into the old wooden barn and climbed up into the hayloft.

Now, spears of sunlight pierced through the cracks and knotholes in the barn's wall. Looking at the angle of the beams of light, Colin thought, *Sun's been up for almost an hour and I can't hear anything moving out there. This has got to be the quietest farm I've ever seen.*

Colin sat down again, dangling his bare feet over the edge of the hayloft, and yawned.

The same dream had woken him almost every morning for the four months since he'd left Sakkara. Solomon Cord chained to a chair, Renata Soliz's family bound and gagged. Victor Cross nearby, talking to Colin on the phone. Telling him that he had to choose whether Cord or Renata's family would die.

And in the dream—as always—Colin chose Cord. Then a man stepped out of the shadows, placed the muzzle of a small handgun against Solomon Cord's forehead and pulled the trigger.

Colin shuddered. *Why do I keep having the same dream over and over? Maybe my brain's just telling me that I made the wrong choice.*

Or maybe it's because I know I did the right *thing. Even though it meant that Sol died, it was still the right thing.*

Colin felt his stomach rumble, and he tried to remember the last time he'd eaten. *Three days ago. The café in Vámospérce. Just before I crossed the border into Romania.*

The owner had been at the back of the café as Colin passed, and he offered Colin a sandwich in return for helping him drag the huge, overflowing bins toward the street.

Good sandwich, Colin said to himself. He glanced down at his bare, unwashed feet. His boots had finally disintegrated over a month before, back in Austria. He didn't need to wear anything on his feet—his skin was more than tough enough to cope with any environment—but an unwashed, shoeless thirteen-year-old boy drew attention, and that was the last thing Colin wanted.

I suppose they're still looking for me. Probably still searching the States. Or maybe they think I went home.

Maybe I should *go back home. See Brian again. God, I wish I'd told him. . . . He must have felt sick every time me and Danny were on the news. His best friends turned out to be the sons of superhumans and we just left him behind.*

Colin swallowed. He didn't want to think about his parents. He wasn't even sure he ever wanted to see them again.

They betrayed me by bringing Max Dalton to Sakkara. How could they not care that he tried to kill me? Dad always said that . . .

He shook his head. *No. Don't think about them. Forget them.*

When Colin was eight years old, two older boys at school had beaten him up. Colin had taken his revenge by stealing a comic from one and putting it in the other's schoolbag. The resulting fight had been so ferocious that it had taken four teachers to pry the bullies apart. Colin had been immensely proud of his act and boasted about it to his parents. Their reaction had not been what he'd expected.

His father had gone ballistic, yelling at Colin, "The ends never justify the means!"

Colin's mother—who was always much more levelheaded than her husband—had taken Colin aside and explained what the problem was. "You stole something. Stealing is wrong. You know that."

"Yeah, but, see, those two used to gang up on everyone, and now they're not even allowed to talk to each other in the playground. Maybe I did a bad thing by stealing, but now everyone else is happier 'cos we don't have to worry about them anymore."

"You stole something. Those two boys might be bullies, but you're a thief. Why is stealing from a bully any better than stealing from a shop?"

"No, but . . ." Colin's argument faltered. "See . . ."

"Colin, you can't do good by doing bad things."

Now, as he lay back on the hayloft in a remote farm in northern Romania, Colin Wagner understood exactly what his parents had been talking about.

Yeah, adults are great at laying down the rules, but they're not always so good at sticking to them. Working with Max Dalton is wrong. I don't care if he's the only ex-superhuman with any knowledge of how mind-control works. Max risked my life and the lives of tens of thou-

sands of innocent people when he tried to use that machine. I know he thought he was doing the right thing, but that's no excuse.

Almost fifteen years earlier, on the day Colin's best friend Danny Cooper was born, Danny's father—the hyperfast superhuman known as Quantum—had received a vision of the future. In that vision, Quantum had seen Danny as a young man leading an army of superhumans against the ordinary people. Billions would die in the war.

Max Dalton knew Quantum well enough to realize that the future he'd seen was likely real—and had to be prevented. Max had used his mind-control on Quantum, forcing him to work alongside the villain Ragnarök to create a machine capable of stripping all the superhumans of their powers.

It had worked. For ten years, there had been no superhumans. And then Danny and Colin—the son of Energy and Titan— reached puberty, and their own powers began to appear.

If only Dad hadn't destroyed Ragnarök's machine just after it was used. . . . Then none of us would have powers. We'd all still be living at home and we'd probably never have learned the truth about what happened to the superhumans.

Once Max had learned that Danny's powers were appearing, he'd attempted to build a second power-damping machine. But without Ragnarök's understanding of how the powers worked, the machine was flawed. It would have killed Colin and Danny and thousands of other people.

We had to stop it, Colin thought. *Even if that means that the war might still happen. . . . You can't sacrifice innocent people just because one half-mad superhuman had a vision of the future.*

Colin sat up and looked around the barn. The shafts of sunlight were at a slightly steeper angle now. *Better get out of here before the farmer comes to milk his cows.*

He froze.

Something's wrong. A farm is never *this quiet.*

Colin pushed himself off the edge of the hayloft, dropped the four meters to the ground and landed silently. *My God! I've gone deaf. But . . .* He shook his head. This didn't seem possible. Before he'd fallen asleep, he'd been able to hear the old farmer snoring in the farmhouse a hundred meters away. Now, there was nothing.

Then Colin turned around and saw the well-dressed man and woman standing right behind him.

Fifteen thousand kilometers to the west a large, sleek, black aircraft descended quickly and almost silently from the night sky, its six turbine engines blowing a large crater in the narrow, moonlit strip of sand that separated the island's dense jungle from the Pacific Ocean.

Danny Cooper couldn't help but admire the skill with which Renata Soliz handled the new StratoTruck's controls; the craft touched down with barely a bump.

The others were already out of the craft and running across the beach by the time Danny had managed to unclip his seatbelt.

This was the farthest Danny had ever been from home: Isla del Tonatiuh was situated five hundred kilometers to the southwest of El Salvador. The island was less than thirty kilometers across and was covered in a thick canopy of vegetation: the perfect place for an international arms-smuggling operation.

Danny silently made his way to the undergrowth, where the five others were waiting for him.

Renata Soliz leaned close and whispered, "How is it that someone who can run as fast as you is always the last one out of the StratoTruck?"

Danny grinned. "It would be a lot easier if whoever designed the seat belts didn't assume that everyone has two hands."

The mission's leader—the former superhero known as Impervia—said, "All right, you know the drill. We move in hard and fast. Danny, you're the scout."

Façade placed his hand on Danny's shoulder. "Ready?"

Danny nodded. He pulled his electronic compass from his pocket and examined it. The tiny screen showed his location and the location of the target. "OK."

Impervia said, "Take no chances, Danny. If they see you, get out of there ASAP. Do not engage."

"Understood. But they won't see me." Danny stuffed the compass back in his pocket, raised his night-vision goggles to his face and turned them on. The goggles had been specially modified so that he could put them on and activate them using only his left hand.

"And keep the scanner going at all times. The target is two kilometers east, but the vegetation is heavy, so keep the noise level down." Impervia looked at her watch. "Now . . . go."

Danny smiled at Renata, then concentrated. Slipping into slow-time was so simple now it was almost second nature. He pushed his way through the bushes.

There were times when Danny was almost pleased that he

was a superhuman. Times like this, when he knew he was doing something good, almost made up for the loss of his right arm. Almost.

Since the start of the year, Danny Cooper, Renata Soliz and Butler Redmond had been involved in over a dozen missions like this one, and each one had been successful.

It'd be a lot easier if Colin was with us, but even so . . . we're not doing too badly.

Danny felt a familiar churning in his stomach. Sometimes, when he thought about the way Colin had left Sakkara, it almost made him ill. *He should have stayed, given us a chance to explain everything. Now he's God-knows-where and his parents are worried sick about him.*

Danny climbed over a rotting, fallen tree and paused to check the compass. Through the night-vision goggles, everything looked green and washed-out. Worse, because he was in his high-speed mode the computer-enhanced images from the goggles flickered maddeningly.

He glanced behind him and saw that his lightning-fast path through the jungle had shaken the moisture from the under-growth, marking his trail with a cloud of droplets seemingly suspended in midair.

Danny continued on his way, wondering how long it would take for Mrs. Wagner to decide that the trip to the jungle would make a good topic for an essay.

That was the worst thing about being a teenage superhuman: He still had to go to school. The previous month, Mrs. Wagner had given him grief about not turning in his geography home-work on time. Danny had tried to argue that he'd been kind of busy saving the world, but the teacher—a former superhuman herself—had simply said, "Danny, you're the fastest human being alive. You could probably *run* to Alaska faster than most people could write an essay about it."

Life at Sakkara isn't so bad, Danny told himself. *Colin should have stayed with us. Max's phone-filter thingy means that Yvonne can't just call us and then use her mind-control, so we're safe there.*

Well, reasonably safe. But Dioxin's locked away and Victor Cross seems to have completely disappeared.

Ahead, Danny could see a point of light. *That's the place.* He lowered his goggles and began to run toward it.

As he ran, a feeling of unease settled over him, like he was being watched. *That's not possible. There's no way they could know we're coming. Besides, I'm moving too fast for anyone to see.*

He stepped out into a clearing and saw a squat, vine-covered, crumbling stone building. Two men in grubby overalls were standing near the entrance. Danny walked around the edge of the clearing, counted all the people he could see, then headed back into the jungle, toward his colleagues.

He could picture the scene: Impervia bossing everyone about, Façade taking no real notice of her and doing his own thing, Renata doing her best to keep as far away from Butler as possible.

Butler Redmond was definitely a little easier to get along with now, ever since he'd had a panic attack during Dioxin's attack on Sakkara. Before that, Butler had swaggered about like he owned the place—now he mostly kept to himself, with only the occasional verbal jab at Danny when he was feeling particularly pleased with himself.

Danny walked out of the jungle a few meters away from the others, and took a moment to look out at the sea. The nearest wave seemed to be frozen in midsplash. Danny concentrated, shifting back to normal time, and the wave crashed to the shore.

"You were gone one hundred and twenty-seven seconds," Impervia said. "Twice as long as you should have been. What happened?"

"Nothing," Danny replied. "I took it easy. I might have been in hyperfast mode, but it's still two kilometers there and two back." He pulled the fist-sized scanner from his belt and handed it to her.

Impervia connected the scanner to the small computer screen built into her uniform's wrist. "All right. . . . We've got twelve hostiles. Four on guard duty, the rest inside the building. Renata, you're on point. Butler will stick close to you. Vaughan? You stay put and monitor. Give us twenty minutes. If we're not back—"

The young soldier said, "I know. Pull out and get back to the transport."

"We keep it quiet until we're on the edge of the clearing, then we take out the guards: Make enough noise to bring the others running. When the compound is secure, I'll set the charges."

Renata asked, "Wouldn't it be easier for one of *us* to go inside?"

"Yes, it would. But what happens if the compound is booby-trapped? You three are too important to lose."

Danny glanced at Renata, who was looking back at him with a familiar expression, and he knew that they were both thinking the same thing: Impervia wasn't a superhuman anymore, but she still wanted to pretend that she was.

Façade turned to the other soldier, Vaughan. "Get the extraction team ready to pick up twelve hostiles. And watch our backs."

"Yes sir."

"Let's do it. Renata, lead the way."

Danny followed Renata into the undergrowth.

He couldn't shake the feeling that something was about to go horribly wrong.

2

THE NEATLY DRESSED MAN SLOWLY
raised his right hand and showed Colin that he was holding a
small device about the size of a cell phone.

Colin stepped back, but the man simply smiled and pressed a
button on the machine.

Instantly, the sounds of the farmyard flooded back and Colin
jumped: He'd been concentrating so hard on his superhearing
that now the sounds were greatly magnified. He could hear
everything: the men's heartbeats, the noises of the animals—
including a tremendous amount of gurgling coming from the
cows' stomachs—birds, insects, the slow ticking of a nearby car's
engine as it cooled down.

"Sorry," the man said. "We knew you'd be able to hear us
coming from miles away so we had to use this. It's a sound-
muffler. It works by inverting—"

"I know how it works. What do you want?" Colin asked.

"We've been tracking you for weeks, Colin."

"Who?"

The red-haired woman gave Colin a warm smile. "Look, we
know you're Colin Wagner. Let's not bother with all that 'I don't
know who you think I am' nonsense, OK? It'll save time."

"We just want to talk," the man said. "I'm Byron, this is
Harriet."

Colin looked them up and down. Immaculate black suits,

white shirts, dark blue ties. Highly polished expensive shoes. "You're Trutopians."

"That's right."

"And you want me to join your organization."

"We just want to talk to you, Colin," Harriet said. "That's all. You're a hard man to track, but we've got people everywhere. You were spotted a month ago outside Budapest, and ever since then we've been concentrating on this area." She paused. "What exactly *are* you doing here?"

Before Colin could reply, Harriet said, "Never mind that for now. Colin, we didn't come empty-handed." She nudged her colleague with her elbow. "Show him, Byron."

"What?"

Harriet rolled her eyes. "What you've got in your pocket, you dink!"

"Oh, right." Byron reached into his jacket pocket, pulled something out and tossed it to Colin.

"A Mars bar," Colin said.

"Yeah. We thought you might be missing some of the comforts of home."

Colin briefly wondered whether the chocolate might be drugged, but somehow he couldn't stop himself from tearing open the wrapper and taking a huge bite out of the bar.

"Reginald Kinsella told us to order that stuff in specially for you," Harriet said. "And your favorite chips."

"You mean crisps," Byron corrected. "Cheese and onion— those are your favorites, right?"

Colin nodded.

Harriet said, "We just want to talk. Mr. Kinsella has been in Munich for the past week, but he's cutting his visit short and he's coming here to Romania specially to see you. Just give him a couple of days of your time, OK? If you're still not interested after that, then that's fine. You know what the Trutopians are all about, don't you?"

"You claim to be interested only in worldwide peace."

"Exactly. We've got a community in Satu Mare, about twenty kilometers from here. It's in the direction you were heading anyway, so it'll save you half a day's walking. How's that sound?"

Colin shook his head. "No."

Byron started to speak, but the woman put her hand on his arm. "Leave it. All right, Colin. We tried." She stepped to one side and pointed at the large backpack that had been behind her. "It's yours. There's enough food for a week, a new pair of hiking boots in your size, a couple of changes of clothes and a portable phone. I've put our numbers on it, just in case."

Byron said, "I suppose it gets pretty lonely out there on the road, so we've also given you an MP3 player. It's got a couple of thousand tracks on it. We weren't sure what kind of music you like, but there's bound to be something there that'll suit you."

Then Harriet reached into her jacket's inside pocket and took out a thick envelope. "Five hundred euro, five hundred U.S. dollars." She handed it to Colin. "And there's a Trutopian credit card in there too. In case of emergencies. It doesn't have a very high limit, so don't go trying to buy a Ferrari with it."

Colin found that his mouth had gone dry. "You're just *giving* me all this stuff?"

Byron nodded. "Yep."

"Even though I said I wasn't interested in talking to you?"

He nodded again. "That's right. Look, Colin . . . This is how Mr. Kinsella put it: You're a superhuman. And more than that, you're one of the good guys. That puts us all on the same side. If we make things easier for you to help people, that makes things easier for us."

"It just seems . . ." Colin shrugged. "Like a bribe or something."

Harriet said, "It's not a bribe. It's what we do, it's what the whole organization is about. We help people who are less fortunate. We've been following you long enough to know that you have no money, no change of clothes, no food, and you haven't had a shower in over a month."

"Actually," Byron said, "we could tell that one even if we *hadn't* been tracking you. But she's right. Sure, the Trutopians want you on board. But if you're not interested, then what are we going to do? Force you to join? That's not our style." He reached down and picked up the bag. "So come on. We'll give you a lift to Satu Mare, and there's no strings attached."

It could be OK, Colin said to himself. *They're not superhuman. If they tried to kidnap me or anything I could just smash open the car door and jump out.* "All right," he said.

"Great!" Byron said. "You don't mind if we drive with the windows down, do you?"

"I'm right behind you, Ren," Butler Redmond whispered.

Renata didn't need to look over her shoulder to know that the older boy was telling the truth: She could almost feel his breath on the back of her neck.

Does he really think that I need protection? she wondered. *I'm twice as strong as he is!*

"Not too far now," Butler whispered.

Through clenched teeth, Renata muttered, "Yes. I know."

"So what we'll do, right, is wait for Danny to give the signal and then we'll rush through, smash into the guys guarding the door, then split up. You take the one on the left and I'll take the one on the right."

"Sure. Whatever."

Butler paused. "Unless *you* want to take the one on the right?"

Renata stopped walking suddenly. Butler almost crashed into her. She turned to face him. "Butler?"

"What?"

"Back off. You're invading my personal space again."

"Right, right." He grinned. "But you have to admit, we're a good team. The way we took down those hijackers last month—that was class!"

Façade caught up with them. "What's the delay?"

"Just working on the plan," Butler replied.

"Leave the planning to Impervia," Façade told him. "You two just do as you're told."

Butler rolled his eyes. "Why are you even *here*, Façade? You're just the pilot. You're a chauffeur, not a soldier."

"I'm here just in case you wet your pants again like you did when Dioxin's men attacked Sakkara." Without waiting for Butler to respond, Façade said, "Now get moving. And stay alert."

Smiling to herself, Renata marched on. *It's Butler's own fault that no one likes him. Before we got to Sakkara the only friends he had were Yvonne and Mina, and they only tolerated him because he was the first person they ever met who was close to their own age.*

Renata swallowed. *God, poor Mina . . .*

For a very brief time, there had been eight teenagers in Sakkara. Then Yvonne had turned out to be a traitor working for Victor Cross, and had used her mind-control ability to put her sister Mina into a coma. Colin had run away. After Solomon Cord had been killed, his daughters Alia and Stephanie had left with their mother.

Now there're just three New Heroes left, Renata said to herself. *And I'm not even sure that I want to be one of them.*

Behind her, Butler crashed through the undergrowth. "Keep the noise down, Bubbles!" Renata whispered.

"Don't call me Bubbles," Butler said. "And it's not my fault. It's these new boots of mine."

They're still not as noisy as that big mouth of yours. Renata knew better than to say that out loud: Butler had a tendency to sulk for days. *This is no kind of life. If it wasn't for Danny . . .* She didn't allow her thoughts to go any further than that.

She knew that later, when they returned to Sakkara, she would lie awake in her sparse bedroom, staring at the blank walls, wishing that she didn't have to stay in that horrible place.

I wonder which idiot thought it was a good idea that we should stay there after Dioxin attacked. General Piers, probably. Grumpy old fool. At least we don't have much contact with him these days. No, we're all part of the military now. Have to follow the blasted chain of command.

Renata couldn't see a way out of her situation: She didn't

want to remain in Sakkara, and she didn't want to go and live with her parents in their Trutopian community.

When Ragnarök's power-stripping machine had been used, Renata had been in her crystalline form. She'd remained frozen for ten years, until an accident during a test-run of Max Dalton's machine had somehow freed her. She'd woken into a world where her younger brother and sister were now adults and had left home, her parents had joined the Trutopian organization and everyone else she'd known had long since forgotten her.

Physically, Renata was still only fourteen years old, but she'd been born twenty-four years ago. That was the argument the Trutopians' lawyer was using: from their point of view, Renata was still a minor. But General Piers wasn't about to give up one of his three remaining superhumans, so the government's lawyers were arguing that Renata's chronological age was what mattered, not her physical age.

They're fighting over me like hungry dogs over a scrap of meat. The Trutopians want me because it'll be great publicity to have a superhuman in their ranks, but General Piers would probably have me shot before he handed me over to Reginald Kinsella and his people.

Impervia's voice whispered through Renata's headset. "Look alive. We're on."

There was a shout from somewhere directly ahead and Renata broke into a run, with Butler close behind her.

She crashed out through the edge of the clearing and ran straight toward the startled guards.

One of them turned and ran—Butler racing after him—but the other whipped a small handgun from his holster and aimed it at Renata, shouting, *"¡Alto o disparo!"*

Renata had grown up speaking Spanish as well as English, and knew what that meant: "Stop or I'll shoot!"

"Tire al suelo su arma!" she shouted. "Drop the gun! Now!"

Oh hell, he's going to fire.

Renata turned her hands and forearms solid and raised them in front of her face just as the man pulled the trigger. The bullet struck her crystalline arms and ricocheted into the jungle.

The man didn't have time to get off a second shot: Renata was on him, swinging her fists. A powerful punch to the left temple and the guard crumpled to the ground.

The door directly in front of her burst open and four other guards rushed out, all armed with semiautomatic weapons. Renata turned her entire body solid and watched with interest as a hail of bullets rattled against her now-transparent uniform.

One day I'm going to have to learn how this power of mine works, she said to herself. *How come I can turn myself solid, and my uniform, but not anything else?*

At first Renata had only been able to solidify her whole body. Since then, she'd learned to control the power with greater precision. Now, she could pick individual parts and change them at will.

It wasn't easy, and almost every time she did it she got a throbbing headache soon afterward, but the trick had saved her life on more than one occasion.

Now, the four guards were staring at her in panic.

They clearly know who I am, so they should be able to guess that I'm not here alone.

Two of the guards were looking around and the other two had stopped to reload.

Renata turned herself back to human and grabbed hold of the nearest two, slamming them into their colleagues.

One of the men recovered quickly and started to scramble away. Renata was about to dart after him when he suddenly collapsed to the ground.

Danny Cooper materialized in front of the guard. "That's it," Danny said. "That's all twelve. Bubbles is around the other side using his force-field to beat up two at the same time."

They turned at a noise from the jungle to see Impervia and Façade approaching. "All done?" Façade asked.

Danny nodded. "Yep." He looked at Impervia. "Though we should check inside to make sure there aren't any others."

"No need," the older woman said. "The scanner says they're all out here." She hit the switch on her communicator. "Vaughan, you can tell the copter pilot to break cover and start coming this way now. I want them to take the hostiles to the nearest U.S. military base for interrogation."

"Acknowledged," the man's voice replied. "That'd be the USS *Ronald Reagan*, out of San Diego. She's currently three hundred kilometers due north of our position, en route for Costa Rica."

"Perfect. Get it done. Butler? You there?"

"I'm here."

"Good. Carry the hostages clear. Fifty meters at least. I'm about to set the charges."

"Wilco," Butler replied.

"You too, Renata."

Renata nodded, crouched down and grabbed two of the unconscious men by the ankles, then started dragging them away from the building.

She was on the way back for a second run when she saw that Danny was trying to use his one arm to move one of the men.

"Leave him," Renata said. "I'll do it."

"I can manage."

"I know you can. That's not what I'm saying." Renata lowered her voice. "Any luck with that intangibility trick?"

Danny shook his head. "Nah. I don't think that one's ever coming back."

Renata paused and glanced toward the building's entrance. "When Impervia opens the door, you think you can get inside without her noticing?"

Danny frowned. "Yeah, probably. . . . Why?"

"If this place is a weapons cache, how come not all of the guards were armed? Why were there only twelve of them? The place should have been much better defended."

"What else do you think could be in there?"

"No idea. But I think we should find out." Peering over Danny's shoulder, Renata could see Impervia opening the door. "Go!"

There was a blur, then Danny was suddenly standing in a slightly different position, a worry line creasing his forehead. "I *knew* there was something wrong here. You were right. There're no weapons in there, unless they're well hidden."

"So what *were* they defending?"

"The place is filled with huge crates of dried fruits, flour, cereals, dried meats . . . all wrapped up in airtight packages. They're just like the emergency supplies we have in the basement of Sakkara. . . . It's food, Renata. We were sent here to destroy food."

3

THE CUSTOMIZED LEARJET TOUCHED down on the runway with such precision that Evan Laurie almost didn't notice they'd landed.

Laurie was thankful that Victor Cross employed such good pilots: He hated flying.

Sitting opposite him, Cross smiled and said, "We're down. You can breathe again."

Laurie felt the tension drain from his body. "Oh, thank God."

"Why are you so scared of everything, Laurie?"

The nervous man shrugged. "Well, when I was a kid, I used to—"

"Wait, wait. Don't tell me," Cross said.

"You've already figured it out?"

"No, I just don't care." Cross leaned toward the window and peered out as the jet taxied to the small terminal building. "All right. . . . Harriet says they've brought Colin to the Hotel Baldigara. He's settled in and seems to be happy enough for the moment."

"What if he recognizes you, Victor? I mean, even with the beard and padding, you're still you."

"Colin's never met me face-to-face, and the real Reginald Kinsella was such a recluse that even the people who worked closest with him haven't been able to tell I've taken his place."

"But even among superhumans Colin is different. We've already seen his powers evolve once. Who's to say that he hasn't developed telepathy?"

"I have thought of that, Laurie. I'm willing to take the chance."

"We've already *got* superhumans. We have you and Yvonne. Why do we need him?"

"Because you just said it yourself: Colin is different. For one thing, he can see the blue lights. For another, he's the child of *two* superhumans."

The jet stopped, and Cross unbuckled his seat belt. "OK. You know what you've got to do?"

Laurie nodded. "Go to Kiev, then catch the cargo flight to Omsk, and from there to Zaliv Kalinina. And don't let Yvonne know where I really am."

"Good. Keep me posted. I'll send you the material as soon as I can."

"This isn't going to work, Victor."

Victor Cross stood up. "Why the pessimism?"

Laurie began ticking off reasons on his fingers. "You underestimated the kids and they destroyed your power-damper. Dioxin got caught. Renata Soliz turned down your offer to join the Trutopians . . ."

Victor laughed. "That's true. But we always get the outcome we want. Look at what I've already achieved—I'm only twenty-one years old and I'm in charge of the largest and most powerful organization the world has ever seen. I've got more money than I can spend. I'm very definitely the smartest man who ever lived. The only person on this planet who could possibly be a threat to me is Colin Wagner, and I'll have him on my side in a matter of days."

"If Colin realizes that you're the man who killed Solomon Cord, he'll . . . Victor, he's got a very strong sense of justice, but I'm not sure that would stop him from tearing your head off."

"It's his sense of justice that's going to persuade him to come over to our way of thinking."

"I still think it'd be easier to just have Yvonne control his mind."

Victor removed his suitcase from the overhead compartment. "It would be easier, yes, but less satisfying."

"You're just doing this to pander to your own ego."

Victor sighed. "I don't know why I let you talk to me like that."

"Maybe it's because . . ." Laurie shrugged. "Actually, I've no idea either, but there must be some part of you that needs me. Otherwise you'd just have me killed, or get Yvonne to control my mind and make me say only what you want to hear."

Cross flipped open his suitcase and checked the contents. "Could be."

Then Laurie said, "Ah . . . I've just realized why you're not letting Yvonne take control of Colin."

"And why's that?"

"Because her mind-control power makes her very dangerous. You're doing this to prove to Yvonne that you don't need her for everything. If she starts to think that she doesn't need you . . ."

Victor nodded, and smiled. "Well done, Mr. Laurie. And as a reward, you get to spend the next five years in the Arctic."

"I really don't want to go, Victor. I don't like the cold."

"I know that. But the work is important. Or it's *going* to be important."

"Victor, I was *asleep!*" Yvonne said. "Do you have any idea what time it is in Wyoming?"

Cross nodded to the guards at the gate and raised the limousine's window. "Of course I do. I know everything. What's your point?"

Their inspection complete, the guards waved the car through: Victor was pleased to see that even though they knew who he was, and they'd been expecting him, they still ran their scanners over the car and checked his and the driver's DNA profiles against the database.

Yvonne said, "My point is that you can't just phone people in the middle of the night and expect them to be waiting for your call."

"Whine, whine, whine. How are things back home?"

"They're fine."

"No sign of Dioxin breaking through your memory block?"

"No. And even if he does manage it, it's not like there's anyone in Lieberstan who'll be listening to him."

"True. We've just arrived in Satu Mare. I'll be heading back to the States in a couple of days, by which time Colin Wagner will be on our side."

"You're certain you can persuade him?"

"Absolutely. Now tell me what happened on the island."

Yvonne paused. "What island?"

"Isla del Tonatiuh. Check your computer." Victor heard Yvonne yawning, then tapping on her keyboard.

"I see it," Yvonne said. "We had a huge cache of supplies there. *Had* being the operative word. The New Heroes destroyed it a couple of hours ago."

"Good."

"Good? Why is it good? Victor, this is the fifth time they've deliberately targeted the Trutopians."

"I know. Who do you think is feeding them the information? You really should be keeping an eye on the larger picture, Yvonne. We trick the Sakkarans into going on these little missions, and they're not going to be around to do normal superhero stuff."

"And the point of that is . . . ?"

"The ordinary people know that there are superhumans again, and they're beginning to realize that these superhumans aren't working for them: They're working for the military. The public backlash will begin very soon."

"Spurred on by you, of course."

"Naturally. All right, we're here." Victor opened the car door and stepped out into the afternoon sunshine. "Time to meet Mr. Wagner and start the conversion process."

Yvonne said, "Victor, if he kills you, can I take over the organization?"

Cross replied, "You *may* take over the organization. Whether you actually *can,* well, that's a different matter."

"I'm thrilled you have so much faith in me."

"Go back to sleep, kid. I'll call you if I need you. Which I won't."

● ● ●

The first thing Colin Wagner did when he arrived at the hotel room was to fill the bath with hot, foamy water, strip off his clothes and lower himself in.

Now, two hours later, he was still in the bath, eyes closed, listening to Alphaville on his new MP3 player.

The last track on the album came to an end and Colin popped out the earphones and set the player down on the floor.

I could get used to this.

The phone beside the bath rang. Colin grabbed for it with a damp hand. "Hello?"

"Colin? It's Harriet. Mr. Kinsella has just arrived, and he'd like to talk to you. When you're ready."

"Sure. I'll be down in a couple of minutes."

Colin hung up the phone and stepped out of the bath. He didn't bother using a towel to dry himself; he just increased his body temperature until all the water evaporated from his skin.

In the bedroom, Colin looked through the spare clothes Harriet and Byron had given him, and chose a plain black T-shirt and a pair of jeans.

So what do I tell this guy? I could string him along for a while, make him think that I might just change my mind. Then I get to stay here.

He dismissed this idea almost immediately. *Better not. For one thing, it'd be wrong. For another, I've got things of my own to do.*

He sat on the edge of the bed and pulled on one of his new pairs of socks. *Should thank him for all the stuff at least.*

Colin looked at the cell phone that he'd left on the bedside table. *I could phone my parents . . . No. They'd only try to persuade me to go back to Sakkara, and that's something I'm not going to do as long as Max Dalton is still there.*

Once he'd put on his new boots and tied the laces, Colin grabbed the room's key-card and made his way down to the lobby.

The red-haired woman—Harriet—was waiting for him. "All clean and shiny?"

Colin nodded. "Yeah. Thanks. I'd nearly forgotten what it felt like to not be covered in dirt."

"Mr. Kinsella's in the restaurant, if you're ready to meet him."

"I'm ready."

Even though it was now lunchtime, the hotel's restaurant was almost completely empty. At the only occupied table, Byron was talking to a tall, slightly overweight bearded man.

So that's him, Reginald Kinsella, Colin said to himself. *The leader of the Trutopians and one of the most famous men in the world, and he came all the way here just to see me.*

Harriet said, "Mr. Kinsella? This is . . ."

Kinsella stood up, and offered his hand to Colin, a big cheesy grin on his face. "Oh, I know who it is! You two take a break. I want to talk to this young man alone."

Byron and Harriet nodded and left the table.

"Sit," Kinsella said to Colin. "You must be hungry."

"I'm OK. I ate in the car. I don't need to eat very much anyway."

Kinsella dropped down into his own chair. "Is that one of your superhuman abilities?"

"I suppose so."

Kinsella nodded. "I read something about you developing similar powers to your mother. I'll tell you, *that* caught everyone out. We all expected you to take after your father."

"So did I."

A waiter darted over and placed a menu in front of Colin. "The special today is—"

"The special today is whatever this young man wants. *Anything* he wants. Do you understand me?"

Colin felt the blood rush to his cheeks. He glanced quickly at the menu. "The lasagna looks nice."

The waiter nodded. "Certainly, sir." He bowed and darted away.

Kinsella sighed. "I hate that. I hate it when people think I need special treatment just because of what I do, or that I'm going to fire them for dropping the bread rolls." He glanced at Colin. "What about you? Is that why you left the New Heroes? Didn't want the fame and fortune?"

"There's fortune?" Colin shrugged. "No, I just . . . There were reasons."

"Understood. You don't want to talk about it." Kinsella placed his elbows on the table and rubbed his temples with his fingers. "Colin . . . Let's be blunt here. You and me are probably the two most influential people in the world. You do realize that, don't you?"

"I don't see myself like that." Colin picked up a breadstick and began munching on it.

"No, you don't. And that's one of the things I like about you. You've got extraordinary abilities, but you're still just an ordinary kid. My people compiled a very detailed report on

Sakkara. Butler Redmond is an ass. Daniel Cooper . . . Between you and me, I think he's dangerous."

"Why do you say that?"

"Because of his father. His *real* father, not Façade. If what I've heard is true, then Quantum had visions of the future. Visions that eventually drove him mad. And Danny's inherited Quantum's speed, so it stands to reason that he might also inherit his visions." Kinsella paused. "That worries me."

Colin didn't know how to respond to that.

"And Renata Soliz . . . I met her, did you know that? I offered her a chance to join us, but she turned me down. So that leaves you."

"I'm sorry, Mr. Kinsella, but I'm not going to join the Trutopians."

"Right. I don't suppose you've been following the news over the past four months?"

"It's not really been possible."

"Dioxin's reappearance scared a lot of people. If you hadn't stopped him in Topeka . . ." Kinsella shuddered. "I don't even like to think about that. But a lot of people realized that they needed greater protection than the police or the military could provide. They joined the Trutopians. Now . . . We're not perfect, and we've never claimed to be. But our people know that they can trust us, because we believe in one thing above all: the truth. There are no secrets among the Trutopians. If anyone wants to find out anything about me, all they have to do is ask. If there are no lies, there are no secrets. Without secrets, no one can deceive the people. The details of *everything* we do are available to the public."

"Don't you *need* to hide the truth sometimes?" Colin asked.

Kinsella shook his head. "No, you don't."

"What if my parents had told everyone that they were Energy and Titan? Their enemies would have known how to get to them. By keeping the secret they weren't just protecting themselves, they were protecting me and everyone else they knew."

"Right. But suppose the Trutopians are successful, and we do manage to—for want of a better way of putting it—take over the world. No superhero would *need* to keep a secret identity, because if everyone always told the truth, then no one would be able to hurt them. In an ideal world—"

"But we don't live in an ideal world, Mr. Kinsella."

Kinsella smiled. "Not yet."

4

SHORTLY AFTER DAWN, RENATA, BUTLER and Danny walked in to Sakkara's infirmary to find Warren Wagner—Colin's father—waiting for them. A former paramedic, Warren was currently filling the role of Sakkara's chief medical technician.

In one corner of the large room, Max Dalton was working at a computer station.

Only one other person was in the room: In the bed closest to the window, Mina looked as though she were asleep.

"So how'd it go?" Warren asked.

"Fine," Danny said. He and Renata had agreed not to mention what they'd found on the island. "Any word from the people in Hungary?"

"Nothing yet," Warren replied. "We're not even certain that the sighting is reliable."

"We should be trying to find him," Renata said.

"We *are*."

"No, I mean *we* should be. Me and Danny, you and Caroline. We know Colin better than anyone else. We can persuade him to come back."

Danny glanced toward Max Dalton and quietly said, "Col won't come back as long as *he's* still here."

Butler yawned and said, "This gonna take long?"

"It takes as long as it takes," Warren said. "But you can go first. Get behind the screens and strip down to your shorts."

While Butler was being examined, Renata and Danny walked over to Mina's bed.

"God. . . . Poor thing," Renata said. "Four months in a coma." She reached out to stroke Mina's blond hair, which had now grown to shoulder-length.

"I wonder if she's dreaming," Danny said, examining the plastic bag of liquid connected via a tube to Mina's arm. "She probably is. I just hope they're not nightmares."

"She *is* dreaming," Max Dalton said, appearing behind them. "At least, according to the EEG readings. And she's not really in a coma. She's just asleep. She moves from time to time, just like everyone does when they're asleep."

He doesn't look well, Danny thought. Max's hair was now completely gray and his once-handsome face was haggard and drawn.

Renata asked, "So the wake-up message didn't work?"

"Obviously not," Max said. For weeks, Max and his team had been scouring through thousands of hours of Sakkara's audio logs, searching for recordings of Yvonne's voice, and singling out the snippets of her voice where she appeared to be using her mind-control. The idea was that they would compile pieces of Yvonne's orders into a "wake-up" sentence for Mina. "It looks like Yvonne's hypnotics can only work when they're issued live. That definitely indicates that it's more telepathic than vocal."

"So what are you going to do now?"

"We've taken X-rays, CT scans, MRIs, ultrasound images . . . There's nothing there. Short of performing exploratory brain surgery, there's nothing else we can do. Not directly. This is where *you* come in, Danny."

Danny looked down at Mina. "What can I do?"

"You can tell us everything about how you regained your powers."

"I don't think I ever really lost them. I think it was the shock of what happened to my arm. I just sort of shut down." To himself, Danny added, *That, and my vision of the future.*

"But the powers came back. If we can figure out how, then maybe we can trigger the same thing for Mina. You said that your powers returned when Renata was trapped in the computer room, after Dioxin's men shot her, right? You're sure there was nothing else before that?"

Danny shook his head. "No."

"Façade said that during Dioxin's attack you insisted on coming back here instead of going to the safe house. Why?"

"I just didn't want to be left behind. I thought I might be able to help."

"And why *did* you think that?"

"Just a feeling," Danny said, shrugging.

Max absently fingered the scar on his neck. "That's how it started for your father. He used to get 'feelings' about things, or he'd know something he couldn't possibly have known. And then the visions started to come."

"Don't ever talk about my father, Dalton. He's dead because of you."

"I know, but . . ." He stopped. "Look, we've already had two cases of superhumans effectively losing their powers and then regaining them, and that's you two." To Renata, he said, "Your recovery can be tied directly to the power-surge from Victor Cross's machine—"

"You mean *your* machine."

"Right. But that's not something we can replicate here. Even if we were to build another one, the power-surge was an unrepeatable accident."

He's never even apologized for kidnapping me and Colin, Danny thought. He glanced at the stump of his right arm.

From the far side of the room, Warren called, "Renata? You're next."

They looked up to see Butler pulling on his T-shirt as he left the room.

As Renata walked over to Warren, Max said to Danny, "You're still blaming me for what happened, aren't you?"

"Who else should I blame? You funded and ran the whole operation. Because of *you* I'm going to spend the rest of my life with only one arm."

"It doesn't have to be that way," Max said. He led Danny to his computer station, and called up a program. On screen, a three-dimensional model of a mechanical arm rotated slowly. "I've been making some modifications to Razor's design."

Danny shook his head. "I don't want to know."

Max didn't seem to hear him. He tapped at the screen with the end of a pencil. "I was going to remove the third and fourth fingers to reduce the complexity, but there've been a few breakthroughs recently in reading and interpreting nerve impulses. We've built a whole array of sensors into the chest harness, and the software is clever enough to be able to differentiate between the nerve signals."

Despite his misgivings about the mechanical arm, Danny couldn't help being impressed with the amount of time and money the government was spending on the project.

"So all you'll have to do is put it on, and within a few seconds you'll be able to use it like it was a real arm. There won't be any feedback, but when we really get a handle on the microminiaturization we should be able to build in thermal and touch sensors." Max stuck his pencil between his teeth and typed a command into the keyboard.

The screen changed to show a wire-frame figure of a man wearing the arm and the chest harness. "It's still just as heavy as it was, but it's much stronger and the harness distributes the weight pretty evenly, so you'll get used to it. I've redesigned it so that you'll be able to put it on without needing someone else's help. And our tests show that when you switch into hyperspeed mode, the arm will too, so it should be able to keep up with you."

Without saying a word, Danny turned and walked over to the window, and stared out.

Why can't they just get the hint that I don't want a mechanical arm? Maybe I should tell them . . .

But Danny knew that telling them wasn't an option. Max and Impervia had known Quantum, and they'd seen how his visions had turned him into a broken man.

Danny didn't want them to know that he had inherited not only his father's speed, but also his ability to sense the future.

It didn't work well, and he couldn't control it, but there were times—like back on Isla del Tonatiuh—when Danny somehow just knew that something bad was going to happen.

And once, shortly before he'd lost his right arm, Danny had seen a vision of himself with a mechanical right arm.

If Quantum's prophecy was accurate, and I'm going to be responsible

for starting a huge war in which billions of people will die, then . . . Then
there's nothing on Earth that's going to make me take that mechanical
arm. If I don't take the arm, then the future I saw can't ever happen.

His thoughts were interrupted by a hand on his shoulder. He
looked around to see Renata standing beside him.

"You OK?"

Danny nodded. "Yeah. Just . . . thinking."

Behind them, the door hissed open and two female guards
entered, one of them pushing an old woman in a wheelchair. The
woman glanced around, spotted Warren and instantly looked
away.

One of the guards put the wheelchair away while his colleague helped her into bed.

"Another interrogation session," Renata whispered.

Danny said, "I don't care if Ragnarök was her son. How can
they treat an eighty-year-old woman like that?"

"I suppose they think Mrs. Duval knows something that can
help them track down Yvonne."

"What could she know? They've never even met each
other!"

Renata shrugged.

Warren walked over, avoiding Mrs. Duval's glare. "Dan? We
need to get you checked out."

"Why do we have to get a checkup after *every* mission?"

"General's orders," Warren said. He picked up the chart from
the end of Mina's bed and flipped through the pages. "Back in
the old days, we just fought the bad guys and went back to our
normal lives. Now, we've got the might of the military behind us.
Like things weren't complicated enough. One superhuman we

can't wake up, one missing in action, one turned against us . . . Only three of you left." He put back the chart and smiled at Danny. "But soon enough, there'll be four."

"You found a new superhuman?"

"Better than that. Razor's team almost has the new Paragon armor finished."

5

EVEN BEFORE DANNY AND RENATA reached the machine room, they could hear a loud pounding echoing through the building. They opened the door and stood on the gantry, looking down at Razor and four other technicians as they worked on what appeared to be the framework of a three-meter-tall bipedal robot.

"All right," Razor said, standing back from the exoskeleton. He brushed his long hair back from his face. "Everyone get clear. . . . Let's try that again."

The robot's motors whined as it straightened itself—then, after a moment, it tilted slightly to the right, then stomped its left foot forward. The robot tilted to the left, then moved its right foot.

Danny grinned. "It's walking! Finally!"

"Shutting down," Razor said. "Take the readings, Mitch." He glanced up at Danny and Renata, and beckoned them down.

Danny was instantly standing in front of the machine, staring up at it. "It's looking good, Raze. Got it flying yet?"

"We're getting there," Razor said. "It can't carry enough fuel to fly more than a hundred meters. That's 'cos it weighs almost a ton."

Renata arrived next to them. "Razor, how on Earth is someone supposed to fit inside that thing?"

"There'll be a lot more space when we tidy all the cables away."

"Maybe someone doesn't need to be inside it. You could fit it with cameras. Then the new Paragon won't even have to go into battle himself."

"We thought of that, but the general feels that the public will have more confidence if Paragon is a person, not a robot." Razor scratched at the three-day stubble on his chin. "That's one of the things we're arguing about. Piers wants the helmet's faceplate to be transparent, so everyone can see there's a person inside. But that'll seriously weaken the helmet's integrity, which is not a good thing considering that the armor will be equipped with shock-bombs."

"What's a shock-bomb?" Renata asked.

"Another of Max's inventions. It's a grenade that only explodes in one direction. You could hold one in your hand when it explodes—they're about the size of a can of soda—and it wouldn't do you any damage, as long as the business end was pointed away from you. And there's no shrapnel."

"Let's see one!" Danny said.

Razor's hair flicked about his face as he shook his head. "They're way too dangerous to fool around with. How did the mission go? Find the weapons?"

"There weren't any weapons. It was food."

"Food? That seems . . . strange. Do you think Impervia knew?"

Renata shrugged. "It's hard to say. She didn't want us going into the building, so maybe she did know. We can't ask her, because then we'd have to tell her how we found out. You know what she's like about us breaking the rules."

Razor asked, "Are you still thinking about leaving?"

"If I had somewhere to go, I'd leave in a second," Renata said. "We should *all* go. Except Bubbles. But we can't take Mina with us, and I really think that one of us should be here for her, if she ever wakes up."

"I talked to Warren," Razor said. "They're no happier here than we are, but they won't leave. He says that this is the best chance they'll have to find Colin. There's something else bothering them, but he wouldn't say what it was. He did say that Sakkara is probably the only place that's safe from Yvonne's influence."

Renata said, "Much as I despised Josh, at least when he was in charge we had some say in the way this place was run. Now if we want anything we have to go through Impervia."

Razor noticed the expression on Renata's face. "You really don't like her, do you?"

"What's to like? She makes us call her by her superhero name even though she hasn't had any powers for over ten years."

Razor's cell phone beeped. "Oh, what *now*?" He flipped open the phone. "Yo . . . Oh, hi Caroline. What's up?" He listened for a moment. "Uh-oh . . . All right, we're coming down."

"What is it?" Danny asked.

"The guys you arrested on the island aren't terrorists. They're security guards. The food supplies belonged to the Trutopians. And they're not happy."

Colin stood at the back of the room as Reginald Kinsella stepped in front of the camera. Kinsella looked annoyed and a little flustered. He cleared his throat, took a sip of water from a glass.

Harriet, operating the camera, said, "We've got the link. . . . Going live in thirty-two seconds."

Beside her, Byron tapped at his laptop computer. "It's coming through fine."

Despite his reservations about the organization, Colin was impressed with how the Trutopians worked. Everything seemed to be done with tremendous efficiency: Even though the community in Satu Mare was quite small and didn't have its own official broadcasting facilities, it had only taken Harriet and Byron a few minutes to track down a digital video camera and a powerful laptop computer and connect them to the Internet.

Harriet counted down the last few seconds, then Kinsella stared into the camera and began to speak.

"Good morning. Or good afternoon or good evening, depending on where you are. . . . As many of you will know, the Trutopian organization does not simply look after itself. Our mission is to help *everyone*, Trutopian or otherwise." Kinsella took another sip of his water. "In a number of different locations we have been stockpiling preserved foods so that in the event of a disaster—an earthquake, for example—we will be immediately able to ship those supplies to the countries in need. Over the past six weeks, fourteen of our stockpiles have been destroyed or irrevocably contaminated by some unknown outside force. A few hours ago, our enemies struck again, on Isla del Tonatiuh, a small island to the west of Central America.

"After the first few attacks we greatly increased our security measures. Our compound on Isla del Tonatiuh was covered with hidden cameras. We have the perpetrators on film." He tilted his head to look past the camera toward Byron, and nodded.

The tall man tapped a few keys on his computer.

Colin walked over to Byron and watched the video footage play out on the laptop's screen.

His heart jumped when he spotted Renata and Butler attacking the guards.

Once the footage was over, Kinsella reappeared on the screen. "Just in case some of you have been living on Mars and didn't recognize them, they were the New *so-called* Heroes, agents of a government that preaches democracy but apparently does not feel compelled to practice it." Kinsella paused. "I can't speak for anyone else, but I personally am not impressed with this new generation of superhumans. At least, not those who are still working for the U.S. military." With that, he cast a quick look in Colin's direction.

"I want answers. I want to know how they can justify an action like that. What if there is another disaster like the flooding of New Orleans? If the U.S. government comes to the Trutopians for help, what will we say? Will we turn them away? No. We will not. We will help them in any way we can, because the Trutopian organization is made up of the people, by the people and, most importantly, *for* the people. Words with which the powers that be in the USA should be only too familiar."

Kinsella stepped back a little from the camera. "I want answers. I want those answers to be honest, complete and without condition. And I want them within the next twenty-four hours." He took a deep breath, and let it out slowly. "To the ordinary people, thank you for watching. And to the governments of all the countries that are opposed to the Trutopians . . . *We* are watching *you*."

6

in the doorway of Ops, watching the monitor over the heads of everyone else in the packed room.

"We're in trouble now," Razor muttered.

At the far side of the room, General Piers hit the remote control to turn off the monitor, then swiveled back to face everyone.

Danny thought he'd never seen the general look so old, so tired.

For a moment, Piers was silent, then he took a deep breath and looked around the room. "Any thoughts?"

Sitting next to him, Maxwell Dalton quietly said, "Someone set us up. And they did a good job of it too." He looked up at Impervia. "You scanned the place?"

The woman nodded. "Twice. Danny did a high-speed pass, then I scanned it again as I approached. Obviously, they've found a way to mask their cameras from the scanner."

General Piers said, "Obviously." He turned to Razor. "How?"

"Probably used fiber-optic cameras. There are models that can run with minimal electricity. The scanners would only pick them up if they were specifically looking for them. You don't set up something like that because you're afraid someone *might* attack. They knew."

At the far side of the room, Caroline Wagner cleared her

throat and said, "I think we're avoiding something here. Why did you go all that way to destroy food supplies?"

Impervia glared at the younger woman. "We didn't. We thought we were going after a weapons cache."

"Either you're lying or you were wrong. If you were wrong, then what else have you been wrong about? And if you're lying—"

"All right, that'll do!" General Piers said. "I've had the secretary of defense on the phone three times already, and our press office has been bombarded with calls from every media source on the planet. I'm putting a hiatus on everything but the Paragon project until we find out who set us up. Maybe it was the Trutopians themselves, maybe it was a foreign power. God knows there are more than a few nations jealous that we have superhumans." He turned his attention to the computer in front of him. "Meeting's over."

As they filed out of the room, Renata and Butler caught up with Danny and Razor.

"I'm really getting sick of this place!" Renata said. "*They're* the ones who messed up, but we get treated like it's our fault."

"Right," Razor said, "and we don't even get paid. I work at least fourteen hours a day, seven days a week, and in return all I get is food and a bed. I got better food and a better bed in Florida, and all I had to do was take out the trash in the mornings."

A voice said, "And if you want to *return* to that life, that can be arranged."

They turned to see Impervia standing behind them. "Razor, back to the machine room. The rest of you . . . Go to your rooms and get some rest. I want to see you in my office in one hour."

In the small town of Moate, Indiana, two teenage girls kept their eyes fixed straight ahead as they approached a large abandoned factory.

Erica van Piet and Karen Zemsty passed the factory every morning on their way to school, and they knew better than to even glance at it. The cluster of half-demolished, graffiti-covered buildings was well-known as a haven for local drug addicts and gang members. This wasn't the worst part of town—there were places where even the police didn't dare go alone—but it was bad enough that the girls knew better than to pass through on their own. There was some safety in numbers.

Erica was tall, slim and dark-skinned, while Karen was shorter and pale-skinned with long red hair. The day they met, Karen had told Erica, "The gangs'll mostly leave you alone, 'less you draw attention to yourself. Never make eye contact. Never carry more than a coupla bucks. You don't want them to think you're worth mugging."

Erica and Karen crossed the barely used, pothole-riddled street and quietly and quickly walked past the gaps in the rusted chain-link fence.

Only a few more minutes . . . Erica thought. Her backpack was slung over her left shoulder, and she kept a loose grip on it.

She sensed Karen stiffen as something moved inside the complex—the faint scrape of metal on stone—and they increased their speed.

Someone should do *something about that place. About this whole stupid town. I wish we'd never come here. I wish—*

From behind, a rough, sneering voice called, "Hey, honeys! Hey, I jus' wanna aks you somethin'!"

"Oh God," Karen muttered.

"Just keep walking," Erica whispered. She glanced around to see a teenage boy striding quickly toward them. He had a red bandanna tied around his head, and something sharp and metallic half-hidden in his hand. "Sorry," she said. "Can't stop. Late for school."

I know I can outrun him, but Karen can't.

Red-bandanna had almost reached them. "Didn't you hear me?"

Erica took a deep breath and clenched her fists.

Then there was another noise behind them, a brief scuffle of footsteps, a muttered swearword from Red-bandanna. Erica glanced back to see a tall, well-built teenage boy racing across the street, slamming the mugger against the chain-link fence. She stopped and stared.

The boy was wearing a ski mask and gloves, and a blue T-shirt with a white lightning bolt painted on it.

Oh no . . .

The would-be superhero plowed his fist into Red-bandanna's stomach, doubling him over.

God, I hope he knows what he's doing. Erica swallowed hard. She knew what was coming next: Two other gang members raced out of the shadows. The one with the crew cut was carrying a short, rusted metal bar. The other was empty-handed, but it was clear to Erica from his muscular, tattooed arms that he didn't need a weapon.

The masked boy elbowed Crew-cut in the face, then yelled to Karen and Erica, "Get out of here! I can take care of myself!"

No you can't, Erica thought. *You're big and strong, but you don't know how to fight.*

She felt Karen tugging at her hand, dragging her away.

"Erica, come *on!*"

But Erica van Piet wasn't even listening. She was watching the gang members: Red-bandanna was holding the young man down while Tattoo was punching him in the face and stomach. Crew-cut was swearing loudly, nursing his bloodied nose.

Erica winced as Tattoo landed a savage kick square in the boy's chest.

I promised I'd keep a low profile. . . . But I can't just . . . They'll kill him!

The boy was on the ground now, on his side, curled into a ball to shield himself from the kicking. Crew-cut approached, slapping the short metal bar against his open hand, waiting for his turn.

"For God's sake, Erica! If they see you watching, they'll come after *us* next!" Karen said, almost screaming.

Little louder than a whisper, Erica said, "There's only three of them."

"*What?* What are you saying?"

The dark-skinned girl slipped her backpack off her shoulder and passed it to Karen. "Hold this." She began to walk back, toward the fight.

"Erica! Are you *crazy?*"

Crouched over the masked boy, Crew-cut raised the metal bar above his head, aiming for the boy's face.

Erica leaped forward, somersaulted in the air, landed on her hands and slammed her feet into Crew-cut's back.

The metal bar dropped from his hands: Erica grabbed it as it fell, swung it upward, hitting Red-bandanna in the back of his knees.

She whipped the bar in the opposite direction, jabbing the end straight into Tattoo's bare upper arm, then spun about, delivering a roundhouse kick that caught Tattoo in the chin.

Erica straightened up.

Red-bandanna was on the ground, clutching his legs. Crew-cut was sprawled facedown across the masked boy, moaning and gasping for breath. Tattoo was flat on his back, unconscious.

Her attack had lasted no more than two seconds.

The masked boy rolled the still-moaning Crew-cut to one side and awkwardly got to his feet.

Deep brown eyes peered from the ski mask with a mixture of shock and gratitude. "I . . . How did you . . . ? What just happened here?"

Erica glanced down at the boy's shoes, then handed him the metal bar. "Next time, leave the superhero stuff to someone who knows what they're doing."

She turned around and walked back to Karen, who had turned even more pale and was starting to shake.

"Erica . . . Where did you learn to do *that*?"

"My dad taught me." She took her backpack from Karen's trembling hands. "Come on. If we're late, we'll get into trouble."

Still staring at the beaten gang members, Karen said, "OK. Trouble. We don't want to get into trouble. . . ." She began to walk backward. "Your dad taught you. . . . What was he? A cop or something?"

"Something like that, yes." Erica put her hand on Karen's face and forced her to look away. "Karen, listen to me, OK? This didn't happen. Got that?"

Karen nodded. "Didn't happen. All right. So what *did* happen?"

"Nothing." They had reached the end of the block and Erica looked back to see that the masked boy had disappeared. "Nothing happened."

They walked the rest of the way to school in silence. Erica was glad of that.

But what about the masked boy? If he starts to wonder about me . . .

She remembered the final meeting with the agent from the Witness Relocation Program: "You must *always* keep a low profile. Your family dynamic is unusual enough that if someone investigates, it won't take them long to put two and two together and come up with the right answer.

"That's the main reason we're putting the girls into separate schools," the agent had told her mother. "There are a lot of people who still believe that your husband was responsible for all those deaths, and since his identity was made public, we must do everything we can to keep you hidden. From now on, your name is Kara van Piet. Your daughters are Tanith and Erica."

At the end of the meeting, the agent had handed each of them a document. "Sign these, please. They're to confirm that you've understood everything I've said."

When the documents were handed back, the agent had sighed.

"Two out of three. Now, *Erica,* see how easy it is to get it wrong? It's *vital* that you remember that from now on your name is Erica van Piet, not Stephanie Cord."

The New Heroes gathered in Impervia's office, a small window-less room situated in the heart of the building. She was already sitting down behind her desk when they entered.

Impervia said, "I know you've been expressing some concerns about how we do things here, but that has got to stop. You have to accept things as they are and trust us. Understood?"

"Yes sir," Butler said.

Renata and Danny didn't reply, but exchanged a glance at Butler's use of the word *sir*—something Impervia insisted upon as a mark of respect to her position.

Impervia sighed and went on. "On a mission, you do as you are ordered. And you do not question those orders, nor specu-late about them. That sort of thing is enough to give any wit-nesses good reason to believe that we are not acting as a unified team. The media are already asking questions about what we do here."

Renata said, "Questions such as, why aren't we actually helping people instead of blowing up the Trutopians' emergency supplies?"

Before Impervia could respond, Danny asked, "*Did* you know what was on the island?"

"No, we did not," Impervia said.

"If you had known, but the general still ordered you to blow it up, would you have?"

"Yes."

"But that's crazy!"

Butler said, "No, it's not. You have to follow the chain of command. Whatever General Piers says, we do. Back when I was in the academy—"

"The academy that threw you out?" Razor asked. "Or was there another one?"

Butler ignored him. "Back when I was in the academy, the first rule we were taught was that people die if you don't follow orders. The commanders know more than the people under them." He looked at Impervia. "That's why *you* were brought in to be in charge of us, right?"

Impervia nodded. "Because I have military experience as well as the experience of being a superhuman."

Renata said, "Kinsella wants an explanation. What are you going to tell him? That it was a mistake?"

Impervia shook her head. "No. We're not going to say anything."

"But they have proof it was us."

"The official word will be that the video was faked."

Renata said, "But the Trutopians know the truth. They'll tell everyone."

"The Trutopians are a dictatorship," Butler said. "They have no elected leaders, and the people don't have a say in what happens. What we ought to do is arrest Kinsella."

"Their members aren't forced to join," Renata said. "They know what they're getting into. Everyone should have the right to make bad decisions, and no one should be allowed to take away that right. Not even us."

"Screw the Trutopians," Butler said "They're nothing but a

bunch of crazies who think that you can save the world just by holding hands and singing about peace and love. That's just bull. There has *never* been peace on this planet. There's never been a time when there wasn't a war going on somewhere. Human beings don't *want* peace."

Razor slowly clapped his hands. "That was brilliant, Bubbles. You're a genius. If only the leaders of the world would listen to you, then everything would be perfect. You should—"

Razor suddenly found himself slammed against the wall, and held in place by an invisible force.

Butler said, "I could tighten my force-field around your skull and crush it to jelly."

Impervia jumped to her feet. "Let him go, Butler!"

Butler took a step back and Razor dropped to the floor, gasping for breath. "You're not worth the trouble, Razor," Butler said. "You're just a thug who got lucky. If you hadn't met Colin Wagner, you'd still be on the streets of Jacksonville, stealing cars and praying that no one tougher came along. The only reason you're here is because Solomon Cord imagined that he saw something in you that was worth saving. Well, Cord's dead and Wagner's run away like a scared little girl. So if you want to *stay* here, you'll keep your big, ugly mouth shut or I will shut it for you. Permanently."

Razor pushed himself to his feet. "You have no idea, do you, Redmond? You don't know what it means to be a superhero."

"Yes, I do. It means that I'm stronger than you are, so just shut up!"

"That's *enough!*" Impervia roared. "The situation is this: We are going to get a lot of bad press because of what happened on

Isla del Tonatiuh, so we need to minimize the effect. That means we have to show the people that we *are* there for them, and that we are united. Are we clear on that?"

"Yes sir," Butler said.

Renata and Razor nodded.

"Danny?"

"Yes. We are clear."

"Good. In a couple of days, you, Renata and Butler will be sent out on standard patrols. This will be a publicity exercise more than anything else. When the armor is ready, the new Paragon will join you."

Renata asked, "And what about the Trutopians? You're really not going to admit what happened?"

"No. It was an accident."

"The way I see it," Danny said coldly, staring at Impervia, "we committed a crime against the Trutopians. It doesn't matter whether it was an accident or not."

"Then it's a good thing you're not in charge here, Mr. Cooper," Impervia said, "because you clearly have absolutely no idea of how the real world works."

"Oh, I think I'm beginning to understand."

7

IN ROMANIA, COLIN WALKED ALONGSIDE
Reginald Kinsella as they made their way through the Trutopian
community. Harriet and Byron walked a few meters ahead, and
a large, expensive car purred along the street, keeping pace with
them.

"You want to know how much the world's governments hate
us?" Kinsella asked. "Last month someone fired a missile at our
jet. We were flying from Zimbabwe into Botswana. No one ad-
mitted to the attack, but you can bet anything that if the missile
had actually hit us, there'd be a dozen different groups claiming
responsibility."

"How did you avoid the missile?"

"Good pilots," Kinsella said. He gestured toward Harriet
and Byron. "And those two are former FBI special agents.
They're good, but they're only human. That's one of the reasons I want you to join us. It's not that I'm afraid of being
assassinated—well, I am, but that's not the main reason. The
Trutopians are the only way to save the world, and if I'm not
around to run the organization . . ."

"One of the newspapers said that no one ever heard of you
until all of a sudden you were put in charge."

Kinsella nodded. "Right. I saw that. When the organization
started back in the 1970s it was really just a cult for the rich. They
had a gated community in San Diego. My parents joined when
I was about nine. Man, I hated the place. The old man who set

up the Trutopians was a narrow-minded bigot. He hated Jews, women, kids and anyone who wasn't white, rich and American. I wasn't allowed to see my best friend anymore, because he was Jewish."

Colin began, "But that's—"

"Stupid, I know. I knew the whole thing was full of crap from the minute I heard about the place, but I couldn't persuade my folks that they were wrong. Then late last year the old man decided it was time to retire. There were a lot of people waiting for him to step down. He called a big meeting, told them they were all far too ambitious, and that he'd chosen me to take his place. I'd only met him once, so I was as surprised as anyone."

By now, they had reached the outskirts of the town, and were approaching a large fenced-off area. Colin could hear a rhythmic thumping sound coming from somewhere inside the compound. "Sounds like marching. . . . This is the army base?" he asked.

"Yep. Thought you might like to see what we have to do to protect ourselves."

Ahead, Byron and Harriet stood waiting at the gate.

Kinsella said, "You know something, Colin? Ever since I took over the Trutopians I haven't had anyone to just, you know, *talk* to. When I was your age, my friends and I would sometimes just bike up to the beach and sit on the sand and talk for hours." He grinned. "My grandfather called it 'star-dancing.' Like rain-dancing, except it's where you talk for so long the stars come out."

"That's a good name for it."

Kinsella nodded to the guard at the gate as they passed through. "Yeah, we used to sit around and solve all the problems of the world. A bit like what we're doing now, I suppose. Except that you and I really can solve the problems of the world. You know why there're so many wars, so much poverty and hatred? Because people have a herding instinct. They believe that they have to protect the herd, their own tribe."

Colin looked around: on the left of the army base was a line of large armor-plated vehicles. To the right, a series of prefabricated buildings. Directly ahead a platoon of soldiers—some of whom didn't seem to be that much older than Colin himself—marched in formation.

Kinsella continued. "It's completely understandable when you're talking about a primitive culture. The trouble is, this is no longer a primitive culture. We don't need to fight over hunting grounds. But the herding instinct is still there. Take a look at any major city and you'll find a Chinatown, or a Latin quarter or a Jewish sector. . . . It's an automatic response, but it's one that the human race no longer needs."

"But you're just creating a bigger tribe. There's still going to be an 'us' and a 'them.'"

"Right. Until the day comes when *everyone* is a member of the same tribe. Then there's no 'them.'"

"I really can't see that happening. It's a great idea, but it won't work."

"It *will* work. The Trutopian organization is the first of its kind in the world. We are bringing people together in a way that was previously only dreamed of. We'll accept anyone—regardless of race, faith or political persuasion—as long as they obey the law. If we can successfully instill the concept of a single nation, then we can disband the armies, dismantle the nuclear stockpiles and divert all those trillions of dollars toward feeding the hungry, healing the sick, free education for anyone who wants it. . . . All the things a decent society should be doing to protect and nurture its people."

Colin nodded in the direction of the marching soldiers. "The Trutopian army is one of the things that bothers me. For an organization that claims to want peace, you sure have a lot of soldiers and weapons."

Kinsella nodded. "Yes. We do. Imagine you're a farmer, and you have a field of valuable crops. Which would you rather use to protect your crops from thieves? A high fence or a sign that reads, 'Please don't steal our crops'?"

"There'll always be someone who can find a way past the fence."

"Perhaps. But we don't have to make it easy for them."

"Suppose you do manage to persuade the whole world to join? What then? Will you really dismantle your armies and trust that everyone will remain peaceful?"

"What would *you* do, in that circumstance?"

"I'm not the one trying to change the world."

"Well, you should be. Everyone should be trying to change the world. I'm just doing it on a large scale."

Stephanie Cord waited until her mother was out of the house before telling her twin sister, Alia, what had happened.

They sat in the kitchen, at the breakfast bar. Alia was meticulously picking the peel off an orange. "God, Steph. . . . If Mom finds out she'll be so mad."

"I had to do *something,* Al! The guy was way out of his depth. They would have killed him."

"What about your friend? What if she talks?"

"She said she wouldn't, but . . ." Stephanie shrugged.

"You didn't tell her Dad was Paragon, did you?"

Stephanie made a face. "How stupid do you think I am? Of course I didn't tell her! Look, I'm not worried about Karen. I'm more worried about the guy."

"You're going to have to find him and talk to him."

"I know. And that's why I'm telling you—if he sees you, he'll think you're me."

"So what do you know about him?"

"He's about six feet tall, big build. Not much older than us— sixteen, maybe. He was wearing faded black jeans, frayed around the left ankle. Old Reeboks with a blue stripe across the toes—the left one has a crack across the stripe."

Alia split the orange into segments, and popped one in her mouth. "His voice?"

"I didn't hear enough to pick up an accent, but the skin around his eyes was very dark. He could be Indian."

"You're sure he's not a superhuman?"

"If he is, he hid it well. But the thing is, he was wearing a blue T-shirt with a lightning bolt across it."

"So?"

"So he clearly wants to be a superhero. And you know whose fault that is?"

Alia rolled her eyes. "Here we go again. God, Steph. You have to let it go. Colin Wagner isn't responsible for *everything* in the world."

"He killed our father."

"No he did *not*! Victor Cross killed him. He was going to kill either Dad or Renata's entire family. He forced Colin to choose between them."

Stephanie said, "He made the wrong choice."

"God, you are so . . . Damn it, Steph! What if he'd chosen the other way around? Renata's family would be dead. What would you think of him then?"

Stephanie glared at her sister. "You're starting to sound just like Mom."

"And you're starting to sound like a complete idiot. You're not the only one who lost him, you know. He was *my* father too."

"Colin promised us he'd get Dad back. Instead, he got him killed. And now, because of him, more people are going to die. That guy in the ski mask . . . If I hadn't been there they'd have smashed his skull in. All because he saw Colin on TV and he thinks he can be a superhero too."

"You don't know that's why he did it. Maybe he did it because he was inspired by Dad, did you think of that? Dad was a super-hero who didn't have any powers."

"That guy is an idiot. Dad was a genius. And he was trained how to fight."

"Just like he was training *us*."

Stephanie sneered. "Us? You almost never showed up for the sessions! You were too scared that Mom would find out. You never even practiced with the armor and the jetpack."

Then a voice from the doorway said, "But *you* did, Stephanie?"

Vienna Cord stepped into the room, glaring at them.

"Mom. I . . ."

She put her bag of groceries down on the kitchen table. "When did this all start?"

Stephanie looked away from her mother, and stared down at the floor.

"When, Stephanie? When we moved to Sakkara?"

Alia hesitated, then said, "That's when he started teaching us about the armor, and how to fly with the jetpack. But the karate started before that. When we were eight."

Mrs. Cord pulled out a chair and dropped into it. "Oh my God. Sol lied to me. He promised me that he was only teaching you karate for self-defense."

"He was protecting you, Mom," Alia said. "He always said—"

"Tell me about that boy. What happened?"

Stephanie said, "Three guys were going to attack me and Karen, and this other guy tried to save us. He was in over his head. They were going to kill him."

Vienna Cord said, "We do not *need* this, Stephanie. If people learn who we really are . . . Well, God only knows what they might do. The Trutopians are furious about what happened on that island, and it's bringing back all the stuff about Dioxin masquerading as your father."

Alia said, "Look, Mom . . . You have to get in touch with the people in Sakkara, tell them what's happening here. Maybe they can move us to somewhere else."

"No!" Stephanie said. "I don't want to have anything to do with them."

"We might not have any choice," her mother said.

For a moment, Stephanie was silent. Then she said, "This is all because Colin found Dad. If he hadn't, we'd all still be in Virginia. None of this would have happened."

Her mother said, "Stephanie, if you're going to go down that road, you might as well say it's all your father's fault for choosing to be a superhero in the first place."

Stephanie found that her mouth had suddenly gone dry. She swallowed. "He . . . he was training me to replace him, and he wanted me to be ready, but I kept putting it off and . . . *You* know. I just wanted to have some fun and I thought that there'd be plenty of time to train. . . . There were real superhumans in Sakkara so I didn't think that I was going to be needed. But if I . . . If I'd tried, if I'd trained harder, like he kept asking me to . . . Oh God, Mom! I'm so sorry! It was *my* fault! If I'd been ready . . . I might have been able to save him!"

In his hotel room in Satu Mare, Colin Wagner had been sitting for hours, watching UNC—the Universal News Channel—on the television.

God, what a mess . . . Colin thought to himself. *How could they have let it get this bad?*

The news channel was now repeating all the footage of his battle with Dioxin over the streets of Topeka. The voice-over said, "And in the four months since, no one has seen or heard from Colin Wagner, the son of Titan and Energy. Eyewitnesses say that he referred to himself by the name 'Power' in this last battle against Paragon."

"Dioxin, not Paragon," Colin said aloud. This particular reporter didn't seem to be able to tell the difference between a murdering supervillain and one of the greatest heroes who ever lived.

The screen cut back to the reporter in the studio. "The rest of the New Heroes—Daniel Cooper, the girl known as Diamond and a young American man whose name has not yet been made public—have apparently been involved in a number of covert operations for the U.S. military, the most recent being yesterday's attack on the small Central American island of Isla del Tonatiuh. With a special report on the island, we now go live to our Central American correspondent Layton Mortimer."

"Thanks, Tom. Isla del Tonatiuh—known as The Island of the Sun God—was discovered in the sixteenth century by—"

Colin muted the sound, then pushed himself out of his chair and began to pace the room.

So what do I do? If Danny and the others really are targeting the Trutopians then . . . What does that mean? Do they know something about the Trutopians? Or is it just that the world's governments are scared of losing power so they want to get at the Trutopians any way they can?

If I had someone to talk to, maybe I could figure it out.

He wondered what time it was in Kansas. *No, I can't phone anyone in Sakkara. They'd trace the call and find me. I suppose I could talk to Mr. Kinsella, but . . . Well, he's not exactly impartial.*

Colin knew who he really wanted to talk to, but he also knew that it could never happen. *She blames me for her father's death. I'm the last person she wants to hear from.*

He looked at the clock on the screen. It was almost eleven in the evening. *It's only nine at home.*

Colin grabbed his new cell phone and keyed in a number from memory. The phone rang three times before a voice said, "Yo."

Colin grinned. "Hey."

There was a pause. *"Colin?"*

"Yep. How are you doing, Brian?"

"You sound different! You . . . What the hell . . . ? Do you have any idea . . . ? For God's sake, Colin! I mean, come *on!*"

"And in English?"

"Where *are* you?"

"Can't tell you that. Sorry."

"You just . . . I find out that you and Danny are superheroes and the next thing I know you're getting into a flying car and I never see or hear from either of you again."

"Yeah. Sorry about that. We didn't really have a choice."

"It was all over the news. There're *still* reporters coming to the door looking to interview me! So . . . What's it like, being a superhero?"

"It's not what I expected."

"On the news they keep saying you've disappeared. Is that true? That you left the others?"

"Yeah. There were some problems."

"When are you coming home? There's still a couple of guys guarding your house. They're just standing there, all day long. You'd think that they might make themselves useful and cut the grass every couple of weeks."

Colin sat down on the edge of the bed. "How are you guys doing?"

"Well, yours truly is now the most popular kid in school. How's that for a turnabout?" Brian paused. "It's not all good, you know?"

"What do you mean?"

"Ever since you and Danny were discovered, there's been a kind of hunt going on. A hunt for superhumans."

Colin didn't like the sound of that. "How do you mean?"

"They're saying that some countries are testing every kid over the age of twelve to see if they have superhuman powers. It's probably not true, but . . ."

"But it might be?"

"Yeah."

"That's not so bad, Brian."

"Well, I heard that there was a girl in Belgium who was pretty average in school but then on one exam she scored top marks, so they took her away and gave her all sort of tests to check whether she was reading the teacher's mind or something. Turned out that she only did so well on the exam because she'd cheated. So then she got expelled and her family had to move to another town."

"I don't know, Brian. . . . That sounds like someone made that story up."

"Maybe. But the kid who died, that was real."

Colin felt his skin begin to crawl. "What was that?"

"How could you not have heard about that? It was on the news a couple of weeks ago. In Newcastle. He tried to prove to his mates that he had superspeed by standing in front of a train. Took the police three days to find all the bits."

"Oh God. That's . . ."

"There've been others. Jumping out of windows and breaking their legs seems to be the most common one. There was a girl who thought she had the powers of a cat and climbed up this really high tree and couldn't get down. They had to get the fire brigade to rescue her. And there was a little kid who nearly drowned seeing whether he could breathe underwater."

Colin felt a trickle of sweat running down his neck. "The boy who was hit by the train. If I hadn't—"

"Don't go blaming yourself for that, Col. You're not responsible for other people's stupidity. Besides, it was Danny he was trying to copy, not you."

That's not the point, Colin thought. "Listen, Brian, I've really got to go, OK? But I'll talk to you again."

"Soon?"

"I don't know. When I can. Take care, all right? And tell your folks and Susie that I said hello."

"Will do. See you."

"I hope so."

Colin ended the call and stared at the phone for a few seconds. *Things are getting crazy out there. I should . . .* He paused. *I should what? Go back to Sakkara and end up working for the American government?*

He glanced at the TV screen to see a photograph of Reginald Kinsella.

He picked up the remote control and turned up the sound.

The newsreader was saying, ". . . who have all, until recently, appeared to be fully supportive of the superhuman program in the United States. But the recent events in Central America, and other attacks on Trutopian communities, have led many of the governments to call on the United Nations to outlaw the use of superhuman operatives outside U.S. soil. These calls have been backed by the Trutopian leader Reginald Kinsella."

Colin muted the TV again and picked up his phone. He selected Harriet's number and seconds later the call was answered.

"Hey, how are you doing, Colin?" the woman asked. "Need anything? I'm staying across town, but if you want I can be there in ten minutes."

"No, I'm fine, thanks. It's just that Mr. Kinsella said something about going back to America tomorrow."

"That's right."

"Can you ask him . . . Well, I know he's busy and everything, but . . . Maybe you can ask him to stay here for a few more days?"

8

IN SAKKARA, WARREN WAGNER OPENED
the door to his quarters to find the blinds closed and his wife lying
on the bed, staring at the ceiling.

"So how are you doing?"

Caroline smiled. "Not so bad. I'm mostly over it, I think. It
wasn't nearly this bad last time."

"Yeah, but you're getting on a bit now."

"*You're* the one with all the gray hairs!"

Warren sat on the edge of the bed and took hold of his wife's
hand. "You've been stressing yourself about Colin, that's all. Just
lie still and take long, slow deep breaths." Then his smile faded
and he found that his mouth had suddenly gone dry. "We're going
to have to leave here. We can't keep putting it off forever. I mean,
we've probably only got a couple more weeks before . . . ."

Caroline squeezed his hand. "I don't want to be here any
more than you do, but . . . It's too much of a risk to leave. This is
the safest place for us. What if someone like Victor Cross finds
out? And what about Colin? We need to be somewhere he can
find us if he needs us."

Warren looked down at the floor. "He doesn't need us. He
can look after himself." He looked back and smiled. "With the
abilities he has, he wouldn't have any problem tracking us down
no matter where we are."

"There's Mina too. Most of them seem to have forgotten

about her. Apart from Renata, I'm the only one who goes to visit her every day."

"Caroline," Warren said, a hard tone in his voice. "We can *not* stay here, and there's no way we can bring Mina with us. We have to put our own family first."

With a sharp hiss, the door slid open and they looked up to see General Piers entering the room.

Caroline looked at him with disgust. "Come in, why don't you?" She turned to Warren. "We have *got* to start locking that door."

"What do you want, General?" Warren asked.

"A few minutes ago your son made a phone call to his friend Brian McDonald. He stayed on the line long enough for us to trace the call to a cell network in northeast Romania. We're having trouble getting the exact location, but it's still the best lead we have."

"Did you record the call? How does he sound?"

"Yes, we recorded it. He sounds good." The old man gave them a warm smile. "There's no guarantee that Colin will come back, but at least we know he's alive and well."

Warren got to his feet. "Let's hear it."

"They're making a copy for you now," Piers said. "I've put Max Dalton on the case. The cell phone networks are different in eastern Europe, but Max is pretty certain that he can track down the number Colin called from. Then you can phone him yourself. After *we've* established contact with him, of course."

Warren nodded. "OK. That's good. Yeah, we can wait a bit longer."

The general nodded, then left the room, closing the door behind him.

Warren sat down on the bed, wrapped his arms around his wife and hugged her close. "When we talk to him, we'll tell him everything, OK? When he realizes how much we're going to need his help, he'll come back. I know he will."

"No, we can't. The general's people will be listening in to the phone call. As soon as *they* know, they'll make sure that we never leave."

Warren suddenly sat back, and grinned. "Hey, was that a kick?"

Caroline took Warren's hand and gently placed it on her stomach. "I think it was!"

Stephanie Cord knocked on the classroom door and opened it.

The teacher looked up from his book. "Yes, Ms. van Piet?"

"Sorry, Mr. Andrews. There's an important phone call for Grant Paramjeet."

The teacher sighed. "Can't it wait? We're in the middle of differential equations here."

Stephanie shrugged.

"All right. Paramjeet, get back here as quick as you can."

A tall, strong-looking boy with a bruised left cheek stood up, his chair scraping on the wooden floor. He followed Stephanie out into the hallway, closing the door behind him. He gestured down the corridor. "In the office, yeah?"

"No," Stephanie said. "Follow me."

With Paramjeet obediently strolling behind her, Stephanie

made her way along the dark corridors and out through the side entrance to the deserted basketball court.

The young man looked around. "I don't get it."

"Thank you for trying to save my life."

"How did you . . . ? I mean, I have no idea what you're talking about."

"You should have picked a better disguise, Grant. Most boys only have a couple of pairs of shoes. I recognized yours when I saw you in the corridor this morning . . . You *idiot*! You could have been killed. What on Earth were you thinking?"

"I saw you were in trouble . . ."

"You're not exactly the sharpest tool in the box, are you?"

Paramjeet took a step back, and folded his arms. "There's no need for that. I do OK." He looked Stephanie up and down. "So . . . Are you, you know . . . ?"

"A superhuman? No."

"But how did you do that? Those guys were twice your size, and there were three of them! Even *I* was finding it tough."

Stephanie stared at him. "Finding it tough? God, you really *are* an idiot. If I hadn't been there, we'd all have a day off school to attend your funeral."

"I was holding my own. I knew what I was doing."

"No you didn't. You don't know the first thing about being a superhero. Your intentions are good, but your methods are lousy. Where was your backup? Did you have an escape route? Did you even know who you were fighting?"

"Well . . ."

"How did you know that they didn't have guns?"

Paramjeet blurted, "I thought there was only one of them!"

"You're not exactly helping your case."

They glowered at each other.

"Look," Stephanie said. "What made you think that you could cut it as a superhero?"

"I have lots of skills! I was the best on the javelin team in elementary school. I know sign language and I can lip-read—my sister is hearing-impaired so I learned the same time she did. I can fight—"

"Not in *my* opinion."

He ignored that. "The New Heroes aren't doing anything to help ordinary people. *Someone* has to do it. Maybe I don't have any powers, but . . . Paragon wasn't a superhuman either, and he was one of the best."

"I know that," Stephanie said.

"He was just an ordinary man who knew that he could make a difference. He always knew that one day he might die, but that didn't stop him. And it won't stop me either. This country needs heroes, and if no one else is going to do the job, then *I* will! No one knows how Paragon died, but I'm betting that he was doing the right thing when it happened. So you can say what you want, but I think he'd be proud of what I'm doing." He jabbed his finger in Stephanie's direction. "And *you* . . . If you won't help me, then you just better make sure you stay out of my way. Because if you try to stop me—"

Stephanie grabbed his finger and twisted it.

Paramjeet gasped in pain and dropped to his knees.

"You were saying?"

"Oh God! Let go, let go!"

"If you had any brains at all, you wouldn't threaten me." She let go, and stepped back.

Paramjeet got to his feet, rubbing his hand. "You're fast." He looked into her eyes for a moment. "I thought I was fast, but you're a lot faster. So tell me the truth, Erica . . . Are you a superhuman? You are, aren't you?"

"No."

"Sure? Maybe you are but you don't know."

"I'm not. And neither are you. You've got to stop trying to be a hero, Grant. Heroes get themselves and other people killed."

"So I should just sit back and do nothing? The gangs own this town now and no one is standing up to them. I'm not going to stop."

"I'm pretty sure you'll stop when they kill you."

A grin slowly spread across Grant's face. "Not if I have you watching my back. That's what we should do—work together. And you can train me, teach me how to do what you did today. I know this town inside out. I know where they all hang out. All the muggers, pushers, dealers, gang-lords . . ." His voice was getting louder now, more excited. "We'll take them all on, one by one. You and me, we'll show them that the ordinary people are not going to sit back and let them destroy our lives and poison our town! Before long it'll be *them* living in fear, not us. And we'll call ourselves the, uh, the . . ."

"The Two Dead Kids?" Stephanie suggested.

Grant's smile instantly faded. "But—"

"Get a grip. The New Heroes can do it because they're superhuman. We're not."

"But we have to do *something*. Erica, if you don't want to work with me, then you can train me. Give me a better chance of making it out there. You'll do that at least, won't you?"

Stephanie regarded him for a moment. "No."

That evening, on the roof of Sakkara, Renata, Danny and Razor sat in their favorite spot, the western side of the low wall that skirted the roof.

Razor peered down over the edge, looking at the pyramid-shaped building's sloping sides. "I need a day off."

"Yeah, that'll happen," Renata said.

"I'm serious. I've been working on the armor at least fourteen hours a day, every day, since I got here."

"And you've *still* not finished it," Danny said, grinning.

"Very funny. I'd be a lot further along if I hadn't wasted ages working on that mechanical arm of yours. I still can't believe it—all the trouble we had designing and building it, and you didn't even thank us. You never even *looked* at it."

Renata said, quietly, "Razor. Stop."

"What?"

"Just don't talk about the arm."

Razor looked from Renata to Danny, and back. "I . . . OK. Right." He paused for a moment. "Why?"

Danny stared out to the west, where the sun was setting over Topeka. For a few seconds, he was silent, then he said, "Nearly fifteen years ago, Quantum had a vision of the future. He saw me leading the world's superhumans in a huge battle against the ordinary people. He said that billions of people were going to die."

"I know about that," Razor said. "But—"

"Last October, in the desert in California, *I* had a vision."

Razor's mouth dropped open. "Seriously?"

"Yeah. I saw myself with some other kids—maybe thirty or forty of them. We were running from a whole squadron of soldiers. I don't know if I saw the same future that Quantum did, but in my vision, my right arm was gone. Replaced by something mechanical."

"God . . . But couldn't that have been just the trauma of losing your arm? I mean, I still see you trying to reach for things with it, and then having to switch to your left."

"I had the vision *before* I lost my arm."

"You should have said. If we'd known, we'd never have built the thing. So you're thinking that if you never take the mechanical arm, then that future won't ever come to pass? There won't be a war."

"Right."

"But the arm itself doesn't have anything to do with the war." Razor frowned in thought. "Quantum never said anything about you having a mechanical arm in his prophecy. You'd think he'd mention something like that. So who's to say you saw the same thing at all?"

"He's right," Renata said. "Just because one vision of the future comes true doesn't mean that they all will."

"Here's a thought: What was your hair like in the vision?" Razor asked. "How long was it?"

"I don't know. . . . About the same as it is now. Why?"

"Never get your hair cut. If you grow your hair long and it doesn't match your vision, then the vision can't come true. Then you can still use the arm."

Danny gave a nervous laugh. "I wish it was that simple!"

"Nothing is simple," Renata said. "Not anymore." She looked across the roof. There were two soldiers standing by the hangar where the new StratoTruck was being checked over by the mechanics. Another two soldiers stood at the top of the stairs, and three more were clustered around one of the helicopters.

Renata knew that there were a lot more soldiers inside the building: at least thirty the last time she'd counted them.

Down below, on the grounds surrounding Sakkara, the makeshift army camp that had been set up following Dioxin's attack was becoming permanent. The ground was covered with precise rows of tents and prefabricated buildings. Military personnel strode back and forth from one building to another. There seemed to be an awful lot of saluting going on.

At the north edge, a platoon of soldiers marched in formation, while toward the south another group was busy completing the five-meter-high electrified fence that encircled the area.

A thought suddenly struck Renata, and she almost jumped.

Danny took hold of her hand. "What is it?"

Biting her lip, Renata stood up, stepped onto the low wall and began to turn in a slow circle.

"You OK?"

Still turning, Renata said, "They've just about finished the fence. How many soldiers would you say are on this base? Including the ones down inside?"

"A couple of hundred, maybe," Danny said, looking over the edge.

"Five hundred and forty," Razor said. "There're also seventeen armored personnel carriers, twenty-four jeeps, eight choppers and in about two weeks we'll be getting some big guns. They're pretty cool. They've got state-of-the-art tracking equipment—those babies'll be able to target a high-speed missile and knock it out of the air before it gets close enough to do any damage. There's no way on Earth anyone is going to get in here without ending up looking like Swiss cheese. Swiss cheese with a *lot* of ketchup."

Renata dropped back to the roof. "And it's all for our protection?"

"That's it," Razor said. "You superhumans don't really *need* protection, but the rest of us do."

"Then let's look at the facts. We're surrounded by hundreds of highly trained soldiers. There's a huge fence that even I'd have a tough time getting past. When the big guns arrive they'll be active at all times, right?"

"That's right," Razor said. "Much as I hate to admit it, this is going to be a very safe place."

"Then you're looking at it wrong, Razor. All that firepower will be great at keeping people out. But it'll be just as effective at keeping people *in*."

Danny swallowed. "I think you're right. Sakkara isn't a fortress. It's a prison."

9

IN HIS HOTEL SUITE IN SATU MARE,
Victor Cross removed his jacket and padded shirt, then detached
the latex potbelly from around his waist and dropped it on to
the bed.

He removed a series of devices from his suitcase, placed one
in each corner of the large room, then sat down on the bed and
dialed a number on his cell phone.

A few moments later, Yvonne's voice said, "Yeah?"

"It's me," Cross said.

"I know it's you. No one else has this number. You sound
different, Victor."

"I'm surrounded by sound-mufflers. Can't risk Colin over-
hearing our conversation."

"So you got him?"

"Yep. Said I would, didn't I?"

Yvonne said, "It would be a lot easier if I just used my mind-
control power on him."

"Colin's powers have shifted before. For all we know, he might
have developed an immunity to your control."

"There's no logical reason for that assumption, Victor."

"Logic has nothing to do with it. If Colin even *suspects* that
you're working with me, we are finished. Eventually, when he's
been prepared, I'll start the process of getting him to sympathize
with your situation."

"And in the meantime I just sit here and wait, is that it?"

"Pretty much. I know you don't like it, but trust me. It'll be worth it." Victor got to his feet. "Right. It's time for Reginald Kinsella to make another broadcast. The Sakkarans have had more than enough time to come up with a good reason for destroying our supplies on Isla del Tonatiuh."

"This is like throwing stones at a wasp hive just to see what'll happen."

"Nest," Victor corrected. "Wasps have nests. *Bees* have hives."

"And both of them have stingers, Victor. Don't forget that."

Warren Wagner pressed his palm against the DNA scanner on the door to Sakkara's interrogation room. After a moment's pause, the door hissed open.

Inside, two guards stood against one wall, carefully watching Impervia and the old woman. Mrs. Duval sat straight in her chair, staring directly ahead.

Impervia stood up, the legs of her chair scraping on the floor. "Warren . . . She's finally agreed to talk, but only to you."

"All right." Warren sat down in the chair, and looked at the old woman. "I'm told you know who I am?"

"Only you," the woman said. "No one else."

Warren nodded, then glanced at Impervia and the others. "Leave. All of you."

"She knows things that are not for your ears. She can't be left unguarded," Impervia said. "General's orders."

"The general can go to hell," Warren said. "Everyone out. Now. I know you'll be listening in, so if anything is said that you don't want me to hear, you can interrupt."

Impervia hesitated for a moment, then she and the guards left the room and sealed the door behind them.

Warren turned back to Mrs. Duval.

"Yes, I know who you are," she said. "I'm old, but I'm not senile. You're the man who killed my son. You're Titan."

"Ragnarök died at his own hand," Warren said. "I didn't want it to happen."

Mrs. Duval pursed her lips, the lines around her mouth deepening. "I'm not proud of what he became. Casey chose the way he lived, and now you tell me that he also chose the way he died."

"That's right."

Mrs. Duval lifted her cuffed hands from her lap and placed them palm-up on the desk. "Look at my hands."

Warren looked; the old woman's hands were covered in calluses and faded scars. "What happened?"

"Thirteen years ago the authorities found out Ragnarök's real name. They couldn't find him, so they found me. Mr. Wagner, are you familiar with the Good Book? Deuteronomy 24:16. 'The fathers shall not be put to death for the children.'"

"I'm familiar with that one, all right."

"I'm imprisoned because of my son's actions."

"Officially, you're not imprisoned. You're under investigation."

Mrs. Duval laughed harshly. "Then perhaps you can tell me why I spent the last thirteen years—"

A siren blared through the room, quickly followed by Impervia's voice. "That is a forbidden topic!"

"All right," Warren said. "Mrs. Duval, why did you choose to speak to *me* of all people? And why wait this long?"

"Because even though you are responsible for my son's death, I believe that you are a good man. And you've also lost your son. But you may get him back one day. That's not something I can ever hope for."

Warren sat back. "That doesn't answer my question. I'm willing to wait as long as it takes for a real answer." He pulled out a small notepad and pen from his pocket and quickly scribbled a note: "They're listening, but not watching." He passed the pad and pen to the old woman.

She nodded and began to write. After a moment, she slid the pad back across the desk.

Warren glanced at the note and frowned. Mrs. Duval had written, "Do you know what is happening in Lieberstan?"

Colin Wagner still wasn't exactly sure what Reginald Kinsella expected of him.

He opened the door to the balcony and stepped out. On the nearby rolling hills he could see large pieces of equipment.

He concentrated his superhuman eyesight on the equipment, forcing it to come into focus. Colin didn't know much about weapons, but they looked like antiaircraft guns to him.

Something went *beep-beep* behind him and Colin turned to see that the television set had come to life by itself. Reginald Kinsella was on-screen, standing in front of a podium.

"My fellow Trutopians," Kinsella began. "Yesterday in southern California a bus crashed off the highway and plummeted down a ravine. Because of the difficulty in securing the bus, it took the rescue workers almost eight hours to recover the bodies of the dead and injured."

Kinsella paused and wet his lips. "Where were the New Heroes? With the resources they have at their disposal, they could have reached the site of the accident a lot sooner than the rescue team. Diamond could have used her strength to secure the bus, while Quantum's son and the boy with the force-field power could have freed the trapped passengers. But because they were not there, two people died needlessly."

Still staring at the screen, Colin dropped into the leather armchair.

"Last October, just before Mystery Day, Maxwell Dalton appeared on television for the first time in years. He said that the age of the superhumans was over. He was wrong: It seems that the age of the super*heroes* is over. Shortly after that, Dalton himself was injured in a mysterious accident, and later indicted for tax evasion. He was supposedly incarcerated in a high-security prison somewhere on the East Coast. Today, my people have uncovered the truth. Max Dalton is *not* in prison. He's in Sakkara, a convicted criminal working with the New Heroes.

"The man running Sakkara—General Scott Piers—appears to be immune from the laws of the nation he's supposed to be protecting."

Kinsella sighed, and shook his head slowly. "But it's clear that the New Heroes are *not* protecting the people. They're being used to attack and destroy facilities run by our organization. They are doing this because we are a threat to their way of existence.

We are building a world without crime, and a crime-free world will have no need for superheroes. You can check out all the facts and figures on our website: The ordinary Trutopian working person—no matter where in the world he or she lives—has a higher standard of living, health and education than anyone in any single country. Crime rates are so low as to be nonexistent. In fact, in the past month only one crime has been committed by a Trutopian: a young man in New Zealand who was driving while drunk. He was fined appropriately, and banned for ten years. Not banned from driving, because he needs to be able to drive to and from his place of work. We have taken the more logical approach of banning him from drinking."

Colin laughed. "Now *that* makes a lot more sense!"

Kinsella continued. "For all the non-Trutopians out there watching this, that's a good example of how this organization works. And it works well. There are now almost twenty million Trutopians, all living without poverty, without fear, without restrictions on their freedom, politics or religion, and without crime. If this sounds like the way you would like to live, then contact your nearest Trutopian center.

"This is how we are going to save the world, my friends. Not with huge armies, or trade embargoes or enough nuclear weapons to destroy the planet a thousand times over. Not even with superpowered humans. The world will be saved by ordinary people like you and me. People who care enough to stand up and be counted. So stand up. Be counted. Save the world."

The transmission ended and the television set automatically turned itself off.

Colin stared at the now-blank screen.

He jumped when the telephone rang, and made a grab for it. "Hello?"

"Colin? It's me," Reginald Kinsella said. "Are you hungry? There's this great place—"

"Hey, I was just watching . . . That was . . ."

"Are you OK?"

"You . . . You're right. We can do it. I don't know how much help *I* will be, but I'm willing to give it a go."

After a moment's pause, Kinsella said, "Colin, I appreciate that, I really do. But you should know that the military—and not just in the States, but all over the world—well, they're not going to respond positively to that broadcast. A world without crime, hunger or poverty will need armies even less than it'll need superheroes. I'm pretty certain that they're all making plans to move against us."

"We'll stop them. You have me on your side now."

"Even if it means . . . ?"

"Yes," Colin said. "Even if it means I'll be going up against the New Heroes."

10

RENATA AND DANNY WERE EATING LUNCH
in Sakkara's dining hall when Razor dragged over a chair and
sat down. He slumped forward until his forehead thumped off
the table.

Renata and Danny continued eating in silence.

"Does anybody," Razor asked, his voice muffled, "want to
know how my day is going?"

"No," Danny said.

"Anybody *else*?"

"Go on then," Renata said. "Tell us."

Razor rolled his head to the side and looked at them. "Slowly.
There's a saying: The first ninety percent of the work takes ninety
percent of the time, and the remaining ten percent of the work
takes the *other* ninety percent of the time."

Danny was about to reply when Impervia approached the
table.

"Meeting in Ops," the woman said. "You're all invited."

Razor lifted his head. "Even me?"

"No. You go back to work on the armor."

"Am I allowed to eat first?"

"You've got five minutes."

Razor groaned and allowed his head to drop down again.

Danny and Renata followed Impervia out of the room and
down to Ops, where they found almost everyone else crowded
into the small room.

"Everything is changing," General Piers growled. "Everything. The media battle we're fighting with the Trutopians is not going well. Kinsella and his people are smart: They know how to use the system and they are shaking the public's confidence. Congress has been talking about us. We do *not* want Congress talking about us." He turned to Danny and Renata. "Tonight's patrol of Topeka is canceled. I want you training as much as possible over the next few days. You're to prepare yourselves for a trip to Romania to bring back your friend."

Danny froze in the act of biting his nails. "You found Colin?"

"Almost. He made a phone call to your friend Brian McDonald. We traced the call to a Trutopian community in northern Romania. We know that Kinsella is also in Romania right now. If he can successfully enlist Colin to the Trutopians, they've won. We have a team scouting it out now, but the Trutopians are making things difficult for us."

"They're not talking?"

"No, worse. They *are* talking. Every one of them who spoke to Colin or even just saw him has come forward and they're telling us everything in extreme detail."

Danny put his hand in front of his face to hide his grin.

"As soon as we pinpoint him, we'll be sending you in to bring him back. The Trutopians won't like that. You're going to have to go in covertly."

Warren Wagner said, "General, it doesn't matter how you approach him. If Colin doesn't want to come back to us, you won't be able to persuade him."

"We will. We have to. Colin is by far the most recognizable

and popular of the New Heroes. We're going to need the good publicity his return will generate, because our strategists are predicting that Kinsella's next move will be to reveal what happened with Mina and Yvonne. The Trutopian spin doctors are going to make it look like the girls were held here against their will."

Renata said, "Well, they *were*! That's no way to treat a human being. Why were they even here to begin with? Yvonne told us that they'd been here all their lives. Why? Superhuman abilities don't show up until you reach puberty. Did you know that they'd become superhuman? Was one of their parents a superhuman?"

Everyone in the room fell silent, watching the general.

He cleared his throat. "Their background is classified."

Danny said, "If we ever encounter Yvonne again, it'd help to have all the information about her. I mean, we all thought she was just very smart and very strong, but it turned out she had mind-control too." Danny realized he was staring at Max Dalton as he said this. "Oh my God. . . . Are you their father?"

Max shook his head. "No."

"Josh, then? Or is your sister their mother?"

"There is no genetic connection between my family and theirs."

"The matter is closed," General Piers said.

Renata stood up. "If you want us to do your dirty work, General, then you're going to have to start treating us better. Tell us everything we need to know about Yvonne or I'm walking out of here. I mean it."

The old man regarded her for a moment. "Yes. I believe you do." He nodded to Impervia. "Tell them."

Impervia said, "Yvonne and Mina were found on the day of the final battle with Ragnarök. Paragon discovered them in one of Ragnarök's hideouts."

Renata's mouth dropped open. "Their father is *Ragnarök?*"

"In a way, yes. We haven't been able to determine the extent of the work Ragnarök did. Our interrogations have proved almost fruitless. All we have really learned is that Yvonne and Mina are the only two who survived. This is why we brought Mrs. Duval to Sakkara. She's the only link we have."

"You've lost me," Danny said. "What do you mean they're the only two who survived? How many children did he have?"

"We believe there were six," Impervia said, "but only Yvonne and Mina survived. When Paragon found them, they were suspended in an amniotic fluid inside artificial wombs. They were about three years old. They'd spent their entire lives in glass jars. Renata, you said that keeping Mina and Yvonne here was no way to treat a human being." She sighed. "Strictly speaking, those girls are not human."

Caroline Wagner said, "Oh my God. They're clones."

"Yes. Ragnarök cloned himself. Four of the six clones failed to gestate, but Mina and Yvonne survived. In fact, they flourished."

"So Mrs. Duval . . . She's their grandmother?"

Impervia nodded. "She is. But she doesn't know that, and she'll never find out." She glanced at Warren. "If she won't talk to you, she's not going to talk to anyone. We've learned everything we can from her. She will shortly be leaving Sakkara."

Façade asked, "Where are you taking her?"

Impervia ignored him. "I trust this matter is now closed and your curiosity about Mina and Yvonne is satisfied. We have work to do, people."

In the heart of the newly built Trutopian community in Wyoming, Yvonne sat in her sealed quarters, staring at the phone, waiting for Victor Cross to call.

She hadn't spoken to him in over a day, and she knew why: Cross was feeling pleased with himself and he didn't want her ruining the mood by reminding him that if Colin learned the truth he could—and probably would—destroy them all single-handedly.

Victor's arrogant to the point of self-delusion, Yvonne thought, running her hands through her long, jet-black hair. *He thinks his way is the only way. And he's willing to step on anybody to prove himself right.*

If I didn't know the truth I'd swear that he *was a Ragnarök clone too.*

Yvonne had been eleven years old when she first realized that she was smarter than her sister. Within two months she was smarter than anyone in Sakkara.

It had taken her a week to hack into Sakkara's computers, and a further week to decrypt some of the data taken from Ragnarök's computers eight years earlier.

And that was when she learned where she and Mina had come from.

Yvonne had entered Mina's bedroom to find her sister sitting on the wide window ledge, her head resting on the sloped glass, staring out at the hills that surrounded Sakkara.

It had been almost six months since they had been allowed outside: their birthday treat the day they turned eleven.

Each day they were allocated an hour of personal time, during which they were free to read, watch television, play games or do anything they liked. As long as it didn't involve leaving the building, eating food that was on the "restricted" list, listening to music that General Piers didn't approve of, being loud or getting in anyone's way.

The rest of the day was spent studying or being subjected to tests by Sakkara's technicians and scientists.

From the little television they had seen, they were aware that normal eleven-year-old girls were allowed to go outside, have friends, eat junk food, go to parties and have sleepovers where they could sit up all night and talk about the boys they liked.

Yvonne and Mina had never met any boys.

As the door hissed closed behind Yvonne, Mina's shoulders sagged. Without turning around, she said, "No luck?"

"No," Yvonne dropped on to the bunk and lay on her stomach, her face and arms dangling over the edge, her fingertips brushing the thin carpet. "I swear . . . General Piers is the most miserable old man in the world."

"He's not letting us out," Mina said. It wasn't even a question.

"He didn't even look at me. Just said, 'No.' Just like that. He didn't even *pretend* to be thinking about it."

"You're smarter than he is. You ought to be able to come up with a way to persuade him." Mina finally turned to face her sister. "They shouldn't be allowed to keep us prisoner here. I mean, it's illegal, right?"

Yvonne raised her head. "Technically, it's not. Cloning is prohibited, therefore anything created through the process of human gene manipulation isn't subject to human status. If we're not humans, it's not illegal to keep us locked up."

"I just wish my superhuman powers would kick in! You've got your enormous IQ, and you're way stronger than me. You'd think that clones would develop the same abilities at the same time."

"People are more than just their DNA: There're a lot of other factors that go into making a person." Yvonne paused for a moment, thinking. "Though I've got a hunch that you *are* developing something . . ."

"Like what?"

"How did you know it was me who came into the room?"

Mina shrugged. "I just knew."

"Maybe you've got some sort of telepathy."

"I don't think so . . ."

Yvonne climbed off the bed. "Just close your eyes for a minute, OK?"

Mina closed her eyes. "Now what?"

"Count to five and then tell me where I am." Yvonne quietly moved toward the door.

Mina counted to five and pointed straight at Yvonne. "There." She opened her eyes.

"You could hear me?"

"No, I just sort of knew." Mina shuddered a little. "I never really thought about it before, but . . . I think this has been happening for a while. I just seem to know where everyone is."

"How does it work? Is it like X-ray vision?"

"Gimme a break. X-ray vision! That'd be weird. I'd be able to see through my eyelids. How would I get to sleep? And maybe, like, I'd forget to open my eyes and be wandering around and people would think I was sleepwalking. Here's a thought, though: If I did have X-ray vision, then wouldn't I be able to see out through the back of my head as well? How would I shut it off?"

And she's off again, Yvonne said to herself. *She's like a dog with a bone when she gets started on an idea.* "Mina, where's the general?"

"He's in his office."

"OK, that's not a good test because you know I just went to see him. How about that new guy, Josh?"

Mina closed her eyes. "I can see you, you're orange, but turning redder. Probably because you're getting annoyed with me. Josh . . . I think . . . I *think* he's heading into the dining hall. Yeah, it's definitely him. Josh has that thing about him, you know? The aspect that only you and me have."

"You've lost me."

"He's different."

"He used to be a superhuman. Would that be it?"

"Could be," Mina said. She opened her eyes. "I'd have to be able to see more people with the same aspect to be certain."

"This is amazing," Yvonne said. She took Mina by the hands. "You can't tell anyone, OK? If they don't know that you're a superhuman, they might let you out one day. It's too late for me because they already know about my intelligence, but you've got a chance."

"I have to tell them, Yvonne. This is exactly the sort of thing they've been looking for."

"They've already got me scheduled for *years* of tests. I don't want you to have to go through that too."

"But they're always asking me if I've noticed any signs that I might be a superhuman. And, well, you know I'm no good at keeping secrets!"

"That's because you talk too much!" Yvonne sighed. "Look, just promise me you won't tell them."

"No, I can't make that promise."

What does it take to get through to her? Yvonne stared at her sister, and—as she spoke—tried to force the words into Mina's brain. *"Promise me."*

Mina nodded instantly. "I promise."

Yvonne stepped back and let go of Mina's hands. *Wow. That was weird.* It had felt as though something invisible and intangible had jumped from her mind into Mina's.

"Why are you looking at me like that?" Mina asked.

"No reason," Yvonne said. *Did that really happen?*

"You're still doing it!"

I have to try that again! "Mina . . . You do talk a lot to the others." Yvonne concentrated as she had before. *"From now on, talk only when it's absolutely necessary."*

Mina nodded.

"Understood?"

Mina nodded again.

She's not responding verbally, because it's not necessary for her to do so. Just like I ordered.

Yvonne moved away, and sat down on the edge of the bed.

Maybe it only works on her, but . . . Maybe it'll work on anyone. I need to check out the files on Max Dalton—he used to be able to control minds.

Yeah, some chance that the general will give me access to the files.

Then Yvonne smiled.

But if I can control people's minds, then he wouldn't be able to stop me.

I could do anything I wanted.

Anything at all.

Now, in her apartment in the Trutopian town, Yvonne thought, *Since then it's worked on almost everyone I've met. Almost.*

Wish it worked on Victor. Then we'd start getting some things done around here.

The phone finally rang and Yvonne grabbed for it. "What kept you?"

"Busy working with Colin," Cross said. "I think he's almost ready."

"Almost? Just let me talk to him, Victor. I'll make certain that he doesn't drift back over to the other side."

"Mind-control isn't the answer to everything."

"But it *is* the answer to the question, 'How do we make sure that Colin Wagner doesn't kill us all?'"

"Colin's not a killer."

Yvonne dropped into her armchair. "Maybe not. But he is a beater-upper when he needs to be."

"So tell me, then. How would you play this out? The whole thing."

"First I'd take control of Colin. Then I'd start making broadcasts on the Trutopian cable network. They'd have to be done live, of course, but if we were careful we'd be able to do it without anyone actually seeing me."

"And what would these broadcasts contain?"

"Instructions for all non-Trutopians to join up."

"Go on."

"Next, I'd contact the heads of state of the most powerful countries. Get them sympathetic to the Trutopians. After that, it'd be easy sailing."

"The New Heroes would never let you get that far. Renata Soliz is immune to your control."

"That's why we need to be certain that Colin is on our side."

"Suppose that they find a way to defeat him? What then?"

"Then I'd break out the secret weapon."

Victor paused for a moment. "Mina's really that powerful?"

"Absolutely. And she has no idea. Her ability to sense auras makes her almost untouchable, and she is immeasurably strong and very fast. I started suppressing her abilities before they could develop fully. . . . There could be even more to her."

"So that's your plan for taking over the world? You could do that in a month. Maybe less."

"I know."

"And then what? You've taken over the world, so what next?"

"Whatever I want."

"Example?"

Yvonne shrugged. "Well . . ."

"Exactly," Victor said. "You don't know. You don't have a plan. *I* have a plan. I know what I want, and I know how to achieve it. Your way might get you the world, but my way will get me something much more precious than that."

"OK, now you're beginning to sound like a crazy person."

Victor laughed. "What do you mean, *beginning*?"

Two months after Yvonne and Mina's twelfth birthday, Yvonne stopped General Piers in the corridor outside his office. "General, can we have access to the Internet?"

He said, "No," and brushed past her.

Yvonne hissed an angry sigh. *Right. That's it!* She marched after him, and shouted, *"Stop!"*

The general stopped walking.

"Give me a computer, and full Internet access."

"I'll get Dalton to set it up for you."

"You will cease all the tests on Mina and me immediately."

"I think you're right. We've done all the testing we can."

"General?"

"Yes?"

"Tomorrow morning, you will resign from Sakkara. You will appoint Joshua Dalton as your successor."

General Piers nodded, stared at Yvonne for a moment, then began to walk away.

Two hours later, Josh Dalton carried a brand-new laptop computer into Yvonne's bedroom and began to set it up. "I don't know what you said to make the old man change his mind, but it must have been good."

"Thanks, Josh."

"So how are you and Mina getting on? Any sign of her developing superhuman abilities?"

"Not yet."

"Maybe it won't happen." He smiled at her. "But don't worry, you might not be the only superhuman. There's a kid in a military academy in Alaska who looks like he might have some extra-normal abilities. It could be a while before we're certain, though."

"Why?"

"Because he doesn't know about it himself. Every year his school plays a friendly football game against one of the rival schools. The guy we're looking at—Butler Redmond, his name is—knocked over another player but wasn't even close to him. I've checked the camcorder footage: The other kid was definitely hit by something invisible, and from the way Redmond was moving, it could only have been him. Some sort of force-field."

"Couldn't you just requisition him?"

"No. Military academies are out of our jurisdiction unless we can prove that someone is superhuman. And that's almost impossible to do if the person doesn't know they've got powers. So we're just going to have to sit back and wait."

"But if he *is* a superhuman . . ."

"I'm sort of hoping that he *isn't*. He's arrogant and obnoxious. A couple more years in the academy should knock the rough edges off him. At least, I hope so. His father's just as bad, so I wouldn't be surprised if Redmond grows up to be a supervillain." Josh paused. "Ah. Sorry. I'm not suggesting that you and Mina are going to turn out bad because of who your father was."

"That's OK," Yvonne said. "We choose our own paths in life."

While Josh returned his attention to the computer, Yvonne watched him carefully.

They all know that we're clones of Ragnarök, so they're never going to really trust us.

I'll talk to them—to every single person in this place—and I'll make them forget where we came from. Get them to change their files, and then forget that they've done that.

Two years later, Yvonne entered Joshua Dalton's office and ordered him to tell her everything about the incident in California.

Josh said, "After they lost their powers ten years ago, Titan and Energy moved back home. They were joined a few years later by Quantum and his wife and son . . . Except that it wasn't Quantum. Façade had been masquerading as Quantum for about a year before Mystery Day."

"Why?"

"He'd been recruited by my brother. Max wanted full access to Quantum's visions of the future."

"How could Façade replicate Quantum's powers?" Yvonne asked.

"He didn't. Most of the time Quantum was still Quantum, but Façade played the role of his civilian identity, Paul Joseph Cooper."

"I've read enough about your brother to know that he wasn't smart enough to build the power-stripping machine on his own. So who was behind it?"

"A man called Victor Cross. He's twenty years old. A genius."

"So he would have been ten when my father's power-damper

was used. If Cross is a superhuman, his own powers wouldn't have appeared for at least another year. Where is he now?"

"Escaped. But not for long. We have a good lead on him."

For a few moments, Yvonne was silent. Then she said, *"You will find Victor Cross and tell me how to contact him, then you will forget all about him."*

11

AFTER MUCH BICKERING, THE TWO
lawyers chose Bloomington, Illinois, as the meeting point, the
city being roughly halfway between Sakkara and the Trutopian
community in Breckin Falls, Cleveland.

Now, with the meeting about to start, Renata Soliz waited
nervously in the small office, chewing her fingernails.

"Don't do that," the lawyer said as he flipped through his
pages of notes.

"Don't do what?" she asked.

"Bite your nails. It's a sign of weakness. When they get here,
just sit still, look like you're paying attention. If there's anything
you don't understand, just pretend you do. OK?"

Renata nodded, then realized that she was already biting her
nails again.

A few moments later, the door opened and a well-dressed
heavyset man entered, followed by Renata's parents.

Renata jumped to her feet and began to move toward them,
but her lawyer reached out and put his hand on her arm. "Don't,"
he said quietly.

Renata hadn't seen her parents in four months. She smiled at
them, doing her best to give the impression that everything was
going to be all right.

"Not a word!" the Trutopian lawyer muttered to Mr. and Mrs.
Soliz, steering them to their seats on the opposite side of the
table.

What Renata wanted to do now, more than anything in the world, was leap over the table and wrap her arms around her mom and dad, and never let go. *Remember what Caroline said,* she told herself. *Slow, deep breaths. Everything will be fine as long as we all remain calm.*

Renata's lawyer shuffled through some of the papers on his desk, and said, "We're all agreed that we can proceed—for this meeting at least—without third-party arbitration?"

"Agreed," the Trutopian lawyer said.

"Fine. For the record, my name is Douglas Landron, representing the government of the United States of America in this initial discussion to determine the custody of Renata Maria Julianna Soliz, also known as Diamond."

"Mackenzie Shoell of the Trutopian Organization, on behalf of Maria and Julius Soliz, biological parents of the child in question."

The two lawyers looked at each other for a moment, then Shoell said, "So how are you doing, Doug?"

"No complaints at this end, Mack. You?"

"Things are pretty good here. So . . . Down to business?"

Landron nodded. "Sure. I've got a copy of Renata's birth record here. As you'll see from the highlighted details, she was born almost twenty-five years ago." He slid a bundle of pages across the table. "I've also got affidavits from three Supreme Court judges that any person over the age of eighteen cannot be considered to be a minor. Therefore, your clients no longer have any legal status as Renata's guardians. Case closed, as far as I can see."

"No, case still open," Shoell replied. "Renata spent ten years in her solidified form during which she did not age and was unaware of her surroundings, and as such cannot be considered to have *lived* during those years. Therefore, Renata is still only fourteen years old. Testifying to that point I have preliminary letters from specialists in genetics, brain functions and"—Shoell gave a slight smile—"philosophy."

"Philosophy? Seriously?"

"The real question in this case is whether Renata was alive during those ten years. The definition of 'life' is of paramount importance."

Renata looked up at her mother and father. They seemed to be just as upset about all this as she was.

Landron said, "A person in a coma will not usually be aware of his or her surroundings, and may not necessarily age in the same way as a person who is conscious. By your definition, such a person would not be alive. That definition is clearly rendered inaccurate by far too many precedents to go into here."

Renata said, "Isn't anybody going to ask *me* what I want to do?"

"Sorry, Ms. Soliz," Landron said. "It would be best if you didn't speak at this time."

Renata rolled her eyes, then slumped back in her chair.

"Sit up straight," her mother said, automatically.

"Maria, please!" Shoell said. "You agreed not to say anything." He looked back at his papers. "The Trutopian Organization will argue that not only is Renata a minor who is being held against the wishes of her legal guardians, but also that Renata has been involved in military action."

"Even if Renata *were* a minor—which she is not—as she is a

superhuman being, Congress allows this under the Extraordinary Circumstances bill. Unless you want to claim that she is not superhuman?"

Shoell shook his head. "No, no. That one we *will* concede. Let me put it all on the table and tell you what we want, Doug. We want Renata out of Sakkara, back with her parents, and no longer working for the military. We are going to fight you every step of the way, so it would be much better all around for you to relinquish your claims to her right now. Sakkara has already had enough bad publicity without the media getting hold of this one too."

"Mackenzie, if you want to try to bring the media into this, feel free. But you won't get anywhere. Renata can be considered to be a military asset. If her identity was to be made public, the security of this nation would be compromised."

"As a minor, Renata is subject to certain laws regarding her care and her schooling. I believe that she is being tutored by one Caroline Wagner, correct?"

"Incorrect. Ms. Wagner is indeed schooling the three other children at Sakkara, but not Renata. She is not a minor and therefore is not legally required to attend school. That she may have chosen to sit in on these lessons is entirely irrelevant."

"And does Ms. Wagner have teaching qualifications recognized by the U.S. Department of Education?"

"Irrelevant. I refer you to the previously mentioned Extraordinary Circumstances bill."

Julius Soliz said, "May I just say something here?"

"I'd rather you didn't, Mr. Soliz," Shoell said.

"Well, tough. Renata is our eldest daughter. I have only seen her once in the past ten and a half years. We thought she was dead. And you two fools are sitting here arguing over her like she was a stolen car or something."

Landron said, "Mr. Soliz, I understand your concerns, but the fact remains that—"

"Screw your facts!"

Landron began to gather up his papers. "Mr. Shoell, if you cannot keep your clients under control, I'm going to call a halt to this meeting. We'll go to court. And we will win. We have the law, the military and the government on our side. What do you have?"

"The Trutopians," Shoell replied. "Twenty million people throughout the world. You want to go to court? Fine. It'll be at least a year before we can bring this case before a judge. By that time, we expect our numbers to have greatly increased. You really want that many people asking questions about the true nature of your work at Sakkara?"

"Mack." Landron sighed. "This case will cost the Trutopians a fortune. It'll drag all your dirty secrets out into the open."

"But we don't *have* any dirty secrets, Doug. I know your people can't make the same claim. The illegal detention of minors—I'm not even counting Renata here, I'm talking about Yvonne and Mina—trespassing on Trutopian soil, destruction of property, illegal genetic experimentation . . . The list is endless. And the money aspect? Not going to be a problem, believe me."

Landron laughed. "You actually think you might win? Seriously?"

"We *will* win," Shoell said. "Sakkara will be disbanded. And rightly so—you're a bunch of thugs using your strength to take what you want. Your people aren't happy that the Trutopians are gaining so much power, so you destroy our supplies. What do you call that?"

"An accident! We were misinformed. And there's strong evidence to suggest that your people set us up. Why else would you have the compound on Isla del Tonatiuh so heavily monitored? You fed us the false information about the island, and then just sat back and watched us destroy the place. That's entrapment."

"And I heard that your official word was that the New Heroes were *not* involved, and that the video footage was faked. Thanks for the admission of culpability."

Renata's head was spinning, and she felt like she was going to throw up. A headache pounded behind her eyes, and was growing by the second.

Her mother was crying quietly, being comforted by her father. *This is harder on them than it is on me!*

"Get lost, Shoell!" Landron shouted. "You know you can't use that as evidence—it's hearsay at best. But you want to play dirty? Fine. By trying to take away Renata, by deliberately leading the New Heroes into an ambush on Isla del Tonatiuh, the Trutopians are acting against the interests of the American people."

Renata said, "Stop! For God's sake! This is crazy!"

Then Landron said, "This isn't about you, Renata. It never was. It's about not letting these people take over the world."

Shoell snorted. "Actually, it's about not letting *you* continue to act as though you already *have* taken over the world."

Landron pulled out his cell phone. "One call from me and the Trutopians will be reclassified as a subversive organization."

Shoell stood up so fast he knocked his chair over. He jabbed at

Landron with his finger. "You try that and we will *bury* you! I'll have Sakkara wiped off the face of the map! We've got enough political power to bring down your entire government."

"That was a *threat*," Landron said, his voice cold with anger. "You have just made a direct threat against the U.S. government."

"You lousy . . . !"

Renata jumped to her feet and screamed, "Both of you, just shut *up*!"

Renata's headache pounded so hard it felt like something had exploded inside her skull. A surge of pain ran through her entire body, and she collapsed back into her seat.

Then she heard her father's voice saying, "Renata? What . . . What have you *done*?"

Dizzy, nauseous, Renata looked up. "Dad? Sorry, I just . . ." She realized that he wasn't looking at her. He was looking at Landron and Shoell.

The two lawyers were still glaring at each other. They were unmoving. Transparent. Crystalline.

12

IN THE SMALL COFFEE SHOP ON MOATE'S main street, Stephanie Cord had finished her latte and was about to leave when she heard someone sitting down directly behind her.

"Don't turn around, Erica," Grant Paramjeet's voice said in a loud whisper. "If people don't know we know each other it'll be harder for them to figure out who we really are."

Stephanie raised her eyes. *Is this guy* ever *going to quit?*

She heard Grant open a newspaper, and knew that he was holding it up in front of his face to hide the fact that he was talking to her.

"Here's what we'll do," Grant said. "My grandma's away for the next two weeks, and I'm supposed to be going over to her place every day to clear out the basement. It's totally packed with junk, but I figure if I work like crazy today and tomorrow, then I can get it all done and that means we'll have it all to ourselves. It's the perfect place for us to train."

Without making a sound, Stephanie put her book and cell phone into her bag, stood up and left the store.

Outside, she felt a tiny twinge of guilt and looked in through the glass door to see that Grant was still talking to himself.

Idiot.

Grant had been pestering her every chance he could. There had been cryptic notes stuffed through the vents in her locker or tucked into her bag as she passed him in the school hallways, a dozen brief but intense conversations and more phone calls, e-mails and text messages than she could count, all pleading for her to train him.

Grant had even set up a website called "The Moate Vigilantes," and it had taken Stephanie threatening to break his arm before he grudgingly agreed that making the website public might not be a good idea.

She was crossing Third Avenue when Grant caught up with her, his rolled-up newspaper in his hand.

But he didn't seem to be annoyed. "Very smooth! I didn't even hear you leave. You're going to have to teach me that one."

Stephanie glanced at him. Grant was walking alongside her, but trying to look as though it was only a coincidence that they were going in the same direction.

A shabbily dressed man moved out of a doorway to block their path. "Spare change?"

"Sorry, no," Grant said.

The man hobbled after them. "C'mon, pal! I just need a coupla bucks to make up the bus fare. I got a job interview lined up, see, an' I need to get to my brother's place so's I can borrow his suit."

"Do I look like I'm dumb enough to believe that?" Grant asked. "Get lost."

"Yeah, yeah, thanks for nothin'." The man turned away.

"Nice," Stephanie said. "How do you know he wasn't telling the truth?"

"He's been using that same line for as long as I can remember. I told you; I know this town inside out."

Stephanie considered this. "So . . . You want to be a hero, but you only want the exciting parts, the whole 'saving the world' trick? There are other kinds of heroes, you know. Cops, doctors, nurses. *Especially* nurses." She pointed across the street to a secondhand clothing store. "See that blue suit in the window? You should buy it, give it to that guy. Looks about his size."

Grant made a face. "Why?"

"It's only sixty dollars. You can afford that, right?"

"Well, yeah, but—"

"Being a hero means helping other people without any direct benefit to yourself. You don't have to fight criminals. You could do charity work."

Grant gave a short, sharp laugh. "Right. Like Paragon would have done that."

"How do you know he didn't?"

"Way I see it, he was kinda busy fighting people like Slaughter and Dioxin."

Stephanie stopped and turned to face him. "If you don't think that helping the needy is worth your time, then you're never going to make it as a hero."

He nodded. "Gotcha. This is part of my training, right?"

Steph gritted her teeth and resumed walking. "Grant, I'm not going to train you. Just get over that idea."

Then she heard running footsteps, and looked back to see that Grant was racing back toward the homeless man. *He's really going to do it . . .*

She knew that she had to get Grant out of her life. She liked him well enough, and every time he talked about Paragon she filled with pride for her father, but she was supposed to be Erica van Piet now, not Stephanie Cord. Grant's presence was a constant reminder of the life she had left behind.

And the people she'd left behind.

Colin woke to find that he was once again sleeping on the floor next to his bed. In the four months since he left Sakkara he'd grown so used to roughing it that the bed just seemed too soft.

Yawning, he stumbled into the bathroom and showered, then stared at himself in the mirror for a few moments. A large red blemish had appeared overnight, just under his left ear.

Colin closed his eyes and concentrated. A ripple of heat and electrical energy ran over his neck and face, zapping the spot and any other bacteria that might be lurking under his skin. He opened his eyes again: already, the spot was beginning to fade.

Colin had just finished getting dressed when Reginald Kinsella phoned. "Mr. Kinsella. What's up?"

"We have a situation that I think you might be able to help with. Interested?"

"What is it?"

"I'd rather tell you in person. You're not too busy, I hope?"

"Not at all."

"Good. I'm already on my way."

Kinsella arrived ten minutes later, a worry line creasing his forehead. He had a small folder in his hands.

"What's the matter?"

"We . . . We found out something . . . Something disturbing. Have you ever heard of a country called Lieberstan?"

"No, sorry. Should I have?"

"It's a pretty small place, used to be part of the Soviet Republic, then it was argued over by some of the newly formed states. . . . That whole area has a convoluted history and I don't really understand it myself. We've got a community there, but the government is putting pressure on us to disband it." Kinsella walked to the window and looked out. "Lieberstan's principal export is platinum. You know anything about platinum?"

Colin shook his head.

"It's one of the rarest elements on the planet, which makes it expensive. What makes it even more expensive is that to get a single ounce of platinum you have to mine and process about ten tons of ore." Kinsella turned around to face Colin. "There is a platinum mine in Lieberstan that's said to be one of the deepest and most dangerous in the world." He removed a photograph from the folder and handed it to Colin. "Satellite image, taken about a week ago."

Colin turned the photo around in his hands. "Which way up? Ah, got it. What exactly am I looking at?"

Kinsella tapped a large, rectangular area, in the middle of which was a dome surrounded by a series of small squares. "This is the mine, shielded by this dome. To give you an idea of the scale, these little squares are buildings, each about the size of the average house. We need to get someone in there."

"Why?"

"I can't tell you, unless you agree to do it."

"What was all that talk about the Trutopians not having secrets?"

Kinsella smiled. "This one isn't our secret. It's theirs."

"You're asking a lot, Mr. Kinsella. How much time do I have to think about it?"

"I told him he had a couple of days," Victor Cross told Yvonne over the phone. He leaned back in his chair and put his feet up on the desk, then scratched at his fake beard.

"Will he go for it?"

"Who can say? Right now, he's checking out Lieberstan on the Internet. All he'll find is the usual tourist stuff about how beautiful the country is."

Cross could hear Yvonne drumming her fingers on the table.

"We *need* him to go," she said. "This is the whole point of finding Colin in the first place."

"I do know the plan, Yvonne."

"Let me talk to him. That's all you have to do. I'll make him want to go. He won't even have to remember that he spoke to me."

"No. It's too much of a risk."

Yvonne said, "Then just tell him the truth about the platinum mine."

"Not yet. Colin needs to think that he's outside the loop. That keeps him off balance."

"But that wouldn't matter if I was controlling him."

"And what if your control doesn't work? What then?"

"It'll work. I'm sure of it."

Cross shook his head. "No. We wait for Colin to make up his own mind."

"This is as much my plan as it is yours, Victor! I'm the one who thought of you taking over the Trutopians. I'm the one who arranged for you to replace the real Reginald Kinsella."

"I know that. And I've never taken credit away from you. But these things have to happen at their own pace. Suppose you do manage to control Colin's mind, but later the Sakkarans find a way to break through that? Then he's our enemy for certain. But if we persuade him correctly, there's nothing they can do to turn him against us. So we play this *my* way."

"And what do I do? Just sit here and wait for you to come back? This is worse than when I was in Sakkara! What's the point of having someone like me on your side when you won't even let me use my abilities?"

"You have to wait until the time is right."

"When will that be? When *you've* done all the work? We're supposed to be a team."

Victor sighed. "I know what you're going through. But you have to be patient, OK? Just trust me. It'll all work out fine."

He said good-bye and hung up the phone.

Cross's superhuman brain allowed him to think about many different things at the same time: Even as he was arguing with Yvonne, he had been considering the best way of dealing with her, how to best steer Colin's opinions, the many different ways Evan Laurie might mess up in Zaliv Kalinina and the nature of the situation in Lieberstan.

She's too dangerous. She's nowhere near as smart as I am, but her mind-control means that if she wanted to she could turn everyone against me.

Maybe it's time to step back. Hand over control of the Trutopians to her. Laurie pretty much has everything set up for the future, and Yvonne's definitely the one to take over here anyway.

Cross stood up and walked to the window. He stared out at the clouds.

But she can't go public just yet. Not until the situation with Sakkara is resolved. And we can't solve the Sakkara problem until we get Colin to Lieberstan.

As long as Yvonne doesn't go completely power-mad, it could work.

He reached for his phone again and dialed a number. After a couple of minutes, the call was answered.

"Hello?"

"It's me, Laurie. How are you doing?"

"Freezing my butt off in this place, Victor." Laurie answered.

"I should have phrased that differently. *What* are you doing?"

"I just told you!"

"You know, I was kind of thinking about the work. Remember the work? The whole point of you being there?"

"We're all set up, ready for you to send us the material."

"Change of plans. I'll be bringing it in person."

"When?"

"Today. Colin will be on his way to Lieberstan within the hour."

"And Yvonne?"

"She's planning to betray me, but that's irrelevant now. I'll leave her to battle it out with the New Heroes."

"What if she wins?"

"Just keep watching the news, Laurie. On the unlikely chance that you ever get married, you'll want to be able to tell your kids what it was like during the last few days before the war."

"I'll do it. I'll go to Lieberstan," Colin said to Reginald Kinsella as they stood on the balcony of Colin's hotel suite. "But I can't promise that I'll get involved in whatever is happening there."

"You're certain you want to do this?" Kinsella asked.

Colin nodded. "You need someone with superhuman abilities, right? Who else are you going to find?"

Kinsella smiled, and looked down over the balcony, resting his forearms on the railing. "There are rumors of a superhuman in Kenya. A seventeen-year-old girl who can transform into some sort of giant cat."

"You think that's true?"

"I wish I knew. We have a few communities there, but none of our people have reported any sightings. I've sent Harriet and Byron to investigate, but I'm not holding out much hope."

Colin was silent for a moment, then said, "Tell me what I need to know about the platinum mine in Lieberstan."

Kinsella straightened up. "We're going to have to send you in alone, understood? We won't even be able to provide much radio support, so you'll be on your own for most of the time. I know I can trust you to do the right thing, whatever you find there."

"How will I get out?"

"The United Nations will send in troops. They'll pick you up."

"How do you know that?"

"Because when the rest of the world finds out what's been going on there, they're not going to have any choice."

13

DANNY COOPER AND RENATA SOLIZ
stood on the roof of Sakkara, sheltering from the heavy rain under an umbrella.

"You're sure you're all right?" Danny asked.

Renata nodded, and squeezed a little closer to Danny as the rain whipped around them. "It's just an ordinary headache now. Barely there at all."

"So Josh was right about you being able to use your power on other objects. . . . I wish I'd been there to see it!"

"I'm just glad that I was able to change them back. What if I couldn't?"

"You're sure there were no side effects?"

"Apart from me getting a splitting headache and them getting the fright of their lives, none that I could see."

"What was the final outcome of the meeting? Any closer to a resolution?"

Renata shook her head.

Danny said, "Look, I know this probably isn't the best time, but there's something I've been wanting to, y'know, talk to you about . . ."

Renata stepped back a little and tilted her head so that her face was only centimeters away from Danny's. "Go on."

Danny swallowed. "I keep telling myself that you've got enough to worry about and the last thing you need is me making your life even more, well, complicated."

"I can cope with complicated," Renata said, smiling.

Danny returned the smile. "Colin and Brian used to think that this was so easy for me." He paused. "I like you."

"I like you too."

"I mean, I like you a lot. More than just—"

Danny heard footsteps splish-splashing across the roof, and turned to see his eight-year-old brother approaching.

He sighed, and muttered, "Perfect timing." He turned to face Niall. "What's up, big guy?"

"Dinner." Niall stepped up to the edge of the roof and peered over the low wall.

He was about to climb up on to the wall when Danny reached out and grabbed the back of Niall's sweatshirt. "No you don't!" Danny said. "You can fall off the wall when someone else is watching you, not me."

"I wasn't going to fall!"

Renata said, "That's true. You probably wouldn't *fall*, exactly. You'd just skid down the side of the building."

Niall nodded. "Right!"

"And land in those bushes. Where the giant rats live."

Niall leaned over the wall again, grinning. "Rats? Cool!"

Danny hauled him back, and pushed him toward the stairs. "Go on. We'll be right behind you."

Renata said, "You know, he looks just like you when he grins like that. It'll be interesting to see how he turns out. You've got different fathers, but Façade was a shape-shifter, so does that mean that Niall will grow up to look like Façade or Quantum?"

"I'm more worried about which of them he *acts* like."

The now-familiar sound of Grant Paramjeet's approaching Reeboks snapped Stephanie Cord out of her daydream. *Oh, not now . . .*

It was early evening, and the small bakery that Stephanie was passing would be open for another hour. She glanced at the display of pastries and muffins in the window, then at Grant's reflection. "You again. You're not tremendously good at getting the hint, are you?"

He smiled. "Anyone would think you didn't love me."

"Anyone would be right." Stephanie resumed walking.

Grant fell into place alongside her. "So I asked that homeless guy if he wanted me to buy him that suit."

"And?"

"And he said he'd rather have the money so he could buy it for himself. See? I told you he was lying. Anyway, I finished clearing out Grandma's basement. And guess what?"

"No."

"I told you my granddad was in the army, didn't I?" Without giving Stephanie a chance to answer, he continued, "Well, maybe I didn't. But anyway, I found his old army kit. Just the uniform and the kit bag, no weapons or anything."

"Good. You and weapons would not be a good mix."

"The bag is huge." Grant stretched out his arms. "Like, *this* big. So I stuffed it with the uniform and a bunch of old clothes and hung it from the ceiling. It makes a great punching bag. You'll see when you come over."

"Grant, I'm busy. Please go away."

"So where are you going?"

"None of your business."

He let out a sigh of exasperation.

Stephanie felt a little pleased with that. It was the first time he'd expressed any sort of frustration at her rejection of him. *Maybe he's finally learning.*

"God, Erica. What can I do to convince you that we have to work together?"

"I want . . . A banana-nut muffin. A big one."

He grinned, said, "You got it!" and ran back toward the bakery.

Stephanie knew that would keep him out of her hair for a while: When she'd looked through the bakery's window she'd seen that the banana-nut muffin tray was empty.

She crossed the street and walked on toward the Shady Oaks Mall, where she found her twin sister Alia sitting on the edge of the outdoor fountain.

Alia looked up, and offered her smoothie cup to Stephanie. "Want some? It's mango and pineapple."

"No thanks. Let's get inside. I had to ditch Grant again."

Alia scooped up her bag and followed Stephanie through the mall's open doors. "I think he likes you."

"He's just obsessed with being a superhero," Stephanie said. "If I can't persuade him to leave me alone we're probably going to have to move."

"I hope not," Alia said. "I'm just getting used to everything in school. Oooh, shoes!"

After Alia had tried on and rejected a dozen pairs of strappy sandals, they bought sandwiches at the mall's food court and sat at the only clean table.

"Oh great," Alia muttered. "Right next to the TV. That means everyone's going to be looking in this direction."

The giant screen loomed over them, silently broadcasting a news report about the rapidly expanding Trutopian organization.

"Hate those guys," Alia said around a mouthful of bread and cheese. "You'd think that the New Heroes would do something about them."

"But they're not doing anything illegal," Stephanie said.

"I know, but still." Alia shrugged. "Dad didn't like them much either, Steph."

"Erica, remember?"

"Right, right . . . But I remember him telling Razor that he thought the Trutopians were dangerous. And he said the same to Colin too."

Stephanie involuntarily cringed at Colin's name. "Don't talk about him."

"You can't blame him forever, Steph—I mean Erica. Colin Wagner didn't kill Dad. Victor Cross did. When Dioxin stole Dad's armor and threw him out of the helicopter, Colin risked his own life to save him."

Stephanie said nothing. She knew that Alia was right, but that didn't make her feel any better.

She knew that sooner or later she'd have to admit that Colin hadn't done anything wrong. But not right now. Now she was still angry. Not just at Colin, but at the whole situation.

She still believed what she had told Grant: Heroes get themselves—and other people—killed.

Dawn was breaking in Romania as a small, sleek-looking un-manned aircraft touched down on the hotel's roof.

"This is a prototype Apache Arbalest," Kinsella said as he and Colin approached it. "It's the only one of its kind, and it is *the* fastest aircraft ever built. It's almost completely invisible to radar and any other tracking device."

"But there's only one seat. . . . I don't know how to fly something like this."

"You don't need to. You just sit back and enjoy the trip. We'll control it remotely. Like I said, it's a prototype—it wasn't de-signed to ever carry a passenger, because no ordinary human could survive the acceleration. It's about four thousand kilome-ters to Lieberstan, but this little beauty has got scramjet technol-ogy. It'll take you from here to Lieberstan in about eighty-four minutes."

"You have got to be kidding me! It's definitely safe, right?"

"For you, yes. Not for anyone else."

"When do I leave?"

"Right now. The Arbalest will drop you off three miles due west of the mine, then it'll depart—we can't leave it waiting around to pick you back up. The mine is huge: Just follow the sounds of the machinery and you can't miss it." He handed Colin a small headset communicator. "This will keep us in touch when you're on the ground, but you won't be able to initiate a call: You'll have to wait until you hear from us. We want to keep radio chatter to a minimum."

Colin nodded and put the communicator in place, tucking

the earphone into his right ear. Hesitantly, he climbed into the cramped cockpit.

"Mr. Kinsella, if what you told me about the platinum mine is true . . ."

"It is. I wish to God that it wasn't." Kinsella reached out his hand, and Colin shook it. "Good luck. And be careful." He took a few steps back.

A moment later, the Arbalest's engines whined into action and Colin felt a sudden, sickening lurch in his stomach as the roof of the hotel began to fall away.

Then the scramjet engines kicked in, and Colin felt as though something hard and heavy slammed into his chest as the aircraft raced toward the rising sun.

14

IN MOATE, INDIANA, STEPHANIE CORD opened the front door of her house to see Grant Paramjeet standing there, smiling at her.

"You can't ditch me that easily," Grant said.

Stephanie frowned. "I'm sorry, who are you?"

His smile faded. "Ah. The wrong twin. Is, uh, Erica around? I wanted to . . . Hold on a second! It *is* you!"

"Worth a try," Stephanie said. "What do you want now?"

"Work with me."

"No."

"Then train me."

"No."

"I'm going to do it with or without your help. People *need* heroes."

"That's what the police are for, Grant. You want to make a difference, join the police force. Become a doctor. Join the fire department."

He stared at her for a few seconds, then said, "I know the truth. I know who you are."

Stephanie swallowed. *No, he couldn't possibly* . . . "What are you talking about?"

"I followed you to the mall. Saw you talking to a girl who looks exactly like you. I figured that either you're clones, or twins." He stared at her face. "You do look a lot like him, now that I know what to look for."

"Now you've totally lost me."

He grinned again. "Right." After a second, he added, "I told you I can read lips, didn't I? My sister lost her hearing when she was six, so we all learned sign language and lipreading. I watched you and Alia in the mall. Your real name is Stephanie Cord, and your father was Solomon Cord. Paragon. The greatest superhero who ever lived. Don't try to deny it. Everyone knows that Paragon had twin daughters, and you're the right age. And I saw your mom coming home from work earlier—she looks exactly like Vienna Cord."

Hesitantly, Stephanie said, "Have you told anyone else?"

"Of course not! What sort of an idiot do you think I am?"

The dangerous sort, Stephanie said to herself. "All right. But if you do tell anyone else, you'll be putting my family in danger." She stepped closer to Grant, and he stepped back. "Understood?"

"I would never do something like that."

"I don't want to see you again, Grant. Not ever. You see me in the hallway in school, you change direction. You look the other way."

"Look the other way . . . Right. That's *your* specialty, isn't it?"

Stephanie glared at him.

"Your father could have done that, but he chose to be a vigilante. He saved hundreds of lives. Maybe thousands. And you could do the same. You *should.* You have the skills. Even if you only save one person, then isn't it worth it?"

"My father had armor, and a jetpack and weapons. I don't have any of those."

Paramjeet's large brown eyes narrowed in anger. "Paragon had something else you don't have."

"And what's that?"

"Guts."

Stephanie swallowed. "Go to hell."

"He had the courage to help people who couldn't help themselves. You think he'd be proud of you?"

Stephanie stepped out into the porch, pulling the door closed behind her. "My father died because someone else was trying to be a hero. Colin Wagner promised me he'd get my father back, but he didn't."

"No, he didn't," Paramjeet told her. "Nothing can get your father back now, Stephanie. He was a great man, and he tried to make the world a better place. But you're willing to sit back and waste your skills because you're trying to convince yourself that Paragon's death was Wagner's fault. Look, all I'm asking is that you help train me. Make me a better fighter. I'm not trying to replace your father—no one ever could—but I'm not just going to sit back and do nothing."

For a long time, Stephanie simply stared at him, then she said, "Tell no one. Leave no record of what we are doing. You'll need some old clothes. Tough material—leather and denim. Strong gloves. Boots. A full-face motorcycle helmet. A baseball bat. Paint everything black. No symbols or insignia. You will do everything I say, when I say it. And you do not go into action until I decide that you are ready. Understood?"

Grant Paramjeet grinned. "I understand. What should I call myself? I've been trying to think of a cool name, but all the good ones are taken."

"This isn't a game," Stephanie said. "You're going to strike at the muggers and gang members and then disappear. No one will ever know who you are."

"But—"

"But nothing! You'll be doing this for other people, not for yourself. *That's* what being a hero is all about."

In her secluded apartment in Wyoming, Yvonne was sitting on the windowsill, staring out at the town below, while she talked to Victor Cross on the phone.

"Laurie and I are on the way back to the States now," Victor said. "Should be there in about nine hours. We—"

There was a burst of static from the phone. Yvonne said, "Victor?"

"What was that? Sounded like . . . Oh hell."

"What's wrong?"

Yvonne heard Victor yelling, "Take evasive action! *Now!*"

"Victor!"

Evan Laurie's voice called, "Cross, there're two fighter jets out there! They look like—"

There was an almost deafening *boom*.

Yvonne nearly dropped the phone. "Victor? What's happening?"

"We're hit! Starboard wing's on fire! Can't see who . . . They're firing again! Oh God . . . Yvonne, we're going down!"

"Who is it, Victor? Who's firing at you?" She could hear the wind howling through the Learjet's cabin.

Victor coughed. "Can't see anything . . . Smoke everywhere!"

There was another *boom* and Victor screamed. "My leg! I'm

trapped . . . Laurie's dead! Oh God . . . I'm sorry. Yvonne, this is not the way I wanted . . . I . . . It's over, Yvonne! It's all over! You have to . . ."

Yvonne swallowed. "Victor?"

The connection went dead.

Yvonne stared at the phone.

Shaking, she let it drop to the floor.

She stood up and walked toward the door of her apartment, opened it and stepped out into the hallway.

She knew that the Trutopians' command HQ was less than a mile away. From there, she would be able to track the path of Victor's jet and find out exactly where it had been shot down.

And she knew that the Trutopians' computers monitored every military operation in the world. She'd find out who it was who attacked the Learjet.

I'll find them and I will kill them. Victor was wrong. It's not over. It's just beginning.

Victor Cross walked through the silent corridor of the hotel and entered the elevator. He pulled off his fake beard, then opened his shirt and removed the padding from around his waist. He straightened his back, adjusting his posture.

By the time the elevator had reached the hotel's lobby, he had completely shed his Reginald Kinsella persona. With his jacket bundled up under his arm, he walked through the lobby and out into the Trutopian community in Satu Mare.

Reginald Kinsella was the one man that every Trutopian knew on sight, but the people on the streets passed him without a second glance.

As he passed a trash can he casually dropped his jacket, beard and padding into it. He knew that the can—like all the others in this perfect and efficient Trutopian town—would be emptied before morning.

Cross walked the short distance to the public parking lot, found the Toyota he'd arranged to be delivered there and climbed in.

He drove to the southern gates and flashed his fake ID to the guards. They scanned it, checked it on their computer and saw that he was a visiting librarian from Budapest.

The guards waved him through and Cross drove north toward the border with Hungary.

After five miles he pulled the car off to the side of the road and flipped a switch on the package under the seat, then walked west across the fields, whistling quietly to himself. Behind him, the Toyota suddenly erupted into flames.

A low, steady whipping sound came from the west, and in minutes the unmanned Apache Arbalest touched down almost directly in front of him.

He squeezed into the small cockpit and activated the radio. "You there?"

"I'm here," Evan Laurie's voice said. "The reports of the Learjet being shot down are just coming in."

"Colin?"

"If he hasn't gotten lost, he should be reaching the mine right about now."

"Perfect. Trigger the news reports about the mine collapsing. I want them fed to every major news source before the Lieberstanian government gets a chance to deny them. Now let's get this chopper in the air. You're sure this thing can cope with the cold?"

"Definitely."

"Good. I don't have superhuman strength, so keep the speed down, got it?"

"Got it. Let's just hope that Yvonne was fooled."

"I'm sure she was. And if not, then . . . Hey, you know me. I always have a backup plan."

Still shaken from the terrifying flight in the Arbalest, Colin Wagner scrambled across the rocky landscape toward the only man-made structure for miles around.

Even though he had seen the satellite photograph, the platinum mine was bigger than Colin had expected. An area that was easily the size of ten football fields had been leveled out. The fifty-meter-high rust-streaked dome in the center of the clearing dwarfed the surrounding buildings. The ground was mostly concrete, poured so long ago that grass, plants and even a few trees had grown up through the cracks.

The entire perimeter was surrounded by a six-meter-high fence. At first glance the fence seemed flimsy, almost laughably inadequate, but Colin could sense the electricity pulsing through it.

Running along the inside of the fence was a three-meter strip of concrete that looked different from the rest: It was clean and smooth, and seemed somehow colder.

By focusing his enhanced vision, Colin could see that the strip wasn't what it appeared to be: It was thin sheets of metal painted to look like concrete.

A pit, probably. God only knows how deep it is.

So how do I get in without being seen?

There were steel poles set at fifty-meter intervals along the fence, each one holding an array of cameras, constantly moving, scanning the area on each side of the fence.

Could be infrared cameras, Colin thought. He concentrated on his body temperature, allowing it to drop to that of the surrounding area.

As he watched, a large door set into the base of the dome rumbled open and a man walked out, followed a few moments later by four others. All five of the men were carrying machine guns.

Keeping as low as he could, Colin moved closer.

Then the mine workers began to emerge, one by one, and Colin knew that going back was not an option.

The workers' hands were cuffed and they moved forward in unison: a slow, half-dead shuffle, forced to march in step because of the heavy chains that linked their ankles.

It seemed to Colin that most of the workers were men and women in their thirties and forties, though he found it hard to be sure of their ages because of the layers of dust and dirt that covered their entire bodies and ragged clothing.

Kinsella was right. It's a labor camp.

One of the workers in particular caught his attention. He was much smaller than the others. Colin focused on him and saw that he was a boy, not more than six years old.

Colin covered his mouth with his hand. He was unable to look away, a sickness churning his stomach as more prisoners filed out. One emaciated woman was missing both of her hands: Instead of cuffs, a thick strap had been fastened around her torso, binding her arms to her sides.

Then Colin realized that there were also people emerging from the surrounding buildings, these groups being led toward the dome. *God, there're hundreds of them!*

One pair of doors in the dome—much larger and heavier than the others—was now rumbling open. A dozen armed men emerged, walking backward, their weapons aimed back through the doorway. Something huge and blue began to move out of the shadows.

Colin adjusted his vision to peer into the darkness . . . And he now knew why he was here, why it had to be him and no one else.

He began to run, straight toward the electrified fence.

An alarm sounded and Colin could hear the whines of the cameras' motors as they all turned in his direction. He leaped at the fence, landed three meters up and felt a surge of electricity ripping through his body, powerful enough to instantly kill any human being on contact.

But Colin Wagner was not a human being. He tore a hole in the fence and pulled himself through. A shower of sparks arced through the air as he landed on the far side of the hidden pit.

He raced toward the enormous dome and, as he ran, concentrated on building up a powerful electrical charge.

The closest prisoners were the first to see him coming, but being chained together, they couldn't do anything to get out of his way.

His feet pounding on the rough ground, Colin leaped over the terrified, stick-thin men and women, landed, rolled to his feet and kept running.

The guards began to panic, aiming their guns toward him, and Colin blasted them with his lightning. He was aware that his charges were powerful enough to cause the men serious injuries.

He didn't care.

15

"I'VE NEVER EVEN *HEARD* OF LIEBERSTAN," Danny said as he and Renata strode toward General Piers' office.

"Me either," Renata said. "The news said that the entire mine has collapsed on itself. There're over a hundred workers trapped and no way to get them out. That's where we come in."

When they reached the office, they found that the door was already open and Façade and Warren were talking to the general.

"What do you want?" Piers barked at Danny.

"We heard about the situation in Lieberstan. We were just wondering when we're being sent in."

"As I was just telling Titan and Façade here, you're not. We've been talking to the Lieberstanian embassy, and they're insisting that nothing has happened."

Renata said, "General, they're lying!"

"They're not. And it's not your concern, Renata."

Façade said, "We've been hearing a lot about Lieberstan lately. Even if the reports of the mine's collapse are false, we should go there anyway. But the general won't let us." He turned back to Piers. "Because he knows the truth. He knows that the mine's output is less than a third of what most people believe. The U.S. government pays Lieberstan three billion dollars a year for platinum that doesn't really exist."

"That's enough!" the general shouted. "Not another word." He slid open a drawer in his desk and placed his hand inside.

Façade ignored him. "No matter what happens there, you're not going to be sent to Lieberstan. The platinum is just a cover for the money changing hands. The Lieberstanian government is actually providing us—and a lot of other countries—with a specific service. They're—"

"I warned you!" General Piers whipped a silver pistol out of the drawer.

There was a blur, then the pistol was no longer in his hand: Danny was handing it to Warren.

"Thank you, Danny," Façade said, his face grim. "They won't send you . . . They won't send you because if you go to Lieberstan you'll find out what's been going on there."

"What do you mean?" Renata asked.

"We found out the truth, and it looks like someone else did too. The mine didn't collapse; it's under siege. It's Colin. We know he was in Romania, heading east—somehow he must have learned the truth about the mine. We've only just confirmed its existence ourselves. Colin attacked the place, and right now he and the workers are fighting the Lieberstanian army. General Piers knows that if you go there, you'll take Colin's side."

He looked at the general. "You're worse than any of the people you condemned to death when you sent them into that place!"

The general roared, "Façade, you will be *shot* for this! This is treason!"

Façade leaned on the general's desk, glaring at him. "You filthy . . ." He stood back, his fists clenched. "Warren. Give me the gun. I swear to God I'm going to ventilate this guy's skull!"

"No," Warren said. "We're not going down that road."

"I've already left," Façade said, leaping forward, his hands grasping for the general's neck.

Then something invisible stopped him, kept him from moving any closer.

Standing in the doorway, Butler Redmond shouted, "What's going on here?"

Renata said, "You heard about the platinum mine in Lieberstan?"

"It's *not* a mine," Façade said, as the force-field dragged him back from the general's desk. "It's a *prison camp*! There are people high up in the government who know all about it. Same with the Canadian government, the Australians, practically every country in Europe, Africa, South America, Asia . . ."

"Is this true?" Butler asked Piers.

"Yes," the old man said, his teeth gritted. "It's true."

To Danny, Façade said, "Have you ever wondered what happened to all the supervillains who were captured over the years? Your real father spent a decade in a secret prison in Nevada. That's because they didn't know who he was, and they considered him to be relatively harmless. But what about the other supervillains? What about Terrain, and Slaughter and Brawn?"

"They're in Lieberstan?"

"They, and a whole lot more. According to our sources, there are almost four hundred prisoners in the camp. Most of them have never even had a trial. Fewer than fifty are actually supervillains. The rest of the prisoners are their associates, and their families. Since the camp was established thirty years ago, eighty-one children have been born there. Born into a life of captivity just because their parents were criminals."

General Piers extended a trembling hand toward the glass of water on his desk. "How . . . How did you find out?"

"Ragnarök's mother," Warren said. "She told me everything, told me where to look. All the details checked out."

Butler said, "But she's just an old woman. How did *she* know . . ." His face fell. "Oh God. She was there too?"

"She was. And right now she's waiting to be sent back there."

"That is absolutely unforgivable!" Renata said. "You can't send an eighty-year-old woman to work in a mine!"

Danny said, "So now Colin's there and he's organized the prisoners in a revolt. Good for him. He's about to get some help. We're going in. We're going to rescue them all, and we're going to shut that place down."

"No you are not!" Piers yelled. "Most of those prisoners are there for a good reason. Have you any idea what releasing them would do to the world's political structure?"

"No," Renata said. "And we don't care."

"Redmond?"

Butler paused for a moment. "I'm . . . I'm sorry, General, but I can't help wondering how long it'll be before you decide that *we're* more trouble than we're worth and we end up in a place like that too. I believe in Sakkara, but what you've been doing in Lieberstan is wrong. I'm with them."

Piers stared coldly at them. Slowly, he said, "With a word, I can have your families arrested. Your friends. Your relatives. Everyone you care about."

"No, you won't, because I've just realized something," Renata said. "I don't know why I didn't see this before. . . . General, you can shout and threaten and order us about all you like, but the fact is you are an ordinary person. *We* are the superhumans here. If it wasn't for us, you wouldn't even have a job. Sakkara is run the wrong way around. It shouldn't be us working for you. It should be *you* working for *us*."

16

COLIN GRABBED THE UNCONSCIOUS guard by the collar and dragged him into the relative safety of the huge dome. He dropped him next to a group of prisoners who were sitting on the ground, chained together.

"One of you search him for the keys. I've got to get back out there."

"Yer a damn fool, kid," one of the prisoners said. He was a weak-looking old man. "Goin' out there and savin' the lives of the men who kept us prisoner here!" The old man spat. "Whose side are you on, anyway?"

"Mine," Colin said. He looked around at the other prisoners. "Any of you strong enough to use a weapon?"

Most of the prisoners didn't even react, but then a voice from the middle of the group said, "I am. No point asking any of these guys, Colin. They've been here way too long."

Colin froze. *He knows my name! And that voice . . .*

Then the man who had spoken stood up. He was bald, with pale skin that was covered in thick red and white scars. He was taller than Colin, with a thin but athletic build.

"Dioxin!"

"Where did you think they'd put me, Colin? In some ordinary prison? This is where the supervillains end up."

He backed away as Colin began to stride toward him, his teeth gritted. "No, stop! Colin, we're on the same side here!"

Colin hesitated for a moment.

"Now, look," Dioxin said. "I know that what I did to you and your family was wrong, but even I don't deserve this."

"You deserve worse. Tell me where to find Victor Cross."

"You're worried about him at a time like this?"

"Tell me."

"Colin, I swear to God I don't know. She . . . Yvonne . . . Put some sort of mental block on me. I know I met Cross, but I don't know where. I can't even remember what he looked like. You should know all this. General Piers had me interrogated for a whole month."

"Who else did Cross have working with him?"

"No idea. It's all been wiped."

"How long did it take you to get from Cross's base to Las Vegas? Which direction were you traveling in?"

"I'm telling you, it's all gone. All I have left are a few fragments of memory. Me and you fighting in the forest, me and my men attacking Sakkara, then you and me fighting over the streets of Topeka . . . That's pretty much it." He held out his cuffed hands. "Free me and I'll help you protect the others."

"You have got to be joking! Cross murdered Solomon Cord, and *you* helped him. You're a killer, Dioxin. You always were and you always will be. You can stay locked up."

"You need me. Everyone else in this place is too old or too weak. Most of them can barely stand."

Colin paused. "If you run, or try anything . . . I will hunt you down."

"I know. Now, are you able to snap these cuffs or not?"

Colin took hold of the short, strong chain linking the cuffs, and squeezed it in his fist. He felt one of the links split.

Dioxin pointed to the chains around his ankles. "And these?"

There was enough space for Colin to insert his fingers into the leg irons and pull them apart.

He stepped back. "I'm warning you, Dioxin. You do what I say, when I say it. Anything else, and you're really going to be sorry."

"Understood." Dioxin pointed to the guard. "Now. The gun."

"I'm not letting you have a weapon."

"Colin, even with a machine gun I can hit a wasp at fifty meters. You don't want me to kill the guards? Fine. I'll shoot to wound."

Colin hesitated for a moment, then reached down and grabbed the guard's gun. He handed it to Dioxin. "Don't even think about turning it on me."

"There wouldn't be any point. I hit you with a volley of explosive rockets and you got up from it. Bullets aren't going to do you any damage."

Colin took a deep breath. "All right. I can hear the army coming back. We need to get the other prisoners under cover before they start shelling us again." He glanced upward: The metal dome was peppered with bullet holes and in one section had collapsed completely.

He led Dioxin back to the doorway. "I just need you to watch my back and provide covering fire if necessary." He pointed. "There're more prisoners hiding behind that concrete bunker, all chained together. I'm going to lead them back here. You see anything—anything at all—just tell me. I'll hear you."

Dioxin carefully leaned his head out through the doorway. "Seems quiet enough now."

"They're regrouping . . ." Colin ran, darting across the open space between the dome and the concrete bunker.

He skidded to a stop in front of the terrified prisoners. "Head for the dome—I don't have time to free all of you!"

The prisoners huddled together, and avoided looking directly at him.

"Move!" Colin yelled. "Now!"

An old man's voice came from the center of the group. "We can't . . . There's . . ."

"What?"

"We don't have the strength to carry the dead."

And then Colin realized that some of the prisoners had not moved at all.

"Colin! Heads up!" Dioxin's voice said. "Incoming!"

Colin looked up. A bright light was dropping from the sky, heading straight toward him.

"Everyone cover your eyes!" he yelled.

He concentrated, focusing his energy on creating a fireball. He could feel the ambient heat of the area soaking into his body, converting itself into flame.

He launched the fireball. White-hot, it scorched the air around it as it streaked upward toward the incoming missile.

The fireball struck the missile, erupting with a ground-shaking explosion.

OK, OK . . . That bought us some time. . . . He looked down at the prisoners, paused for a second, then began snapping their leg irons.

The first was a woman about his mother's age.

"Don't just stand there!" Colin yelled. "Get moving! *Run!*"

One by one, the prisoners were freed, and shuffled back across the open compound.

He took one last look at the bodies. An elderly man lay staring up at the sky, his chest covered in blood, his eyes still open.

He . . . He's the one who told me that some of the others were dead. He was dying himself.

They'd all still be alive if I hadn't come here.

Dioxin's voice said, "Colin? You hear me? Get over here!"

Colin turned and ran, trying to push the images of the dead out of his mind.

As he reached the dome, Dioxin said, "Got some others coming in through the east door, but it doesn't look good out there. They said that the big guy is still alive, but he's pinned down."

"Show me."

Dioxin led Colin through the dome. This was the first real chance he'd had to look around. Enormous pieces of machinery were fastened to the ground with bolts larger than his head. Ten-meter-long cams and pistons rose from deep pits. The place had the stench of scorched metal and there was so much rock dust in the air that Colin could feel it grinding between his teeth.

As he passed a woman lying against one of the machines, gasping for breath, he stopped and stared. The woman had gray, mottled tentacles in place of her arms, and a series of narrow slits in the side of her neck that looked like gills. *She must have been like this when she lost her superhuman powers, but she didn't change back . . .*

Dioxin said, "Calls herself Loligo. Been here about fourteen years. Caught sneaking around an Italian battleship, trying to sabotage it."

Colin crouched down next to the woman. "Are you all right?"

"Can't . . . Can't breathe . . ."

"She needs water," Dioxin said. "And lots of it."

"Where?"

"Over that way. There's a tank."

"Take her," Colin said. "Make sure she's all right."

Dioxin backed away. "We've got more important things to worry about."

"You will help this woman. Understood?"

Dioxin stared at him for a moment. "You're the boss. But don't blame me if these guys turn on you."

Colin felt something strange touch his hand, and looked down to see that the woman had pressed one of her tentacles against him.

"*Grazie . . .*"

Colin nodded, then turned and ran for the east door, leaving Dioxin as he attempted to lift the woman into his arms.

He heard a series of gunshots and a loud, almost deafening bellow.

Directly ahead, one of the guards was standing in the entrance, shooting at something off to the side.

As Colin ran he tried to generate another lightning bolt, but creating the fireball had almost drained him of energy. Instead, he picked up speed, heading straight for the guard. He leaped the last ten meters and crashed into the guard, sending him flying. And finally he got a good look at the guard's target. The enormous, half-glimpsed blue creature he'd seen from the hillside.

The four-meter-tall man was covered in bullet wounds, but somehow still found the strength to stand. He staggered over to Colin, the ground trembling under his bare feet.

Colin looked up at him. "You've lost a lot of blood."

"Tell me about it," the giant said, his voice rumbling. "Thanks for the save, kid." He reached down and patted Colin on the back, the blow almost knocking him over. "I owe you one. I suppose you know who I am? Or has the outside world forgotten me in the past ten years?"

Colin followed him into the building. "Forgotten you? How could anyone forget someone like *you,* Brawn?"

Yvonne stood on the control gantry that overlooked the monitoring room in the Trutopian headquarters.

She felt her stomach tighten as she read the information on the screen in front of her. The broken, burned-out shell of the Trutopian Learjet had been found crashed into a mountainside in Poland, twenty-four miles south of Rzeszow. There were no survivors. Under Yvonne's orders, a team was currently en route to the crash site to examine the wreckage.

So far, the Trutopian military strategists hadn't been able to determine who had shot down the jet.

They've covered their tracks well. Whoever did it knew we'd be searching for them. They're scared of us. And they should be.

Yvonne looked down into the large, dark room. The dozen

military strategists worked feverishly at their stations, overseeing the training of the Trutopian armies. The strategists didn't talk to each other. They didn't take coffee breaks. They didn't look up from their work, or even stop long enough to stretch.

The wall directly opposite Yvonne was one giant monitor, currently showing a map of the world. The Trutopian communities were highlighted in green.

She turned her attention back to her own computer and began tapping at the keyboard. The Trutopians had hacked into every major news source and communications network.

Yvonne's computer informed her that the New Heroes had left Sakkara and were currently on their way to Lieberstan. Right now they were in a high-speed transport—a second-generation version of Max Dalton's StratoTruck—flying over Kazakhstan.

The U.S. defense forces had been put on high alert, but no one seemed to know exactly why. Yvonne puzzled over this, probing through the reports and analyzing the incoming data, until she found the reason: a video message from Sakkara to the headquarters of the United Nations.

Yvonne played the video, and Danny Cooper stared out of the screen. Standing behind him were Renata Soliz and Butler Redmond.

"My name is Danny Cooper. I'm sure most of you know all about me. And some of you probably know why I'm contacting you now. Many—if not most—of your countries have been involved in the prison camp in Lieberstan.

"There are innocent people there, persecuted simply because they have a connection to someone you consider to be a threat.

Many of those innocents are *children,* born into slavery. You are supposed to be civilized people, yet you have knowingly allowed this place to exist.

"The New Heroes are going to Lieberstan. You will give us the support we need to put an end to the situation there with as little loss of life as possible. The prisoners are to be given their freedom, reunited with their families and fully compensated. I'm sure that some of the prisoners do deserve punishment, but not there, not like that.

"These are your instructions: You will immediately contact the government of Lieberstan and order them to withdraw their troops from the area. If they refuse, you will send in your own troops and you will *force* the Lieberstanian army to withdraw. After we have freed your slaves, the whole story will be made public. Do not doubt me on this: We will conduct a full investigation and we will name everyone involved. Those of you responsible cannot hide from us. You will have to answer to the people of your own countries.

"I want to make this very clear: This is not a negotiation. We are *telling* you what to do. The situation in the Lieberstanian platinum mine is intolerable and unforgivable. It ends here and now."

The video blanked out, and Yvonne stepped back, still staring at the screen.

Good for you, Danny.

The Trutopians are everywhere. We're poised and ready to go. It's like a chain of dominoes; Victor Cross and I spent a long time setting up the pieces, but in the end it all comes down to a single push.

And you've just provided that push.

17

Dioxin told Colin, "My guess is that they're keeping the airstrikes to a minimum because if they destroy the mine then they lose the only real asset this country has."

Colin nodded. "That's something at least. What about chemical weapons?"

"Then they'd lose the prisoners. The rest of the world pays Lieberstan a lot of money to keep us here."

Dioxin led Colin to the heart of the dome, where most of the prisoners had been gathered. They had raided the food and water supplies, and for the first time in years they were able to eat enough to fill their stomachs.

"How badly are we doing?"

"At least twenty-three dead," Dioxin said. "Another fifty or so wounded."

"Out of how many?"

"About four hundred, I think."

A voice shouted, "They're coming back!"

"Brawn! Dioxin!" Colin yelled. "Get them all inside the safest structures you can find!"

As the prisoners were rounded up, Colin turned and ran from the dome, reached out with his senses. He could feel the heat radiating from the approaching engines of the tanks. *They're close.* He slowed a little. *No, it's not that they're close—there're* hundreds *of them!*

He pulled off the headset communicator and examined it. It seemed to be working, but why hadn't Kinsella contacted him? *Maybe I need to get to higher ground.*

Colin ran toward the western gate, darted outside, then turned and began scrambling up the side of the dome.

From the dome's apex, he could see the tanks approaching from the east, surrounded by a massive cloud of dust. He turned. More were coming from the north, and the west. The mountainous terrain to the south prevented them from approaching that way.

There's no way I can defeat them all on my own.

Brawn is the only one of the prisoners who has any superhuman strength, and that's just due to his size. If he was as strong as he used to be, then maybe we'd have a chance.

Colin heard a low humming coming from the west, and looked up to see a dark aircraft streaking across the sky.

A roughly spherical object dropped from the aircraft, spinning and tumbling so fast that even Colin's enhanced vision couldn't make it out. Whatever the object was, it was glistening in the sunlight.

The object crashed into the side of the dome, bounced off and hit the ground rolling.

Colin chased after it.

He skidded down the side of the dome, landed heavily on his feet and reached the object just as its surface shimmered, becoming opaque, and human.

It stood up, and swayed a little. "Whoa! That was fun!"

Colin almost tripped over his own feet. "Renata?"

She grinned, and looked over to the huge dent she'd left in the side of the dome. "That was the coolest thing ever! Did you see that?" She jumped at Colin and wrapped her arms around him. "God, I've missed you!"

"What are you doing here?"

Renata stepped back. "Helping you. I see your hair's grown back."

"Dioxin's here."

"I know. You're keeping him locked up, right?"

"Well, not exactly. I—" Colin heard a scream coming from directly above, and jumped back. "Someone's falling!"

"Ah, he'll be fine."

As Colin watched, he realized that the falling man wasn't screaming: He was laughing. At about forty meters above the ground, his fall began to slow, cushioned by some invisible object.

Butler Redmond touched down with a slight bump. He raised his right hand to the communicator attached to his ear. "We're down. And Colin's here." He nodded to Colin. "Long time no see, stranger. You've got the entire Lieberstanian army on the way. What's the status with the prisoners?"

"Most of them are not really in any condition to fight. Brawn is here and he's still four meters tall—and still blue—but he's been shot about a dozen times."

Butler said, "Colin, from what we can tell, so far you've just been putting out fires, right? Dealing with the attacks as they come. We need to go on the offensive. My force-field can withstand practically anything, but there's no way I can make it large enough to shield the entire dome. We have to get all the prisoners into one place, the smaller the better. I'll protect them while the rest of you deal with the Lieberstanians. We just need to hold them off long enough for the UN peacekeeping force to get here with the rest of the team."

Colin said, "Where is Danny?"

"Right here," Danny Cooper said, suddenly standing next to Colin, a cloud of dust settling around his feet. "These two might be able to survive jumping out of the StratoTruck, but I wasn't taking that chance." He smiled. "So you phoned Brian, but you couldn't find time to phone *me*?"

Grinning, Colin slapped his friend on the shoulder. "I heard a rumor that the four of us are superheroes. Let's find out if that's true."

They began to run toward the dome. Danny was already waiting for them next to the nearest doorway.

Colin's headset communicator buzzed. "Finally! Hello?"

"Hello, Colin," a female voice said.

Colin frowned. "Who's this? Where's Mr. Kinsella?"

"Reginald Kinsella is dead, Colin."

Colin stopped running. "What?"

"Someone shot down his jet. We're not yet certain who it was, but all the signs point to the New Heroes."

Colin looked toward the dome, where Renata, Danny and Butler were entering through the doorway. "No way! That's impossible! They'd never kill anyone! Who *is* this?"

"You will keep listening until I say otherwise."

"Oh no . . ."

"Oh yes, Colin. This is Yvonne, your former teammate. The New Heroes are your enemies. *Destroy them.*"

18

"DANNY, WE NEED YOU TO SCOUT THE area," Renata said as she looked around the dome. "Get back to the hills and see what you can do about disabling some of those tanks."

"Will do."

Butler said, "There's a large platoon approaching on foot from the northwest. You should be able to slow them down a bit too."

"OK. Which way is that?" Danny asked.

Butler sighed, and pointed. "*That* way. Weren't you ever a boy scout?"

"No."

"Just go," Renata said. "And don't get killed."

Danny winked at her and was gone.

"Butler?"

"I know. Round up the prisoners and protect them."

"Not yet. . . . The east side seems to be their strongest point, so you go that way—see if you can use your force-field to flip over some of the tanks, create a barricade." She turned around. "Colin can help you . . ."

Colin was standing in the doorway, silhouetted against the light, his hands by his side. Tiny electrical sparks crackled across his fingers.

"What's the problem?" Butler asked.

Colin took a step closer. "You are." He raised his hands—and bolts of lightning arced out toward Renata and Butler.

Renata ducked to the side. "That almost hit me, you idiot!"

At the same time, Butler yelped and ripped the communicator from his ear. It was now nothing more than a lump of melted plastic and metal. "What did you do that for?"

Walking toward them, Colin said, "I don't want you contacting the others."

He leaped forward and lashed out with his fist, hitting Butler square in the jaw. The older boy flew backward and crashed against one of the giant pistons.

Instinctively, Renata rolled out of the way, spun around and slammed Colin in the back of the head with a crescent kick. "Have you gone nuts? Why are you attacking *us*?"

Without a word, Colin sprang to his feet and launched himself at her, catching her around the waist.

Renata crashed to the ground and Colin crouched over her, pounding his fists into her face and stomach.

Renata felt her lip split and she grabbed hold of Colin's wrists. *I'm stronger than he is* . . . She began to force him backward. "Damn it, will you just *listen* to me!" Renata shouted.

Colin didn't reply: He just kept straining to get to her, his eyes mad with fury.

Then Renata noticed a tiny electrical spark run over one of Colin's hands.

Oh no . . .

She jerked her head to the left milliseconds before Colin's powerful lightning bolt arced into the ground. A smell of scorched hair filled the air. *That could have killed me!*

Colin struggled to break her grip; Renata solidified her hands and arms, and forced Colin onto his back.

"Why are you doing this?"

Finally, he spoke. "These prisoners . . . Some of them are only children!"

"I know! We're here to help you!"

"Liar!" Colin spat. "You're like all the others—you'll do or say anything to get what you want."

Renata let go of Colin and jumped back from him. "We're your friends, Colin!"

Colin stood up. "My friends? No, you're not. Real friends would never betray me, never go behind my back and start working with Max Dalton. Your people killed Reginald Kinsella!"

Freeze him! Renata told herself. *Like you did with the lawyers back in Bloomington. Never mind how much it's going to hurt—just do it!*

But Colin was already charging at her again, his powerful fists coated in white-hot flame.

Renata leaped aside, ran for the dome's superstructure and began to scramble up the girders.

A bolt of lightning plowed into her leg, the pain rippling through her entire body. Renata watched with horror as her hands spasmed, letting go of the girder. She fell.

She turned herself solid seconds before she hit the ground, and could only watch, unmoving, as Colin raced up to her, lifted her over his head and threw her.

Her crystalline body tore a ragged hole in the side of the dome and crashed to the ground outside.

She had landed on her side, facing the dome's entrance, and now Colin came racing through, straight toward her.

Then he stopped, shuddered and started moving backward, struggling against the invisible force.

What the . . . ? Colin thought. *Got to be Butler. His force-field.*

Colin was lifted off the ground and pressed against the side of the dome.

Butler walked up to him. "Talk to me, Colin. What's going on here?"

"You're about to be defeated."

Colin was slammed back into the ground, immobilized. He tried to break free, but the force-field was holding him down too tightly.

Butler was right in front of him, raging. "You fool! You've sided with the enemy!"

"You New Heroes are the enemy, Redmond! The Trutopians only want peace . . . but you brought war. You murdered Reginald Kinsella because you know the Trutopian way is right."

"You've joined those nutcases? Well let me tell you this, Wagner. *We* didn't start this conflict. You did."

"He's right, Colin," Renata said, approaching from the side. "I don't know what's got into you, but this ends right now."

Burn them, a voice inside Colin's head said. He concentrated, channeling all his energy into heat.

The ground around Renata and Butler was starting to steam and scorch. The concrete blackened.

"Back away, Redmond! I know you have to drop the force-field every few minutes so that you can breathe—if you open it now the heat I'm generating will burn the air from your lungs!"

Then Colin found himself lifted up, the invisible force-field wrapped around his entire body like a shroud, and thrown high and far into the air.

He spun about as he fell, crashed through the branches of a tree at the edge of the clearing and dropped into the coarse undergrowth.

Before he could recover, the force-field gripped him again, squeezing him so tight that his radio headset was crushed against his skull.

Colin reached up, pressed his fingers into the force-field and began to pull as hard as he could.

He heard Butler gasp and the force-field's pressure increased.

Colin concentrated on the ambient heat from the area, from Butler and Renata themselves. He drew the heat into himself and channeled it through to his fingertips.

Renata said, "Butler, he's doing something! It's getting colder!"

"I *know*!" Butler grunted. "Turn yourself solid!"

In seconds, Colin's fingers were glowing white-hot. He redoubled his strength, and pulled.

The force-field ripped apart soundlessly.

Colin leaned over, gasping for breath. He could hear Butler saying, "Not possible . . . Not possible!"

He looked up to see Butler on his knees, his hands clutching his head. A thick layer of frost covered the area. Butler was almost blue with the cold.

Colin charged at Butler, kicked out wildly. His foot hit

Butler's chest, and sent him crashing against the same tree he'd slammed Colin into. The frozen tree shattered, and Butler fell to the ground, unmoving.

Colin looked around to see that Renata was curled into a ball, solid, covered in frost and ice.

He walked toward her.

Renata instantly turned human again and started to scramble backward, her feet skidding on the frozen ground. "Colin, please! You have to stop!"

"*I* have to stop? You chose to side with the warmongers, Renata! You had your chance to join the Trutopians. Now stand down, or I will *make* you stand down!"

Renata hesitated. "You have to fight *with* us, Colin! Everything has changed in Sakkara. We came here to help you, not to attack the prisoners." She pointed toward the hills. "It's those people out there you should be fighting."

He strode forward. "That was your last chance. You wasted it."

With a sudden lunge, Colin leaped at Renata. She blocked his punch with her left arm, and with her right fist landed a powerful blow square to his face.

Colin staggered back and stared at her. He used the back of his hand to wipe the blood from his mouth.

"I swear to God, Colin, I am on your side!"

But Colin wasn't listening: He was aiming his hands at her.

Renata threw herself to the side just as a lightning bolt seared the air.

She dropped to the ground, pivoted on one arm and swung her legs at his stomach. Colin doubled over.

Can't stop now, got to make sure he's unconscious!

She surged upward, forcing Colin back. He let fly with another lightning bolt that struck her in the shoulder. The pain was excruciating, but Renata knew she couldn't let that stop her: She charged at him.

Then Colin turned and fled, racing toward the electrified fence, leaping at it. He seemed oblivious to the shower of sparks as he scrambled over the fence and dropped the six meters down to the other side, and continued running.

Renata pounded after him. *I'm not immune to electricity, but maybe if I—*

The ground gave way beneath her, the thin sheets of concrete-colored metal buckling and splitting.

Renata instantly turned herself solid, plummeting into the darkness.

He tricked me!

Oh God, it's too dark . . . I can't see anything!

When she was in her solid form, Renata could feel nothing. Not heat, or cold or pressure. Not even the sensation of movement.

How will I know when I've stopped falling?

That's two down. Colin scrambled back up the fence, leaped from the top and easily cleared the three-meter-wide pit.

A part of him felt guilty for attacking Renata, but he reminded himself that she was the enemy. *If she didn't want to fight me, then she chose the wrong side. They all did.*

No, it's me. I'm on the wrong side! Yvonne is working with the Trutopians. They used me! He swallowed. *They're still using me . . . They made me attack my friends!*

No, the New Heroes are the enemy. No matter what they try, I'll fight them and defeat them. They're the ones who murdered Kinsella.

Yvonne's controlling me and I can't do a damn thing about it!

Colin found Butler half-buried under the frozen splinters of the shattered tree. He waded through the debris and lifted Butler to his feet. The older boy was clearly concussed, shivering, blood seeping from a gash in the back of his head.

Can't leave him here to die . . .

Carrying Butler over his shoulder, he began to run, back across the open space toward the dome.

There was a sudden roar of jets, then a huge metal figure sailed over the dome, and set down directly in front of Colin. It was almost three meters tall, bristling with weapons.

Stunned, Colin stepped back, allowing Butler to drop to the ground.

The armored figure strode toward Colin, moving with a grace and fluidity that seemed impossible for something this size.

It stopped in front of him, then a voice boomed out: "You're in an awful lot of trouble, son."

Colin stared. "Dad?"

19

INSIDE THE NEW PARAGON ARMOR, Warren Wagner looked down at Colin. "I don't want to have to hurt you, son. Stand down!"

Colin's rage-filled eyes stared back at him. "No."

"Colin, what do you think is happening here today?"

"I'm here to free these prisoners, and you are trying to stop me."

"You're wrong. We only just found out about this place ourselves. We came to help you protect the prisoners from the Lieberstanian army."

"How can I trust you, after what you did at Sakkara? You took the side of the man who tried to kill me. You chose Max Dalton over *me,* Dad! I'm warning you: Take your people and leave this place right now."

"Fine. That's exactly what we *want* to do. But you're coming with us. We need to find a way to deprogram you."

"I'm not leaving."

"Then . . . we're going to have to do this the hard way."

Colin smiled. "Renata and Butler tried and failed. You really think you can take me?"

"Yes," Warren said. He held out his right hand: He was holding one of Max's shock-bombs, aimed directly at Colin. The bomb activated: There was a deafening *boom*, and Colin instantly shot backward.

Colin skidded across the rough ground and stopped only when he collided with the concrete wall of one of the bunkers.

He jumped to his feet, but Warren was already on him, locking one huge mechanical hand over his face, and forcing him back against the wall.

Warren pressed his free hand palm-first against Colin's chest. There was a brief, intense flash of light from his palm, then he stepped back, letting Colin drop.

Before Colin could recover, Warren unclipped a weapon from his forearm, aimed and fired. The fist-sized canister exploded against Colin's face, enveloping him in a thick cloud of orange gas.

Scrambling backward out of the gas cloud, Colin began to choke and cough, then collapsed on to his back.

Warren flipped Colin over onto his face, pulled his hands behind his back and sprayed them with a thick, clear liquid that instantly set. He bound Colin's legs in the same way.

Warren stood back, disgusted with himself for what he'd had to do to his own son. He activated his communicator. "Razor? I've got him. He's immobilized. Get the StratoTruck over here."

"Is he OK?"

"Just get here, will you? What's the status with the Lieberstanian army?"

"They're retreating. The UN forces are on the way."

"Good." Warren reached up and opened the visor of his helmet. He crouched down beside Colin. "You conscious?"

Colin stirred, but said nothing.

"I'm sorry, Colin, I truly am. I had no choice. I know you're more powerful than I ever was, but there's no substitute for experience. When Solomon Cord designed this armor he made sure that it would be powerful enough to stop a renegade superhuman. We never thought it would be you."

The roar of the StratoTruck's turbine engines approached.

"We're going to take you back to Sakkara, OK? We'll find a way to help you." Warren sighed. "Your mother and I were worried sick about you. You shouldn't have just taken off like that! But we're going to sort you out, and we'll be a family again."

The StratoTruck soared over the hills, and touched down close to Warren and Colin.

Half a dozen soldiers jumped out, followed by Razor.

Razor looked down at Colin. "My God. Warren, what did you do?"

"What I had to do." He turned to the soldiers. "Someone go and pick up Butler, and check out that pit; see if you can find Renata."

Razor crouched down. "Hey, Colin . . . Col? Can you hear me?"

Still bound and blindfolded, Colin nodded. "I hear you, Razor."

"You're going to be OK. Man, I'm glad you're back with us. There's stuff happening at Sakkara. . . . But more important than that, it looks like the Trutopians are gearing up for war." He patted Colin on the shoulder. "But you can do it, right? You're strong enough to beat them, aren't you?"

Again, Colin nodded. "Yes, I'm strong enough to stop the Trutopians. But . . . what makes you think that I *want* to?"

Colin tensed his arms. There was a loud *crack* from the solidified binding material.

Warren Wagner darted forward, grabbed hold of Razor's arm and pulled him back from Colin. "Run! Get the others into the StratoTruck and take off!"

He stepped back from his son. "Colin, you've got to listen to reason."

Colin tore his arms free from the binding fluid.

Oh Jesus, the look on his face—he's going to kill me! "You just stop right there, young man!"

Colin paused.

Warren had used the tone of voice that had always worked on Colin when he was a child.

Then Colin grinned. "What are you going to do? Ground me?"

Warren tried to take another step back, but at that moment the armor's motors stopped working, and the display projected on to the inside of the helmet disappeared.

"I can control electricity, remember?" Colin said.

He charged forward and struck, plunging his hands right into the armor's chest plate.

Colin tensed his muscles and pulled.

He tore the armor apart, showering the area with fragments.

The ruined exoskeleton staggered, then tumbled backward to the ground.

"For God's sake, Colin! You've got to stop this! Can't you see what you're doing is wrong?"

Colin pulled his father out of the damaged armor and threw him aside toward the wall of the dome.

Warren raised his arms in front of his face. He felt the bones in his left hand and arm snap as they hit the wall. He fell to the ground, landing heavily, breaking his right leg. The leg that Ragnarök had broken over ten years earlier.

He watched, unable to move, as Colin used his lightning to fuse the armor into a pile of useless scrap.

Colin strode up to him. "The UN forces will take care of the prisoners. Against my orders, I'm going to let you all live. But if you ever come after me or my people again, I might just change my mind on that. Do you understand me, Dad?"

Warren nodded. "I . . . Colin . . ."

"Tell Mom I said hello."

"Please. Son. You can't do this. Don't leave us again!"

"I know I'm only thirteen and a half years old, but I don't need you anymore. I'm leaving."

Then a voice behind them said, "No. You're not. Not if I have anything to say about it."

They turned to see Danny Cooper standing close by, staring at Colin with revenge in his eyes.

20

THERE WAS A LONG MOMENT OF SILENCE, then . . .

Colin charged forward.

Danny shifted into slow-time, but Colin was still moving incredibly quickly.

He darted past Colin, heading for the doors of the dome to lead him away from the others.

Colin's arm whipped out at the last second, but Danny ducked under it, rolled and came to his feet behind Colin.

Concentrating as hard as he could on his speed, Danny shifted even further into slow-time.

Colin seemed to be moving sedately now, almost gracefully, as Danny rushed up to him and landed a powerful punch across Colin's jaw.

Another punch, and another. Danny knew that from Colin's perspective the three punches all landed in less than a tenth of a second. He continued pounding, over and over with his one arm, not caring about the shock of pain that ran up his arm with each blow.

Colin staggered back from the assault.

I can do this, Danny thought. *But even if I do manage to knock him out, what then? He's too powerful; there's no way we can keep him locked up!*

Danny made another charge, but as he raised his fist Colin

launched a lightning bolt. Danny could see the bolt coming, but couldn't move fast enough to get out of its way. The bolt hit his arm, the shock sending him skidding across the ground and in through the dome's entrance.

He grabbed a discarded metal chunk and flung it at Colin, knowing that in real-time it was moving faster than a bullet. It struck Colin's left arm and buried itself in his flesh.

Danny pressed home the advantage. He darted around Colin, and charged at him from behind, ramming his shoulder into Colin's back. Colin was shoved forward against the solid stone wall of one of the dome's interior buildings.

Colin collapsed to the ground facedown.

Danny switched back to normal time. "Stay down, Colin!"

Colin didn't reply. He pushed himself up off the ground, somersaulting over backward to land on his feet.

They stared at each other for a moment, then Danny shifted back to slow-time and charged.

He saw Colin concentrating, the same look he got when he was building up to a lightning bolt. Danny dodged to the left, out of the line of fire.

Or so he thought: Something erupted from Colin's body, an expanding shock wave of fire and lightning that rippled out in all directions.

Danny was caught in the explosion, the heat searing his skin, the light almost blinding him.

His entire body wracked with pain, Danny stumbled backward and fell to the ground.

Didn't know he could do that . . . Danny did his best to ignore the pain; he put all his effort into moving at the fastest possible speed; he knew that he needed more time to recover than Colin was willing to give him.

From Danny's perspective, Colin would take almost thirty seconds to reach him.

Slowly, the pain began to subside. *What can I do? He's almost as fast as me, and he's practically invulnerable. He won't listen to reason!*

Colin let loose with a white-hot fireball that scorched the ground along its path. Danny rolled to the left, but the fireball adjusted its trajectory to match.

He's controlling it!

Danny scrambled to his feet and ran, the fireball gaining on him.

Got to do something he can't anticipate!

Danny stopped, turned and raced toward the fireball, leaping over it at the last possible moment.

He kept going, straight toward Colin.

He saw Colin brace himself for the blow—and then Danny dropped to the ground and collided feetfirst with Colin, easily dodging his swinging fists.

Colin was knocked over like a bowling pin, but even before he landed, Danny was up again. He launched a powerful kick at Colin's stomach. It felt like kicking a concrete pillar, but it had an effect: Colin visibly winced when he hit the ground.

I've got to slow him down. But how? He's way too strong for me to just knock him out with a punch, and with only one arm I can't exactly strangle him.

Danny frantically looked around for something he could use as a weapon, but there was nothing.

Now, Colin was getting back up. Danny charged at him, knocking him onto his back once again.

Then he ran: straight out of the dome, back to where Razor was lifting Warren to his feet.

Without stopping, Danny snatched up a steel bar from the remains of the Paragon armor, and raced back inside to where Colin was getting to his feet.

God forgive me for this . . . He swung the steel bar.

It struck Colin hard across the back of his head. Colin barely reacted.

He raised the bar for another swing, but Colin managed to get his arm up and block the blow. For a moment, the two stood locked in combat. Then Colin grabbed the bar with his right hand and swung at Danny with his left, a low punch that hit him square in the stomach.

Danny collapsed on the ground, heaving. He flipped over onto his back and saw that Colin was standing over him, the steel bar in his hand.

Danny swallowed. *If he hits me with that thing I'm dead!*

Then Colin crouched down beside Danny and grabbed his arm to prevent him from moving.

He's saying something. Danny shifted back into normal-time in order to hear him.

". . . ever see you or any of the others again, you'll regret it. Do not interfere with Trutopian matters! You understand?"

Danny nodded. "Yes, but—"

Colin slammed down with the bar, right for Danny's face.

Danny rolled his head out of the way just in time; the end of the heavy steel bar plowed into the ground less than an inch from his right ear.

Colin picked Danny up with one hand and flung him out through the hole in the dome that Renata had made when he threw her.

In the air, Danny moved into slow-time.

He looked down and saw the ground approaching. *Even though I'm in slow-time, I've still got the same mass. . . . If I hit the ground at this speed I'll be liquefied. And there's nothing I can do about it.*

Danny swallowed, and could feel himself starting to panic. *If I can twist around so that my legs touch down first, then maybe I can start running. . . . No, that's crazy!*

Now, he could see his own shadow zipping over the ground to meet him.

Then, only meters away from collision, Danny suddenly felt his body turn rigid. His vision dimmed, and he could no longer hear anything.

He crashed into the ground and bounced three meters into the air, spinning. He tumbled to a stop, faceup. In the corner of his vision, he saw the StratoTruck approaching with Renata at the controls. Crouched on the vehicle's open ramp was Razor. With one hand, he was gripping the doorframe. With the other, he was holding on to Renata's arm.

As the StratoTruck touched down, Danny's vision cleared, his hearing returned and he found that he could move again.

He pushed himself to his feet and painfully made his way over to the StratoTruck.

Renata—shaking, her face drained of color—wrapped her arms around him. "I didn't know if I'd be able to do that!"

He smiled. "I'm glad you tried. Are you all right?"

She buried her head in his chest. "I . . . I'll be OK."

To Razor, Danny said, "How's Butler?"

"He's unconscious, but I don't think he's badly hurt," Razor said. "We just totally got our butts handed to us, Danny. What in the world do we have that can stop him?"

Then they heard the screech of tearing metal and turned to see something burst through the roof of the dome, moving straight upward.

Danny slipped into slow-time to see the object more clearly. *Oh no! As if this wasn't difficult enough!*

He shifted back to real-time.

"What *was* that?" Renata asked.

"That," Danny said, "was Colin's lifelong dream finally coming true. He's learned how to fly."

21

CROUCHED ON THE EDGE OF A ROOFTOP overlooking a quiet street, Stephanie Cord handed the small pair of binoculars to Grant Paramjeet. "Do your lipreading thing."

Three stories below, a heavyset man in a baseball cap was holding a thick package while he watched the approach of a woman wearing an expensive-looking overcoat.

Grant adjusted the focus of the binoculars. "OK. She's just said, 'What do you have for me?' . . . Can't make out what he's saying. 'How much? . . . I can give you two now, and the rest tomorrow . . .' Now he's handed her the package, and she's giving him the money. She's moved! Can't see her lips now." He lowered the binoculars. "Got to be cocaine."

"What makes you think that?" Stephanie asked.

"It's a rich person's drug. And she's rich. Look at her coat, her clothes, the way she carries herself. Plus that's a Lexus SC 430. Costs over sixty thousand dollars."

Stephanie nodded. "OK. Well spotted. What else does the car tell you?"

Grant raised the binoculars again. "Can't make out the license plate. . . . Wait, there's a sticker on the windshield. I don't recognize it, though."

"I do. It's a parking pass for the Donaldson Golf Club. And I see the edge of a child's seat in the back. So we know that the woman's married, with at least one kid."

Grant frowned. "How does the parking pass tell us she's married?"

"Because the Donaldson Golf Club doesn't admit women."

Below, the woman was walking back to her car.

"So do we follow her," Grant asked, "or the dealer?"

"We *should* follow the woman, but that's not an option."

"Why not?"

Stephanie raised her eyes. "Because we're on foot and she has a car."

"Right, right. So the guy, then?"

"We definitely don't follow him. You're not ready yet. Besides, it's almost five, and we have to be in school in a few hours."

They waited until the woman and the dealer had departed, then quietly climbed down the fire escape.

Despite her protests, Grant insisted on walking Stephanie home, even though of the two she was the one who least needed protection.

When they reached the door to Stephanie's house, she turned to him. "All right, I'm safe now. Go home, get some sleep—" She stopped. Grant was staring over her shoulder.

Stephanie turned to see her mother standing in the doorway, arms folded, a blanket around her shoulders.

"Get in here!" Vienna Cord whispered. "Right now!"

"Oh great." To Grant, Stephanie said, "I'll see you in school."

Grant nodded and left at a run.

As she stepped into the hallway, Stephanie said, "So now what? I'm grounded?"

"Where were you?"

"Out." Stephanie unzipped her jacket and pulled it off.

"It's six o'clock in the morning, Stephanie. Why don't we save time by skipping all the shouting and me telling you how worried I was? Tell me everything. Who was that boy?"

Stephanie followed her mother into the sitting room. *I could tell her that I've been seeing him. . . . No, she's too smart to believe that.* "That's the boy I was telling you about. His name's Grant Paramjeet. He wants to be a superhero. If I don't train him, he's going to do it anyway, and he'll get himself killed."

"He's not your responsibility."

"Mom, I—"

"Sit down." She picked up the remote control and turned on the television set, switching it to UNC, the Universal News Channel. "You have to see this. They've been repeating the same report all night long."

Stephanie sat down and pulled off her boots as she watched.

The screen showed a view of a large, dark area covered in lights. Stephanie couldn't figure out what she was supposed to be looking at. The reporter's voice said, "Details are sketchy as to the exact nature of today's incident, but there is no doubt that the New Heroes were involved. It is believed that earlier today Daniel Cooper—the son of the legendary superhuman Quantum—contacted the United Nations and presented his findings on the platinum mine. The UN immediately moved into action, freeing the trapped mine workers. . . . I'm told that we can now go live to the scene."

"That was the disaster we heard about last night?" Stephanie asked.

The screen cut to some shaky footage, as though the camera

operator was running over rough ground. The camera was moving toward the base of a large, rust-covered metal dome, where Danny Cooper had emerged from a doorway, surrounded by soldiers. Danny was covered in cuts and bruises, his black New Heroes uniform ripped and torn.

A reporter shouted, "Danny? What happened here today?"

Before Danny could reply, Butler Redmond stepped in front of him. "We have no comment to make at this time."

Danny glanced at Butler, and muttered, "Heck with that."

He was suddenly standing in front of the camera. "This thing have its own light? Turn it on."

Danny moved out of shot, then the camera bobbed a little, and Danny's voice said, "I won't break it. I just want to show everybody something."

The camera zoomed around the soldiers, through the dome's doorway and into a large, open area between some of the dome's inner buildings. Hundreds of people, all wearing gray, torn rags, were being treated by medical personnel. Danny's voice came from offscreen. "This is what happened here. These people were not mine workers. They were slaves."

Someone shouted, "Get that camera out of here!"

The camera zoomed closer, right up to where Renata Soliz was crouched next to an emaciated little girl with a filthy bandage on her left forearm. "I was talking to this girl earlier. Nine years ago she was born here. This is the only life she's ever known. Her name is Estelle."

Then the camera was knocked to the side, and a gruff voice said, "Cooper! I told you to get the camera away. You have to . . ."

Renata got to her feet and moved out of shot. There was a loud *thump*, then Renata crouched down again.

"Thanks," Danny said. "Something broke on one of the machines they use to process the platinum ore. It took a chunk out of Estelle's arm. It was treated by wrapping it in these bandages and waiting *fifteen days* for the doctor to make his monthly visit."

A voice in the distance shouted, "Cut the transmission! I don't care how you do it. Shut down the feed."

"They're going to cut us off," Danny said. "But before they do . . . ."

The camera pulled back from Renata and Estelle, then zoomed away again. When it stopped, it was out of focus, an indistinct blue shape filling the screen. "Hold on. . . ." The camera moved back a little, and the four-meter-tall man came into focus.

Brawn grinned at the camera. "Hi Ma! If you're watching, sorry about . . . uh . . . well, everything, I guess."

The screen went blank.

After a moment, the screen cut to the news presenter. The woman looked pale and shaken. "That . . . Uh . . . That was . . ." She glanced briefly off-camera. "And now over to Tom with the weather."

Vienna Cord hit the remote control's mute button. "When I realized you were missing, I tried to phone Sakkara. Eventually they put me through to Façade, who told me everything. Danny was right about the mine being a prison camp. A lot of the old supervillains are there. And . . ." She paused for a moment. "It looks like the Trutopians found out about the place, and sent in someone to free the prisoners."

"Who?"

"Colin. He's working for them now. He attacked Danny and the others when they tried to help him. He almost killed them."

Sitting in the control room of the Trutopians' headquarters, Yvonne stared at the bank of monitors. At first, as the news reports began to trickle in from Lieberstan, she had been stunned to discover that the New Heroes were still alive.

She had ordered Colin Wagner to kill them all.

He defeated them, but he left them alive.

Yvonne realized that she had been staring at the screens for hours, not taking in what the reports were showing. She sat back and blinked rapidly.

I ordered *him to kill them! No one has ever disobeyed one of my orders!*

She knew that there were some people who were completely immune to her control, but she had never expected that someone might follow her orders only partially.

Once, in Sakkara, she had ordered a man to stand up and sit down at the same time. The man had almost gone mad trying to obey the conflicting instructions.

The New Heroes should have been killed. That had been the plan. Yvonne had everything set up to follow that, and even had the press release ready to go. It explained how the world's most powerful governments had established the labor camp in Lieberstan, how the Trutopians had discovered it and asked Colin to investigate, and how the New Heroes had been sent in to stop him, and had not proved equal to the task.

But instead, Colin had left them alive. Now there was no way the people would believe that the New Heroes had known about the camp all along.

It's not over, Yvonne said to herself. *They're alive, but I still have Colin on my side. Even if I can't force him to kill them, he's still far more powerful than all of them put together.*

The phone beside her keyboard beeped once and she picked it up. "Speak to me."

"This is Clements in Strategics," a man's voice said. "We've tracked down a direct line to the UN commander in Lieberstan."

"Connect me to her," Yvonne said.

The phone rang for almost a minute before a woman's voice said, "Stonebridge."

"Commander, you will obey my orders. Do you understand?"

"I understand."

"You will issue an order that the prisoners are to be taken immediately to Sakkara. Only the superhumans and the children and teenagers. The human adults will remain in Lieberstan. If your superiors question this, you will explain that the children are potential superhumans, therefore Sakkara is the only facility equipped to deal with them."

"Understood."

"You will tell no one about this call." Yvonne hung up the phone.

There was a *thump* from somewhere down on the work floor. Yvonne leaned over the rail to see that one of the engineers had collapsed at his station, landing facedown on his keyboard.

I suppose I'd better let these people get some rest before they all die on me.

22

THE RADIO HEADSET THAT KINSELLA HAD given Colin had been destroyed in the fight with Butler, so he had no way of contacting the Trutopians. He also had no real idea how to get from Lieberstan to the United States of America. He was aware that America was to the west, but that was about all he knew.

He still couldn't believe it: He was flying, racing westward, catching up with the sun. Back at the platinum mine in Lieberstan, he had somehow *known* that he could do this. Flying was almost effortless: All he had to do was concentrate, will himself in the direction he wanted to go, and he went.

He had left Lieberstan at a little after one o'clock in the afternoon, local time. By the time he reached Portugal, the sun was low in the sky behind him.

As he approached the U.S. coast, moving westward but facing the opposite direction, Colin Wagner witnessed something that very few people have seen: the sun setting in the east.

He stretched his arms out and spotted the dried blood on his knuckles. The sight of it made him feel a little queasy, but at first he wasn't exactly sure why.

I could have killed them. I beat the hell out of them and only stopped when they couldn't fight on. God, what have I done?

No! They deserved it. They were part of the whole conspiracy to keep those people in slavery. Every stupid country in the world was part of it. That's why Kinsella was right: There shouldn't be separate countries. That only leads to war.

The Trutopian way is the only way. Peace above all. That's one of their mottoes. Peace above all.

But . . . Surely not peace at any cost?

On the StratoTruck, Renata Soliz felt like she was going to collapse from exhaustion, but she forced herself to stay awake. With Warren Wagner injured, she was the only one who could pilot the craft. *We should have brought Façade with us,* she thought.

Razor climbed into the copilot's seat. "Danny and Butler are asleep. You holding up OK?"

"Not really. That place . . . God, have you ever *seen* anything like that?"

Razor said, "Yeah. I have. But this isn't the time to talk about it."

"How's Mr. Wagner?"

"Stop worrying about other people," Razor said. "You need to get some sleep."

"Just tell me."

"He's on one of the copters. His right leg is broken pretty badly. His left radius and ulna are fractured, as are a lot of the little bones in his hand. He told me the names of them but I can't remember. He's got serious burns on his chest and stomach. But he'll live. He kept telling the army medics that they were doing everything wrong, so he can't be that bad." Razor looked out of the cockpit window. "Hold on. . . . Which way are we going?"

"North. Up over the pole and then down through Canada and into the States. It's the shortest route."

"The UN copters can't go this way."

"I know. And they don't have the range. We'll get to Sakkara long before them."

"I still don't think it's a good idea bringing the prisoners there. Especially not Dioxin."

"Yeah? Well when you're in charge, Razor, you can make the decisions."

"Look, I know you're upset, but you don't have to take it out on me."

Renata sighed. "Sorry. It's just . . . that little girl. Estelle. How could anybody treat another human being like that?"

"They don't see them as human beings, that's how." Razor was silent for a few seconds. "I did a lot of bad things. I never killed anyone, or anything like that, but . . . I stole cars, robbed from stores, burgled a couple of houses. I even mugged someone once. I was able to justify it to myself because I was living on the streets. I was telling myself that I was only doing what I had to do to survive."

Renata glanced at him. "You mugged someone."

"Yeah. I was fifteen, desperate for money. I saw this guy coming out of his office late one night, and I just walked up to him and told him to give me his wallet. He looked rich. Well-fed. I hadn't eaten in two days."

"And he just handed his wallet over to you?"

Razor shook his head. "He tried to run. But like I said, he was well-fed. Overweight. There was no way he could outrun me."

"Did you hurt him?"

Razor paused. "Yes."

"God . . . You beat up a man just for a couple of dollars."

"Actually, he had nearly four hundred bucks on him. That's a lot of money to someone living on the streets. I could have fed myself for two months on that."

"But that poor man! That could have been his wages. He might have *looked* rich, but that could have been all the money he had in the world."

"I know. But I didn't care. I was only looking out for myself, just like the guy who mugged *me* two minutes later was only looking out for *him*self."

"There you go. That's poetic justice."

"It didn't feel very poetic when he was beating the crap out of me. But you know what happened after that? The guy—the one I mugged in the first place—saw me lying on the ground and he came back."

"Even after what you did to him, he helped you?"

"No, he spat in my face and kicked me in the nuts."

Renata burst out laughing. "Sorry, but *that's* poetic justice!"

Razor grinned. "Yeah, it probably is. But that's how my world worked. I had to be the biggest and the toughest, otherwise people would walk all over me. And then Colin Wagner arrived in the shelter one day and changed everything. He was stronger than me, smarter and a better person. I owe him and Solomon Cord my life."

"And now Colin's back, and he's the enemy. Why do you think he's like that now?"

"You know the old saying: power corrupts. Absolute power corrupts absolutely."

"You think that's what it is? That Colin's turned evil?"

"No, that's not in his nature. I think someone is controlling him. There's only one person we know who has that ability: Yvonne."

Danny Cooper walked down the StratoTruck's ramp and stepped on to the roof of Sakkara.

A short, gray-haired, bespectacled woman in a business suit was waiting for him. "Mr. Cooper?"

"That's me."

She glanced past him toward Renata and Butler. "I need to speak to you. Alone."

"And you are?"

"My name is not important. Come with me, please."

The woman walked away toward the far edge of the roof.

"Better see what she wants," Renata said.

Danny walked over to the woman. "What can I do for you?"

"Your actions have had serious consequences, Mr. Cooper. Do you understand that?"

"I helped free a lot of people who were wrongly imprisoned, if that's what you mean."

"The president is . . . upset with the events of the past two days."

"So am I. Did he know about the labor camp?"

"No, he did not. If he *had* known, he would never have allowed that place to continue to exist. He has ordered a full investigation into the matter. General Scott Piers has been placed under arrest. He will be interrogated to determine which of his superiors—if any—knew of the situation."

"So what do you want me for?"

"The president has asked me to convey his personal thanks to you for your help, but . . . he feels that your approach was flawed. By threatening the leaders of the United Nations you have put us in a very difficult position. By broadcasting that footage of the prisoners you have exacerbated the situation. We have no doubt that your intentions were noble, but the outcome is very serious. This could topple the government."

Danny shrugged. "So? Your government changes every four years when you have an election, right? What's the difference if it happens a little early?"

The woman sighed. "Mr. Cooper . . . Politics is not about elections, or about power. It's about trust. The people need to feel that they can trust their leaders. Your actions have given them reason to doubt that trust."

Danny stepped back. "*My* actions? I'm not the one who put those people there and left them to rot!"

"We are on the brink of a third world war, Mr. Cooper. Did you know that?"

"Are you serious?"

"The Trutopians have been systematically undermining every country on the planet. They are united, they are trained and they are armed. Is it true that Colin Wagner has joined their ranks?"

"That's what it looks like."

"And you New Heroes were unable to defeat him."

Danny bit his lip. "What's your point?"

"My point is that you have shown the Trutopians that they are stronger than we are. If they should conclude that the world's powers have been weakened sufficiently, they will attack."

"No, they won't. Reginald Kinsella only talks about peace, not war."

"But Kinsella died yesterday. Even now the Trutopians are beginning to redeploy their troops. Our experts are certain that unless we can change the tide of events, the war will begin in a matter of days."

"So what do you want us to do?"

"We want you to make a public statement. You will appear on public television and you will tell the world that the labor camp was organized by the Trutopians."

"But that's totally not true!"

"Nevertheless, that *is* what you will say."

"I will not!"

"If we have to, we will do it without you. It won't be as effective, but we don't have any other option."

"No. When I contacted the United Nations I told them that I would tell the truth about the labor camp. That's what I'm going to do."

"Then you have condemned us to war."

23

As they watched the troop carriers set down on the grounds around Sakkara, the New Heroes argued over what their next move should be.

Butler said, "These people need us."

Razor nodded. "Much as I hate to agree, Butler's right. We can't just take off."

"I'm not staying here a minute longer than I have to," Danny said.

Renata pointed down toward one of the copters. "Hey . . ."

Far below, a dozen of the freed prisoners—all teenagers and children—were standing in a line on the grass while a corporal handed them black one-piece uniforms.

"At least they're getting a change of clothes," Razor said.

Renata pointed, "No, not them. Over *there*!"

They looked to see an entire platoon of soldiers quickly moving into formation around a Boeing Chinook helicopter, then the copter's ramp opened and Brawn crawled out.

"I actually kinda like him," Danny said. "I know he's one of the bad guys, but some of the other prisoners said that he looked out for them."

Butler said, "But he's not actually a superhuman anymore, right?"

"No, just big. When they all lost their powers the ones who had a physical change stayed that way. He's only as strong as any ordinary thirteen-foot-tall man would be."

"And there's Dioxin," Butler said. "They're not taking any chances with him. I wonder who else they've got. Terrain, maybe. What about Slaughter? They did catch her after Ragnarök's last battle, didn't they?"

"I think so," Razor said. "So what are we going to do?"

"Find Colin," Danny replied.

"But where do we even begin looking for him?"

Butler said, "The Trutopians. They—"

Façade's voice came over Danny's radio. "You kids better get down here to Ops—"

Danny shifted into slow-time and ran, leaving the others behind. He darted down the stairs and zipped past a soldier who had just opened the main door, then along the corridors and into Ops.

Façade was saying, "—because there's a message coming through that we're probably not going to like." He jumped when he saw that Danny was already standing next to him. "God, it creeps me out when you do that."

"What's happening?"

Façade pointed to the monitor. "See for yourself."

The screen showed the flag of the Trutopians, with the words STAND BY. After a few seconds, the flag dissolved into footage of a small, burned-out jet.

A woman's voice said, "Yesterday, an aircraft carrying the Trutopian leader Reginald Kinsella was shot down over Poland. All six people on board were killed. DNA analysis of the bodies has confirmed that Reginald Kinsella is among the dead. No one has yet claimed responsibility for the attack, but we cannot deny the rumors that the attack was orchestrated by the New Heroes.

They have long been opposed to the Trutopian ideals, and assassinating our leader is not beyond their capabilities."

The screen cut to aerial footage of the platinum mine. "Less than one hour ago, officials from the United Nations uncovered a mass grave next to the Lieberstanian labor camp. It is estimated that almost a hundred bodies are within, many of them children. The English philosopher Edmund Burke once said that the only thing necessary for evil to triumph is for good people to do nothing. We Trutopians strive to be good people. Therefore, we will *not* do nothing."

Razor, Butler and Renata appeared at the doorway, just as the screen changed to show a burned-out high school. "We closed our doors once before, when our communities were being attacked by the former supervillain Dioxin, using the armor he stole from Paragon. Since then, we have attempted to foster stronger relations with our host nations. We cannot in all conscience continue to do so. We cannot exist alongside the same governments who have knowingly enslaved innocent people in Lieberstan, and therefore we will no longer support them.

"All Trutopians who are currently outside their communities are urged to return home as soon as possible. The people who assassinated Reginald Kinsella undoubtedly did so in an attempt to break the Trutopians. But they are about to learn that we do not break so easily. From this moment on, the Trutopian communities are one unified state. We do not belong to any other nation. Any attempt to breach our borders, or to in any way subjugate our people, will be considered to be an act of war and will be met with appropriate force."

The screen went blank. Danny collapsed into a chair. "Just great."

"We'll find a way to sort this out, Danny," Façade said.

"How? They've got Colin on their side. He's stronger than any of us!" He looked at Renata. "You might be able to stop him, if you use your power to solidify him."

"I don't know. . . . I nearly collapsed from the pain when I turned you. If I lost consciousness, then he might turn back."

"Well, *I* can't do it," Danny said. "He's almost as fast as I am, and way stronger."

Butler said, "He tore my force-field apart."

"Then you'll have to start acting as a team," Façade said. "Hit him together."

Renata said, "Even if we do manage to stop him, how can we contain him?"

"There's also the matter of how to catch him in the first place," Butler said. "He can fly now."

Then Razor said, "I don't know how you're going to catch him. But if you *can* get him on the ground, I have an idea. But you're really not going to like it."

In Wyoming, Colin slowed as he approached the Trutopians' specially built town.

Yvonne had been feeding him directions for the past two hundred miles, and now—finally—he would see her face-to-face for the first time since her betrayal of the New Heroes.

He wanted to tear her apart, but knew that he wouldn't be able to get within arm's reach of her.

She directed him to the roof of the tallest building, and he saw that she was already waiting for him, standing next to one of the four huge automated sentry guns that were mounted on the corners.

He landed just as a set of large hangar doors were closing at the far end of the roof. Colin couldn't see what was inside.

He wanted to throw himself at Yvonne, to hurt her for what she had made him do, but he could only stand there, waiting for her to speak.

"You left the New Heroes alive. Why?"

"They're my friends. My father."

"I ordered you to kill them. Why didn't you do so?"

"I'm not a killer."

She began to slowly walk around him. "Most people aren't, but they would kill if I ordered them to. Why not you?" Without waiting for Colin to respond, she said, "Do you understand that you have been used?"

Colin nodded.

"And how does that make you feel?"

"Angry. Betrayed."

"You thought that Reginald Kinsella was your friend, right?"

"Yes."

Yvonne smiled. "Now here's the bit you're *really* going to hate. Kinsella died months ago. The man who took his place—the man you met in Satu Mare—was Victor Cross."

"No!" A wave of anger and hatred surged through Colin, staggering him. His knees weakened and he slapped his hand over his mouth as he felt the bile rising through his throat.

Yvonne gave him a thin-lipped smile. "He played you for a fool, Colin. All of you. Victor and I orchestrated this whole thing. From the moment I made contact with him, the New Heroes were doomed."

"You're lying! That's not possible!"

"There was no way we could predict everything that would happen—we really thought that Dioxin would be able to kill you—but it's all worked out the way we wanted. And everything led to this moment. The world's governments are about to fall. They have the New Heroes on their side, but we have you. And you're more powerful than any of them. There is only one way that this is going to end."

"Why are you doing all this?"

"You saw what was happening in Lieberstan. *We* didn't set that up: the so-called civilized nations did. Human beings have proven over and over that they are incapable of living in peace. For any one nation to be comfortable, others must suffer. That's the way it has always been. We will put an end to that by creating only one nation."

"That's what Kinsella—*Cross*—kept telling me."

"He was right."

"Maybe he was. But who are you to decide how other people should live their lives?"

"I'm a superhuman. I'm smarter than everyone else."

"I'm a superhuman too. And I'm more powerful than you can even imagine. So by your logic *I* should be the one in charge, not you."

"But I can control you."

"Not perfectly."

Yvonne sighed. "Many cultures share myths and legends, did you know that? Even cultures that seem to be very different often have the same roots to their folklore. One of the most common is the story of the flood. You've heard of that, I take it?"

"Noah and the ark, and all that. Yes, I've heard of it."

"The basic story exists in almost every culture. The world is filled with corruption and evil, and God—or the gods, depending on what you believe—sends a great flood to wipe out most of the human race and start again. That's what we're doing here."

"Killing innocent people to save other innocent people. You can't justify that."

"History will prove me right."

"I'm sure that Adolf Hitler believed the same thing. If you want to save the world, why can't you just use your power to order everyone to be nicer to each other?"

Yvonne's face contorted with disdain. "Oh *please*. Even you can't be that stupid. Human beings are like sheep. They spend their lives worrying about money and transient comforts while they ignore the real problems of this world. Overpopulation, pollution, corruption, crime, poverty . . . All of these problems can be solved, but the humans don't do anything about them. Not because they can't, but because they won't. Sure, maybe I could order everyone to be nice, but then they'd be no better than zombies. I want them to *choose* to be nice."

"You can't always get what you want."

Yvonne raised an eyebrow. "*I* can." Then she smiled again. "Besides, the humans owe me. They owe me big-time. I spent the first three years of my life in a glass jar, and the following decade imprisoned purely because of who my father was. General Piers was desperate to find out whether Mina and I were superhuman. Every day there was a new test, and the tests were not always painless. No matter what happened, I was never going to have a normal life."

"But—"

"They could do anything they wanted to us, and the law was on their side because technically and legally Mina and I are not human beings." Yvonne looked out over the town and spread her arms. "But despite all that, look what I'm doing for the humans. I'm going to create a whole new world for them. A better world, a stronger world." She glanced back over her shoulder. "Of course, to do that I have to get rid of the old one first."

"You're mad."

"By whose standards?" She walked to the edge of the roof and peered down. "This place is not what it appears to be. There are no civilians here. We built it to look like an ordinary town, but it's not. It's a fortress. We have weapons that can track and take down even the most advanced missiles before they get close enough to do any damage. And if the military tries to approach over land, they'll discover that most of the buildings on the outskirts are actually disguised heavy weapons. Nothing short of a nuclear strike is going to penetrate our defenses, and even then this building is strong enough to withstand that."

"They'll stop you!" Colin said.

"Let them try. The more firepower they direct at this location, the less they'll have to defend the rest of the world against our troops. I want you to familiarize yourself with this town and its defenses. Your friends will be coming here."

"How do you know that?"

"Haven't you figured it out by now?" Yvonne said, turning toward the open hatch. "I know everything." She smiled again. "The world is filled with corruption and evil, Colin. Here comes the flood."

Stephanie Cord pulled the remote control from Grant Paramjeet's hand and switched the channel to UNC.

"Hey!" Grant tried to snatch it back.

"My house, my remote."

On-screen, the female news anchor said, "Related news coming in from Monticello, Arkansas: According to witnesses, several dozen armed members of the local Trutopian community have raided a supermarket and cleared the shelves of supplies. This could be in retaliation for the earlier attack on the Trutopian community in nearby Jefferson County. Tom?"

The male news anchor said, "That . . . uh . . . that seems unlikely, Diana. The attacks happened within minutes of each other, and it looks very much like the Trutopians were provoked. It's understood by all Trutopians that the only way forward is through peace."

Grant said, "It's started."

"Don't be ridiculous!" Stephanie said. "No one's that stupid." She switched to the local news channel. It displayed nothing but a card reading, WE ARE EXPERIENCING TECHNICAL DIFFICULTIES. PLEASE STAND BY.

"That's probably just a coincidence," Stephanie said.

Alia came into the room. "The guy on the radio just said that the Trutopians have been declared illegal. If they don't disband, the army's going to be sent in. And there's a curfew. No one's allowed out on the streets until further notice." She glanced at Grant. "You'll have to phone your parents, tell them you're staying here."

Stephanie switched the TV back to UNC. The female news anchor was saying, ". . . getting literally dozens of similar reports from all over the world. The Trutopians are said to be heavily armed and more than willing to use their weapons against their enemies. Fifteen people are confirmed dead, with upward of a hundred injured. It's believed that—"

Her companion interrupted her. "Diana, we're getting a transmission from the new leader of the Trutopians."

The screen changed to show a teenage girl walking up to a podium that displayed the Trutopians' logo. There was a flurry of camera flashes.

"Oh my God! It's Yvonne!" Stephanie stabbed at the remote control's mute button.

"Hey! I want to hear that!" Grant said.

"No you don't," Alia said. "She's got the power to make you do anything she says."

They watched in silence as the camera closed in on Yvonne and she began speaking.

"What's she saying, Grant?" Stephanie asked.

Grant began to recite Yvonne's words: "The governments of the United States of America, Brazil, Germany . . . something . . . and Poland have all declared their intentions to invade Trutopian territory. We will not allow this to happen. I have a message to all the Trutopians listening. You all understand that what we're building here is a utopia, a perfect world. But it's not logical to build a perfect world on imperfect foundations. The old world has to be destroyed before the new one can begin." He turned to Stephanie. "My God!"

Stephanie pointed to the TV set. "She's not finished!"

Grant continued: "Something . . . didn't get that . . . Now it's time to stop talking about peace, and start making it happen. Some people say that fighting for peace doesn't make a lot of sense. They're wrong. It makes perfect sense. You will fight and kill anyone who is not a Trutopian. You will keep fighting until we are triumphant."

Yvonne simply turned and walked away. The camera panned to a shocked-looking reporter.

Stephanie hit the mute button again.

"Tom, Diana . . . I . . . I don't know what to say. We've just heard what sounded very much like a call to arms issued by this unnamed teenage girl who, it is claimed, is the new leader of the Trutopians."

Someone shouted off-camera and the reporter looked around wildly. The camera shook and began moving, bobbing and swaying as it followed the reporter. Breathlessly, he said, "Don't know if you're still picking this up. . . . We've just been told that we are trespassing on Trutopian soil. We've been given five minutes to evacuate the building or we will be declared prisoners of war."

The screen cut back to the two news anchors.

The woman said, "Well, Tom, it appears that the president was right to call the Trutopians an evil, illegal organization, especially if they've appointed this young girl as—"

Tom lashed out with his fist, knocking the woman to the floor. "*You're* the ones who are evil! You broadcast lies and slander about us!" He leaped to his feet, picked up his chair and was about to bring it down on her when a security officer darted in from off-screen and tackled him to the ground.

A voice shouted, "Go to commercial! Go to commercial!" and the screen was suddenly showing an advertisement for coffee.

Stephanie swallowed. "OK . . . *Now* it's started."

24

IN THE COOPER FAMILY'S QUARTERS IN
Sakkara, Danny watched as Façade carried his pajama-clad
brother Niall into the sitting room and sat him down on the sofa,
next to his mother.

Rose Cooper was wrapped up in her dressing gown, and
looked blearily at them. "So what's wrong now?"

"We're leaving," Façade said. "Not all of us. Just myself, Danny
and Renata. Warren's still recovering from surgery and can't travel,
so he and Caroline are going to stay. Plus there's Mina and the baby
to consider. Butler still believes in Sakkara, so he's staying too."

"What about Razor?" Rose asked.

"He's definitely staying," Danny said. "And we want you to
stay too." He crouched down next to his mother. "This is probably
the safest place for you. Sakkara is practically impregnable, you've
got the U.S. Army camped outside, and Butler has promised to
make sure you'll be OK."

Niall looked up at his older brother. "So you're going off to
do superhero things?"

"Yep."

"OK then. Just don't get killed or anything stupid like that."

"I'll do my best."

Rose said, "You don't have to do this."

"Somebody has to."

Then the door to the apartment opened and Impervia strode
in, followed by six armed guards. "No one is leaving."

Façade asked, "And how do you know what we're talking about?"

"After the attack on General Piers we started monitoring everything. I'm surprised you didn't figure out we'd do that."

Façade smiled. "Oh, we did."

"This situation is too volatile for us to allow you . . . to . . ." Her shoulders sagged. "Where's Danny?"

Danny Cooper arrived on the roof of Sakkara to find that Renata had already taken care of everything: She stood on the StratoTruck's ramp, surrounded by unconscious soldiers.

"Let's go," Renata said, racing up the ramp.

She jumped into the pilot's seat to see that Danny was already sitting next to her. "I wish I could do that," she muttered. "All right. . . . Razor, you hear us?"

"Loud and clear. It's all set. The equipment's stored in the back, and you've got enough fuel for about six thousand kilometers."

The StratoTruck's turbine engines whined into life and the vehicle rose sharply into the air.

"You're sure you know how to fly that thing?" Razor asked.

"Yep," Renata said.

"I hope so, because you're now officially on the wrong side of the law."

Renata laughed. "Hey! Doesn't that make us supervillains?"

The morning sun rose over the Rocky Mountains, illuminating Colin Wagner as he floated in midair. He adjusted his eyesight to compensate and resumed scanning the sky.

"OK, Control. I can see a fighter, moving fast. It's going from north to south. It's pretty far away."

"Identify the make and model of the craft," the Trutopian mission analyst said over the radio.

"Let's see . . . It's got the letters JSF on the side, near the pointy end."

"Joint Strike Fighter. That's an F-35 Lightning, Colin."

"Are they dangerous?"

"Very. Anything else moving?"

"A lot of activity on the ground, but nothing close. How goes our completely illegal and immoral war? How many innocent people have we killed so far?"

Yvonne's voice said, "Colin, I'm listening to everything you say. *Do not speak about the war like that again.*"

Automatically, Colin answered, "Understood."

He closed his eyes and listened. This high above the ground, it seemed that every sound reached him: He could hear gunfire, screaming, the rumble of tanks and the roar of helicopters and jets.

A new sound appeared and Colin opened his eyes to see that the F-35 had changed course, banking toward him.

"Uh-oh. The fighter's seen me . . ."

"Get out of there, Colin!" Yvonne said. "F-35s have got HPMs."

"What?"

"Directed-energy weapons—high-powered microwaves that could fry your insides. Move! Do *not* let him get a direct line on you."

Colin zoomed up and out of the path of the aircraft.

"Destroy the fighter, Colin!"

Colin pitched himself up and forward, and increased his speed, aiming to come down on top of the F-35. The noise of its engines was almost deafening and Colin had to almost completely shut down his hearing to be able to concentrate.

The pilot saw him coming and sharply banked the jet away from him; Colin increased his speed to match.

The F-35 went into a sudden three-hundred-and-sixty degree roll, and pitched up sharply as it emerged.

Colin streaked past it, unable to slow himself in time. *This guy's good. . . . But he can't keep it up forever.*

Colin darted after it, but again the jet managed to shift its course, throwing him off. *He's probably been flying for years—I've only been doing it since yesterday.*

He swooped down behind the craft, then came up directly beneath it. His fingertips brushed the fuselage just as the jet pulled up once more. *I'm going about this the wrong way,* Colin thought.

He hovered in place as he watched the jet zoom away, flip over and resume its attack. Colin dropped, plunging feetfirst toward the ground, then reversed direction just as the F-35 passed overhead. He smashed through the rear of the plane, shattering its engines.

The F-35 began to drop like a stone.

He watched it for a moment, then launched himself after it, catching up, coming close enough to see the pilot frantically grabbing for the ejection seat's lever.

The fighter's canopy was blown off, and the seat was launched. Almost instantly, its parachute was deployed.

Colin and the pilot both watched the F-35 crash into the

ground and break into thousands of pieces. Colin drifted toward the pilot and floated down alongside him, only a few meters away.

The pilot removed his oxygen mask. "What are you going to do to me?"

"Nothing. As soon as you land you're free to go."

For a moment, the pilot just looked at him, then he grabbed his handgun and aimed it at Colin's face. "*You're* not. You're under arrest. You attacked a U.S. Air Force plane, endangering the life of the pilot and threatening the security of the nation."

"But you attacked me first!" Colin looked at the gun. He'd never actually been shot before. His father had been bulletproof, but Colin still didn't know whether he'd inherited that trait, and wasn't too anxious to find out. "All right. Arrest me. It's going to take your people hours to get here. Do you really believe that you can hold the gun on me all that time? I mean, just one lapse in concentration and I'm out of here."

"Why are you people doing this?"

"I'm doing it because I'm being controlled by a superhuman who can make anybody do anything she wants. *She's* doing it because she wants to destroy our civilization so she can start a new one."

"You know what you're doing is wrong, but you're doing it anyway?"

Colin nodded. "Yeah. On the positive side, for some reason she can't order me to kill. But pretty much anything else she tells me, I have to do."

The pilot lowered his gun. "Man, that *sucks*."

"I know."

A gust of wind caught the parachute, and the ejection seat began to drift. Colin moved to keep pace with it.

"So this girl . . ." the pilot said. "How are you going to stop her?"

"I don't think I can. But there are others, the New Heroes. Trouble is, if they get anywhere near her, she'll order me to fight them."

"Where is she?"

"The Trutopian base in northeast Wyoming. The new town."

Yvonne's voice came in over Colin's radio. "Colin? You dealt with that fighter yet?"

"Yes, it's been destroyed."

"Good. Then get back here. I have another job for you."

"OK." Colin turned to the pilot. "I've got to go." He pointed to the east. "Nearest road is that way. There's nothing around here, so you'll be safe until your people come to pick you up. I hope they don't make you pay for the fighter."

"We'll send the Trutopians a bill."

Colin smiled and rose into the air. *God, I hope they win.*

Carrying two steaming mugs of coffee in his gloved hands, Evan Laurie nudged the door open with his shoulder and walked into the dark, freezing room.

The room had been carved out of solid ice. Even through his boots, thick socks and the rubber matting on the floor Laurie's feet were aching with the cold.

He stepped over a bundle of cables that snaked across the floor and carried the mugs over to Victor Cross's workstation.

"I hate this place," Laurie said, as he handed one of the mugs to Cross.

"So you keep telling me," Cross said. He nodded toward the monitor. "The U.S. Army is moving on the Trutopian HQ."

Laurie dragged over a chair and sat down next to Cross. "You know that this could be the biggest mistake of your life, don't you?"

"You should know by now that I don't make mistakes," Cross said. "Everything is going according to the plan. With Colin on her side, Yvonne will win this war."

"Right. And then she's going to figure out that we're not dead. She'll come looking for us."

"She won't figure it out. The DNA analysis of the bodies confirms that we died in the crash."

Laurie said, "You should arrange for the bodies to go missing in case she wants to examine them herself. Because if she does she'll spot that they're not real bodies, just charred lumps of cloned flesh and bone."

A message popped up on the screen. Cross frowned. "That's not right . . ."

"What?"

"Danny Cooper and Renata Soliz have left Sakkara. They've stolen the StratoTruck."

"They could be going after Yvonne," Laurie said. "Renata's immune to Yvonne's mind-control, and if Danny's moving fast enough he won't be able to hear her. She won't be able to control him either. What's their trajectory?"

"Uncertain. The StratoTruck's transponder has been disabled. But it doesn't look like they're heading for Wyoming."

Cross leaned back in his chair, staring at the monitor. "I don't get this. I've taken everything into consideration. I know these New Heroes better than they know themselves. I know their strengths and their weaknesses. I know how they think and how they react. Right now, they *should* still be trying to work out a way to stop Colin."

"Then that means . . ." Laurie paused for a moment. "Victor, it means that they've thought of something that you haven't."

Cross shook his head. "That's impossible. The plan . . ."

"It looks to me like they've got plans of their own."

25

IN SAKKARA, BUTLER REDMOND STOOD
at attention in Impervia's office as she interrogated him.

"You don't know where they've gone?"

"No, sir."

"Are you lying to me, Butler?"

"No, sir."

"Why didn't you go with them?"

"Sakkara is a likely target for the Trutopians. There are civilians here. I stayed to help defend them."

"What did Renata and Danny take with them?"

"Unknown, sir."

Impervia nodded slowly. "You understand that I cannot possibly trust you, Butler?"

"Sir?"

"You sided against a commanding officer. That's a court-martial offense. The only reason you're not in irons right now is that we might have need of your talents. When this is over, you *will* face a full investigation."

Butler swallowed. "I understand that, sir."

"Now get out of here."

Butler saluted, turned on his heel and marched out of the office. He made his way down to the machine room, where Razor was working at his bench.

"She didn't ask me if I knew what they were doing," Butler

said. "That's good. I didn't want to have to lie to her. You know that there's no going back from all this, don't you? No matter what happens, our lives as we knew them are over."

"What choice do we have? Sit back and let the Trutopians take over the world?"

"But this plan of yours, Razor. . . . Danny could be killed."

"I know that."

"Steph? Wake up."

Stephanie Cord turned over in the bed and mumbled. "Just another five minutes."

"*Now*, Stephanie!"

She opened her eyes. *I know that voice!* She sat up and stared at the young man standing next to her bed. "Danny?"

"Razor told us where to find you," Danny said. "Your sister let me in."

"What do you want? Shouldn't you be out there fighting the Trutopians?"

"That's where we're going. And that's why we need you. You can fight."

Vienna Cord leaned in through the doorway. "Daniel Cooper. I hope you have a good explanation for this!"

"Mrs. Cord . . . Hi. I was just—"

"Come with me. Now."

Danny followed Mrs. Cord outside, and Stephanie quickly pulled on her T-shirt and jeans, trying not to listen to her mother shouting at Danny.

She picked up her boots and went out into the sitting room,

where Alia was sitting on the couch, her legs tucked under her, as she ate a bowl of cereal. Grant Paramjeet was asleep in an armchair, snoring quietly.

"They're in the kitchen," Alia whispered. "So what does he want?"

"I don't know yet."

Alia shrugged and turned her attention back to the cartoons playing on the TV.

In the kitchen, Mrs. Cord was still giving Danny hell while at the same time she was putting a plate of scrambled eggs and bacon in front of him. "We saw it on the news, Danny! If you had just gone to the UN without threatening them, then . . . Well, I don't know. But that would have been the better thing to do."

"I know that now. But . . . We were annoyed." Danny picked up a fork.

Stephanie sat down and pulled on her left boot, then glanced up to see that Danny had already finished eating and was putting his fork down on the empty plate.

"Thanks. Who's the guy in the other room?" Danny asked.

"A would-be superhero," Stephanie said. "Long story. But he can't go home yet because of the curfew."

"Superhuman?"

"No."

"Then he's no good to us," Danny said. "Renata's waiting in the StratoTruck. For all we know, they might have a tracking device on it that Razor wasn't able to detect, so they could be coming for us. We have to get out of here as fast as we can."

Mrs. Cord said, "Stephanie is *not* going with you."

"They need me, Mom! I can't just turn my back on them."

"I promise we'll keep her safe," Danny said.

Vienna stared at him coldly. "No. Do not make promises like that. Stephanie, I *forbid* you to do this."

"I know, Mom. But I have to do . . . I have to do the right thing."

As the StratoTruck soared into the air, Renata glanced over her shoulder at Stephanie. "Good to see you, Steph. Are you ready for this?"

"I don't know that I'll be any help."

Danny said, "Yes, you will. Follow me." Steadying himself by grabbing on to the backs of the seats, Danny led Stephanie to the rear of the StratoTruck, where two large crates had been stored. "Can you open those? You need two hands to do it."

"Sure." Stephanie unclipped the nearest crate, and pulled the lid off. "Oh."

"Yeah. . . . Try the other one."

The second crate contained a helmet, a large object wrapped in canvas and one of the New Heroes' black uniforms.

"It's your size, I think," Danny said as Stephanie held up the uniform. "Bulletproof, fireproof, insulated . . . Everything you'll need. The helmet has an audio filter that will strip out the controlling frequencies from Yvonne's voice. Just don't forget that she's still very smart and incredibly strong."

Stephanie dropped the uniform and stepped back. "You're kidding. You want me to go up against Yvonne?"

"Not alone. But the more people we have the better. Butler's stayed behind in Sakkara, because he has the best chance of protecting the others. So it's just the three of us." He pointed to the canvas-wrapped object. "You'll need that too."

Stephanie reached into the crate, removed the object and unwrapped it.

"Razor gave it a complete shakedown; it's in perfect working order. You know how to use it, don't you?"

"Yeah. . . . Where did you find it?"

"Some guy picked it up off the street in Topeka, tried to sell it on eBay a couple of months back. General Piers's men tracked him down and made him an offer."

"What, they threatened to break his legs or something?"

"No, I mean a real offer. Like, they gave him twenty thousand dollars for it."

Stephanie paused. "I'm not sure I'm ready for this."

"You're more ready than anyone else. Your father trained you for years. I think he'd be pleased to know that his daughter was using his jetpack."

26

YVONNE STARED AT THE GIANT MONITOR in the Trutopian control room. It showed a map of the Earth overlaid with thousands of blue, red and green dots.

The blue dots indicated where a battle was taking place. The green dots—far fewer than Yvonne would have liked—showed where the Trutopians had won their battles. Their losses were indicated in red.

"Show me the enemy's movements," Yvonne ordered the man standing next to her.

"Actual or projected?"

"Both."

A series of yellow and orange arrows began to appear on the screen, showing the position and directions of the enemy armies.

There're an awful lot of them heading this way, Yvonne thought.

The door below opened and Colin walked in. He didn't bother climbing up the stairs to the gantry: He flew instead.

"So how are we doing?" he asked, hovering in the air on the other side of the railing.

"They're converging on our location. Our defenses should be strong enough to hold them back."

"Should?"

"That depends on whether or not they have Danny and Renata with them. Our last report says they stole the new StratoTruck from Sakkara and disappeared with it."

"Then it doesn't seem likely that they're coming here."

"Perhaps not, but I'd like to know what they're up to." Yvonne finally took her eyes from the screen. "Whatever happens, do not let them get close to me. Understood?"

Colin nodded.

"According to the projections, their first strike craft could be here within minutes. Our surface-to-air missiles will deal with them."

Colin said, "Yvonne, you can put an end to this now. No one else has to die."

"But I don't want to stop it, and I don't care whether people die."

Colin paused for a moment. "You do know that if I can find a way to break your programming then it's all over for you, right?"

"That won't happen."

"You can't order me to kill. I'm able to resist that, so maybe I'll develop a resistance to the rest of your programming."

"Then I'll just have to go to Plan B."

"And what's Plan B?"

"I call it the Colin-Killer Plan." She smiled. "You don't get to be as intelligent as I am without having a lot of backup plans."

"Like Victor Cross did?"

"Exactly."

Someone on the floor below shouted, "We've got two radar blips incoming from the north!"

"Activate the defenses!" Yvonne ordered. "Shoot them down!"

Colin could only watch in silence as the large screen showed a pair of white points streaking toward the Trutopian base, to be met with a barrage of missiles. The white points disappeared.

"Targets are down," the man next to Yvonne said. "Pilots ejected. They'll land just outside the perimeter."

Yvonne shook her head. "No, they won't land at all. Target the pilots!"

At the StratoTruck's controls, Renata Soliz said, "Acknowledged, Razor. I'll report back."

Stephanie asked, "So?"

"The army is definitely concentrating their firepower on the Wyoming base. They tracked Colin there, so they're going to forget about the rest of the country until they find a way to stop him."

"Then we have to get to him first," Stephanie said.

"They've already shot down over a dozen fighters," Renata said. "We'll never get close enough."

Danny said, "We get as high up as we can, I'll jump out and you solidify me before I hit the ground."

"Danny . . . I don't want to use my powers on anyone else. I'm not even sure I should be solidifying parts of my body—every time I do it the pain gets worse."

"OK. Just fly us toward their base and we'll try to come up with something else. But that might be our only option."

Colin didn't know much about military tactics, but he was pretty sure that one of the most important things a warrior could do was cause the enemy to panic. A scared soldier would fight harder, more desperately, but a *terrified* soldier would be much more likely to make mistakes, or simply drop his weapon and run.

Yvonne had ordered him to kill the attacking soldiers, but so far he'd managed to avoid doing that. *How is it that I have to obey all her other orders, but not that one?*

One of the gunships came roaring up over the roof of a deserted multistory parking lot, straight toward him.

Colin aimed his right arm and a powerful lightning bolt arced out and struck the copter. It shuddered and began to drop, and Colin could see the pilot struggling with the controls.

He resisted the urge to blast the copter again. Instead, he ran toward it. The gunship crashed to the ground, its rotors still spinning.

Immediately, a team of five soldiers leaped out and opened fire on Colin.

He felt the bullets pounding against his chest; they hurt, but they didn't do any damage.

Yeah, I'm definitely bulletproof now.

He charged at the soldiers, who scattered and ran.

Colin leaped at the helicopter's cockpit and punched his fist through the glass. The pilot was desperately fumbling with his seat harness's release catch, muttering, "No no no no no . . . !"

"Relax!" Colin yelled. "I'm not going to hurt you!" He swung his fist again and punched another hole in the glass, then grabbed hold of the joystick and ripped it out through the cockpit.

The pilot finally managed to free himself and scrambled from his seat.

"Well done. Now, run away." As the soldier ran after his colleagues, Colin jumped back from the copter, and rose high into the air.

All around the perimeter, the U.S. soldiers were encroaching. Strategically placed heavy weapons covered every possible approach.

Yvonne had told him that there was no way that the Trutopian defenses could be breached. *She was wrong about that,* Colin thought, *because they're definitely getting in.*

Half a block away, enemy soldiers smashed through the blockade with an armor-plated half-track truck. The huge vehicle easily scrambled over the debris and headed straight for a platoon of Trutopian soldiers.

Colin saw this and swooped down to ground level, darting through the streets.

He blasted the half-track with a bolt of lightning, but it had no effect. The vehicle hit one of the Trutopian guards, sent him spinning into the air and kept going.

Colin raced after it, but before he could catch up with it he heard the roar of a second engine.

He turned to see an even bigger and faster vehicle bearing down on him. A missile streaked from the armored car, straight toward him. Colin dodged to the left, clipped the side of a building, hit the ground and rolled. The missile slowed, turned about and aimed itself at him again.

The vehicle charged past, and a second missile was launched at him. Colin ran, and glanced over his shoulder to see that both missiles were right behind him.

Heat-seekers!

As he ran, he concentrated on his own body heat, forcing it to dissipate into the surrounding air.

The missiles were still coming.

Maybe they're not *heat-seekers—some sort of image-recognition!*

Then the vehicle fired again, and a fourth time. Ahead, Colin spotted an unfinished office building. He crashed through the glass door and raced through the lobby, up the wide stairwell.

He focused his hearing on the armored vehicle. A man was saying, "I see him! He's heading to the upper floors!"

Another voice said, "He's trapped. Detonate the missiles!"

Colin raced up the stairs four at a time, and smashed through the wooden door leading to the roof.

A deafening boom erupted from somewhere on the ground floor, and the entire building quaked.

He made a run for the edge of the roof, and jumped just as the office building collapsed beneath him.

He caught hold of a window ledge on the building opposite, and in one move pulled himself up and through the window. He realized as he was falling that the building didn't have any interior walls or floors. It was an empty shell.

Colin landed in a shower of glass fragments and rolled to his feet. One of the walls was clearly fake and the large track marks on the ground showed that the building had recently housed one of the Trutopians' heavy weapons.

The soldiers think that there are civilians here, so they're not using their heavy guns!

The building shook as something exploded against the outer wall.

Colin flew up to the roof and crashed through a window, then allowed himself to fall straight down, landing feetfirst on top of one of the armored cars. He dropped to the ground and ran, making sure that the enemy soldiers were following. *If I fly, they'll know they can't follow me and they'll give up the chase. I have to lead them away . . .*

Yvonne's voice came over the radio. "Colin?"

"Bit busy getting shot at!"

"Never mind that. We've got something incoming. We don't know what it is, but it's big and fast. We've hit it with everything we have, but it's still coming. It should hit just south of Pythagoras Square."

"I told you, I'm busy!" A bullet ricocheted off the back of Colin's head. "Ouch! Man, that was a good shot."

"This is an order! Find out what that falling object is!"

27

RENATA HAD TAKEN THE STRATOTRUCK as high as it could go, flown it directly over the center of the Trutopian town, then pitched it straight downward and rammed the engines to full speed.

Seconds before they were in range of the Trutopians' weapons, Renata turned the StratoTruck solid, as well as herself, Danny and Stephanie and everything inside the vehicle.

Now, as the vehicle screamed toward the ground, Renata Soliz felt like something was hacking through her brain with acid-covered knives.

This isn't right! I'm solid, so I shouldn't be able to feel anything!

She had hoped that by turning herself solid at the same time as the StratoTruck and her friends, she would be able to avoid the murderous headache.

Oh God, I hope I have the strength to turn us all back!

A barrage of missiles exploded against the side of the crystalline StratoTruck, knocking it off course. It plowed through the side of a building, demolished a large sculpture and smashed into the ground, showering the area with fragments of paving slabs.

We're down! Renata thought. *Change back, change back!*

The sun exploded behind her eyes as the StratoTruck and its crew rippled, changing from invulnerable crystal back to their normal state.

The StratoTruck's engines—which had been running before the change—were now inactive.

Renata slumped in the pilot's chair, blood pouring from her nose, ears and eyes.

As if from a great distance, she heard Danny's voice calling her name, but she was unable to answer.

"She's alive," Stephanie said, "but . . . she's not in a good way."

Danny stood looking down at Renata. "Oh Jesus. . . . Then we have to abandon the plan and get out of here."

Renata stirred. "No . . ." Her voice was weak, and cracked. "No. I'll be fine. Danny, you have to do it."

"I . . . I know. But you're not in any state to move."

"I'll turn myself solid. If I change only myself, I'll be OK. There won't be any pain." She gave him a weak smile.

A sensor light on the dashboard began to flash. "They're coming," Stephanie said. "Danny?"

"Just give us a minute, OK?" he snapped.

"We don't *have* a minute!" Stephanie moved toward the back of the StratoTruck, picked up her father's jetpack and clipped it on. She opened the second crate.

Danny crouched next to Renata, and put his hand on hers. "We'll stop him, then we'll get Yvonne, OK? When you're feeling up to it, come find us and kick their butts, got that?"

Renata nodded.

Danny said, "Look, about what I was saying before, that time on the roof of Sakkara when Niall interrupted us . . . ? I know this *really* isn't the right time, but—"

She pulled him closer and kissed him. "I love you."

Danny grinned, "Funny, I was just—"

Renata shimmered, and turned solid.

"Just about to say the same thing," Danny finished. He paused for a moment, then took a deep breath, and moved closer to Stephanie.

"She'll be OK."

"I hope so." Danny nodded. "Let's get this over with."

Colin turned left, vaulted over a burning car and darted around the corner into a wide, tree-lined market square . . . and straight into a squadron of four enemy soldiers.

He leaped into the air just as they opened fire, soaring over their heads to come down directly behind them.

Colin spun about, aiming a kick at the nearest man's back, knocking him into his colleagues.

One of the soldiers remained standing: He aimed his rifle at Colin's head and pulled the trigger just as Colin launched a fireball at the gun.

The rifle exploded, knocking the man to the ground.

Cautiously, Colin moved forward to check on the man . . .

. . . And was suddenly flying backward through the air. He collided with the trunk of a large oak tree.

What the . . . ?

He tried to sense the energy patterns around him.

Something invisible smashed into the left side of his face, knocking him to the ground.

He was hit again, this time across the back of the head. He rolled away, flipped over on to his feet and looked around. There was nothing.

Colin felt something wet on his chin. He put his hand up to his mouth and it came away covered in blood.

A sudden pain ripped into his side. He stumbled.

Something caught him in the upper arm, spinning him about. The invisible force crashed into his stomach, then immediately hit him in the back of the head, almost knocking him to the ground.

Doesn't feel like Butler's force-field—whatever it is, I'll freeze it. He focused on the heat around him, drew it into himself. In seconds his breath was misting in the air and frost was forming on the ground.

Colin was hit again, square in the face. He toppled backward, his head cracking off the concrete. He rolled aside, tucked his feet under him and jumped up. *Got to fly . . .*

He had barely risen off the ground when something powerful snatched his leg, pulled him back, slammed him facefirst into the ground. *Concentrate! Whatever this thing is, it has to use energy. I should be able to—*

Another hit, this one to his throat. Colin gasped, and began swinging his arms wildly.

His left hand collided with the invisible force, and a shock of pain ran up his arm.

Got to get some distance! Cold didn't work—maybe lightning will.

Colin turned and ran, charging across the market square. He sensed something brush past him, but before he could react he was hit once more, the blow to his chin sending him reeling backward.

The invisible object slammed into his chest, then his left side. A sharp blow to his right arm left it momentarily numb and useless.

Then the rain of blows turned into a storm: Colin staggered under the onslaught.

Every part of him was being targeted. His head, arms, chest, stomach and legs were being hit so fast that he didn't have time to react to each blow before the next one landed. The skin on his arms and chest began to erupt in cuts and bruises.

No, this is wrong! This can't happen to me! I'm one of the good guys!

Then a small part of his brain added, *If I'm one of the good guys, what am I doing working for Yvonne?*

Colin crumpled to the ground, unable to take anymore, and the pounding stopped.

I've sided with someone who doesn't care if she kills thousands of people.

He wiped the blood and tears away from his eyes.

I attacked my friends . . . I nearly killed my dad!

"Go on then!" Colin said. "Whatever you are! Finish this! After what I've done, I *deserve* to die!"

Then a figure materialized into existence, silhouetted against the midday sun. Colin blinked rapidly, trying to focus his eyes on the half-man, half-machine standing before him.

"What kind of creature *are* you?" he cried.

The figure said, "Jeez, that's a fine thing to say to your best friend."

28

DANNY COOPER HAD NEVER FELT MORE powerful than he did now. Or more ashamed.

He looked down at the mechanical arm that was attached to his body by a complex harness. With this weapon, he had beaten his best friend almost to a pulp.

Now, Colin was slowly, painfully, getting to his feet.

"Stay down," Danny said.

"Danny, I . . . I can't help myself. I have to fight you."

"You stopped a few minutes ago. You just gave up."

"That's because I didn't know what I was fighting. Yvonne ordered me to fight the Trutopians' enemies. She didn't tell me to defend myself." Colin leaped forward, at the same time blasting at Danny with a powerful lightning bolt.

Danny immediately shifted into slow-time, and dodged to the left. As Colin passed, Danny slammed down on the back of his head with his metal arm.

He switched back to normal-time, and watched Colin crash to the ground. "Just stop, Colin. You can break her programming."

"You think I haven't *tried*?"

"She ordered you to kill us before, back in Lieberstan, right? You had plenty of opportunities, but you didn't do it. If you can break that part of her programming, you can break all of it."

Colin wiped the blood from his nose and mouth. "Not that easy, Dan." He began staring at the mechanical arm.

Danny could feel the arm growing hot. "What are you doing?" He switched to slow-time, and examined his arm, flexing its artificial joints. It seemed to be working fine, but a couple more seconds and Colin could have melted it.

I'm going to have to beat him into unconsciousness, Danny thought.

He ran around to the opposite side of Colin, raised his arm and brought it down hard on his friend's head. He struck again, and again.

As before, it was like pounding a stone wall with a hammer. But no matter how tough the wall, sooner or later, it was going to crack.

Then, as Danny watched, Colin turned his head and stared at him.

He shouldn't be able to do that! I'm in slow-time!

Colin grabbed hold of the man-made arm with his left hand and hauled himself to his feet.

Danny tried to pull away, but Colin's grip was unbreakable.

Colin clenched his right hand into a fist and pulled it back.

No! Danny did the only thing he could: He grabbed for the harness's quick-release catch and ran, leaving behind the only chance he had of beating Colin. He'd sprinted six blocks before he risked looking back.

Colin was twenty meters behind him, flying along just above ground level.

Far ahead, Danny spotted the StratoTruck. *Can't go that way, don't want Colin to try to use Renata against me.*

He changed direction, put on another burst of speed, heading south, away from the StratoTruck. He wished that he was still able to move as fast as the day he'd lost his powers—and his arm. That day, he was sure, he'd moved faster than the speed of light. Somehow he knew that he'd never be able to move that fast again.

Danny risked a quick glance over his shoulder. The street behind was empty. He turned left at the next corner. He slowed down, shifted into normal-time, and looked around, hoping to spot a familiar landmark. *There!*

The mechanical arm lay on the ground almost directly ahead. He raced toward it, snatched it up, and had just clipped it into place when Colin was suddenly on him, crashing down from above, knocking him to the ground.

Stephanie Cord adjusted the jetpack's controls to set her down on the roof of a large apartment building next to the Trutopian town's main square.

I must be mad, doing this. It's been ages since I used the jetpack, and I've never been in combat.

She activated her helmet's radio. "Razor?"

"Steph? What's your status?"

"I don't think I've been seen yet. I'm trying to home in on Yvonne's position, but I'm not exactly sure which building she's in."

"Danny and Renata?"

"Renata's not doing so well. It hurt her a lot to change us. Now she's turned herself solid to try and wait out the pain. I don't know where Danny is. He went after Colin."

"Steph, we've got to put an end to this soon. The Trutopians are fighting like maniacs. You've got to get to Yvonne and force her to order them to stop."

A small crater appeared in the roof close to Stephanie, showering her with tiny fragments of concrete.

"What the . . . ? Someone's shooting at me!"

She hit the jetpack's controls and soared into the air, spinning about in the hope of spotting the sniper.

A bullet plowed into her side, knocking her off-balance. She immediately dropped down and checked her abdomen. The bullet hadn't penetrated her uniform, but it felt like she'd been punched in the kidneys. *God,* that's *going to leave a mark.*

As she looked, a red dot of light appeared on her stomach.

Stephanie hit the jetpack's afterburners and shot straight up. She switched her helmet's visor to infrared mode, then looked around again. Almost directly ahead of her, on one of the other rooftops, was a bright human-shaped image.

Stephanie darted to the right, curved around one of the larger apartment blocks, dropped down to ground level and headed straight toward the sniper's building. *Can't hit me from this angle . . . I hope.*

When she reached the sniper's building she executed a perfect ninety-degree turn, heading straight up, only inches away from the side of the building.

Ahead, she could see the muzzle of the sniper's rifle protruding over the edge of the roof.

She reached out her hand, adjusted her course a little and grabbed hold of the barrel, snatching it from the sniper's grip.

Stephanie set down on the roof a few meters away from the astonished sniper.

The man made a grab for his sidearm, but Stephanie was already striding forward, his own rifle trained on him. "Don't even think about it."

The man froze.

"Now . . . Thumb and forefinger only . . . Remove your weapon, drop it and kick it over to me. That's it. . . . Put your hands on top of your head and turn around. Walk to the edge."

The man shook his head.

"Do it!"

He slowly turned around, and took three steps. The toes of his boots were over the edge of the roof. "Don't kill me!"

"Where's Yvonne?"

The sniper pointed. "That apartment block. The top five floors are the control room."

"Defenses?"

"Automated weapons on the roof. Anything that gets closer than thirty yards will be shot down. What are you going to do to me?"

Stephanie jabbed the butt of the rifle into the back of his neck.

The sniper pitched forward and Stephanie grabbed the collar of his uniform, pulling him back. He dropped to the roof, unconscious.

Stephanie activated her radio. "Razor? I've pinpointed Yvonne's location. Trouble is, I won't be able to get close to it."

"All right. Just send me the . . . Aw hell!"

"Razor? What is it?"

In Sakkara's machine room, Impervia placed the muzzle of her gun inches from Razor's head. "You are *so* under arrest."

"Don't do this, Impervia. We're fighting your battle for you."

"You're using our resources to do it. Who were you talking to?"

"No one."

"Where are Danny Cooper and Renata Soliz?"

Razor straightened up. "I'm saying nothing."

Impervia lowered her gun and leaned back against Razor's bench. "Damn it, Razor! Why didn't you just come to me?"

"We don't trust you to do the right thing."

"What are you talking about? We're trying to stop the war."

"Yeah, and at the same time you want to get rid of the Trutopians."

"They're the *enemy*, you stupid little punk!"

"No, they're being controlled. They're just innocent people. We're trying to get to Yvonne, force her to put an end to the fighting. If she's killed then she can't reverse her order, and the Trutopians will keep fighting until every last one of them is dead. Or every last one of *us*."

Impervia's radio beeped. "Commander? We're picking up a lot of activity outside the base. Better get down here."

"Give me details."

"They're coming from the north and west, upward of twenty heavy APCs, hundreds of foot soldiers . . . Don't know how they got this close without us spotting them."

"Put the base on full alert and remove all nonessential personnel from the perimeter. Anything tries to breach the fence, terminate with extreme prejudice. Understood?"

"Understood."

Impervia glared at Razor. "You've got forty minutes to get your people to Yvonne. If you fail, and if it doesn't look like we're making any progress, I'm going to order a full retreat from the Trutopian town. Do you know what that means, Razor?"

"You're going to surrender?"

"No. We're going to do the only thing we can do to ensure that Yvonne is taken care of. The Department of Defense has given us permission to end the war by any means necessary. If we have no other choice, we will kill Yvonne and fight the rest of the battle the hard way."

"How are you going to do it?"

"After the last battle with Ragnarök it was decided that the world could never again allow a superhuman to become so powerful. There is a plan. Razor, very soon now I will be told to put that plan into action. Once I give the order a twenty-minute countdown will begin. That's how much time you'll have to withdraw your people from the area."

Yvonne checked through the reports coming in from the other Trutopian communities throughout the world.

The news wasn't as good as she'd hoped. Nowhere near as good.

The communities in Lesotho had completely fallen to the South African National Defence Force. The New Zealand communities were about to be defeated, and the Peruvians had apparently managed to quell the fighting without any loss of life.

Yvonne estimated that close to thirty thousand Trutopians had already died.

Her monitors showed her that Colin Wagner and Danny Cooper were still slugging it out, only a couple of miles from her position.

The Trutopian guards had found Renata Soliz: She was in her solidified form, still in the StratoTruck. The troops had set motion-sensitive mines all through the vehicle: If Renata turned back to human, she'd be blown apart.

So there's only Butler to worry about, Yvonne said to herself, *and he's back in Sakkara, protecting the civilians and the kids they rescued from the platinum mine.*

Yvonne sat back and studied her monitors. *It's time to put Plan B into action.*

She reached for the phone, dialed a number. Seconds later, a man's voice said, "Hello?"

"You will listen to me."

"I . . . I'm listening."

Yvonne smiled. "You put a device on all the phones in Sakkara to filter out the controlling frequencies from my voice. Very clever, Mr. Dalton. But you should have anticipated that we already had people inside Sakkara. Two months ago one of them swapped your cell phone for an identical, unfiltered model."

"Oh my God!" Max Dalton yelled. "Somebody—"

"Shut up. You will not call for help. Where are you now, Max?"

"Fourth floor. The infirmary."

"Good. You're exactly where I want you to be. Put your cell

phone into loudspeaker mode. Walk over to the bed next to the window."

"I'm there."

"Place the phone on the pillow."

"It's done."

"Good." Yvonne took a deep breath. *"Mina. Wake up."*

29

DRIFTING ABOVE THE DEBRIS-COVERED town, Colin knew that the battle was a stalemate. He could fly up and out of Danny's reach, but then Danny simply kept dodging his fireballs and lightning bolts.

This is the way it should be, Colin thought. *If Danny's keeping me busy, then I'm not hurting anyone else.*

His heightened senses scanned the area, searching for the telltale signs of movement. When Danny was moving at top speed, Colin couldn't see or hear him, but he still left a trace: a sudden rush of wind, tracks in the concrete dust, objects appearing and disappearing.

The problem was that Colin couldn't tell where Danny was, only where he had been.

Colin paused. He knew what he had to do to draw Danny out.

He darted away, skimmed over the roof of a small shopping mall and touched down in the large triangular area known as Pythagoras Square.

Colin walked to the edge of the impact crater and looked down at the StratoTruck.

He drifted down into the crater and hovered in front of the vehicle. Through the canopy, he could see Renata's crystalline form.

Then something plowed into his side, knocking him away from the StratoTruck, out of the crater.

As Colin skidded on his back, ripping a channel through the broken paving slabs, Danny materialized in front of him. "You stay the hell away from her!"

Feeling disgusted with himself, Colin rose into the air and flew straight toward the StratoTruck.

Danny raced forward, his artificial arm outstretched toward the back of Colin's neck.

Faster! Go to get to him before he . . .

Colin reached the StratoTruck and smashed through the canopy.

Danny saw a small octagonal device attached to the dashboard turn red, then white, and slowly begin to blossom. A similar device on the hatch did the same, then a dozen more scattered throughout the vehicle.

Mines!

Danny reversed direction, and ran for cover as the mines bloomed into white balls of fire.

Slowly, almost gracefully, the StratoTruck was ripped apart by the huge explosion.

Danny felt the ground shake and ripple under his feet. The buildings around him began to shudder, their remaining windows fracturing, the glass splintering inward.

He jumped aside as a head-sized chunk of the StratoTruck's fuselage passed by, shot straight through an abandoned car and buried itself in the wall of an apartment block.

Renata . . . I hope she can survive this.

Metal, concrete and glass shrapnel rained down on Pythagoras Square as Danny raced forward.

The StratoTruck was gone, the impact crater it had made upon landing now double in size.

Danny shifted back into normal-time. The sound of the explosion was still echoing through the town.

In the center of the crater, Renata's solidified body was perfectly intact.

Danny almost cried with relief. *Thank God! But where's Colin?*

Something heavy thumped to the ground nearby, and Danny scrambled up the side of the crater to see what it was.

Colin Wagner lay unmoving on the ground.

Danny walked up to him and nudged him with the mechanical arm. "Col?"

Colin groaned once.

Danny stepped back and activated his radio. "Razor? It's me. Colin's down. At least, he is for the moment, but—"

"Danny!" Razor's voice said. "Get back to Sakkara as fast as you can. We're under siege here. The Trutopians are breaking through the perimeter and . . . Mina's awake!"

"How?"

"Never mind how—just get here! Butler's trying to hold her back but she's . . . God, I've never seen anything like it."

If Razor said anything further, Danny didn't hear it: He was already in slow-time, racing toward the town's southern gate.

Sakkara's a thousand kilometers away, Danny thought as he dodged around a scared-looking platoon of young U.S. soldiers. *But that's only in a straight line. . . . The roads don't go in straight lines.*

He darted back to the marines, pulled a map from the hands

of one of the soldiers and resumed running. *Right. Got to find Interstate 90, go east until* . . . The wind shredded the map, leaving a trail of paper confetti behind him. *Just perfect* . . .

Stephanie Cord had never felt so alone—or so scared—in her life. She'd been unable to reestablish contact with Razor, and several times she'd had to resist the urge to simply fly away from the Trutopian base.

Now, she was crouching on the balcony of an apartment building, using the telescopic mode built into her helmet to watch a squadron of soldiers who were pinned down by a Trutopian armed with a rocket launcher.

She was thankful that so few Trutopian troops were on the streets. *They've put too much faith in their automated weapons,* she thought. *And they definitely underestimated the U.S. military.*

There was a sudden *whoosh* as another rocket streaked toward the soldiers' position. It exploded against the thick wall they were using for cover.

Stephanie grabbed the balcony's railing and pulled herself over, only activating her jetpack a few meters above the ground.

She followed the rocket's dissipating smoke trail back to its source—a hundred-meter-high radio mast situated in the west side of the town.

Her infrared visor showed a strong heat source at the top of the mast. She could make out two human figures.

There was a sudden bright flare as another rocket was launched, this one heading straight toward her.

Stephanie dodged to the left, and could feel the heat of the missile as it missed her by less than a meter.

These guys are good.

Two more missiles were simultaneously launched at her. *Oh fantastic! They've* both *got rocket launchers!* She dropped down to street level and darted to the left, then right. The missiles blew large craters in the asphalt, showering Stephanie with fist-sized chunks.

Directly ahead, she could see the base of the radio mast. It was at least five meters across, a complex network of reinforced steel girders set into a heavy concrete base. *Or maybe there's another way . . .*

Stephanie ramped the jetpack up to full power, zooming toward the radio mast's base.

She passed through a gap between two girders, immediately pulled back on the controls, then angled her flight upward, aiming straight toward the top of the mast.

They'd have to be incredibly stupid to use their rocket launchers now, Stephanie thought as she dodged and weaved between the girders, *so I should be able to—*

The two Trutopian soldiers fired. The first missile struck one of the girders above her, shaking the whole mast. The second missile streaked toward Stephanie.

She shifted aside and the missile shot past her and exploded against the base, shattering the concrete.

The radio mast creaked and shuddered. One of the soldiers lost his balance and fell.

Stephanie darted out from among the girders and grabbed hold of the terrified man's right arm. "Hold tight!" she yelled. "I'm going to get your friend!" She angled back toward the top of the mast, her arm straining, the jetpack slowing under the extra weight.

But the other soldier wasn't willing to be captured so easily: He pulled out a handgun and began firing at Stephanie.

A bullet clipped Stephanie's leg, another ricocheted off her helmet. To the man she was carrying, she shouted, "I can't grab him. Need one hand to control the jetpack. You'll have to do it."

The man didn't respond. Stephanie glanced down to see that he was hanging limp, barely conscious. One of his colleague's bullets had struck him in the chest.

Then the radio mast buckled. A hundred tons of steel girders toppled to the ground, completely crushing a small hotel and the office buildings around it.

Shaking, Stephanie flew toward the U.S. soldiers' location, and lowered the wounded Trutopian fighter to the ground, carefully placing him on his back. She pressed her hands over the bullet wound and looked up as a U.S. soldier with sergeant's stripes on his shoulder ran toward her.

"The other one!" Stephanie said. "He could still be alive."

"My men will check on him. How's this one?"

"There's a lot of blood."

The sergeant placed his hand on Stephanie's arm. "OK, miss. You did good. Now step back and leave it to us. We'll take care of him from here." He crouched over the Trutopian soldier and examined the wound. "Doesn't look too bad. I think he'll make it. Good thing his friend hit him, though."

"*What?* These men aren't evil, sergeant. They're being controlled!"

"So I've heard," the sergeant said. "But look at this . . ." He pointed.

The unconscious Trutopian soldier was holding a pistol in his left hand.

"A couple of seconds later and he'd have blown your head off." The sergeant stood up. "So. The big question: Who are you and what are you doing here?"

"My name is Stephanie Cord, I'm—"

"One of Paragon's daughters." He smiled. "All right, Ms. Cord. Thanks for the assist. Now this war is over for you. Get yourself out of this town and back behind the line."

"No." She activated the jetpack and rose slowly into the air. "My friends are still here. They need my help."

The sergeant said, "Just like your old man. The apple doesn't fall far from the tree, does it? All right, Stephanie." He pulled the Trutopian soldier's gun from his hand, and passed it to Stephanie. "You'll need this."

"I don't use guns. My father never did."

"Your father had weapons built into his armor."

Hesitantly, Stephanie dropped back down and took hold of the gun. "All right," she said. "Just in case."

Back at Sakkara, Razor and Max Dalton struggled to carry the unconscious Warren Wagner up the stairs and onto the roof.

"She just woke up, like nothing had happened," Max said, almost shouting over the noise of the battle. "Didn't say a word. She got out of bed, pulled on her uniform and then . . . I don't know. I can't remember."

Something exploded against the side of the pyramidal building, trembling the roof. Razor stumbled, almost lost his grip on Warren. Ahead, Façade was helping Mrs. Cooper into a helicopter.

"She's fast," Max said. "Not as fast as Danny, but athletic. Bouncing off the walls, spinning . . ."

"Dalton!" Razor said. "Focus on what you're doing! Forget about Mina—Butler can take care of her."

"He doesn't stand a chance."

Running toward them, Façade shouted, "Move! The Trutopians got through the fence—they're swarming into the compound! Razor, I'll take over. You go see who's left."

Razor stepped away from Warren, then took the stairs three at a time and rushed into the corridor, where he saw Caroline Wagner and Niall Cooper running toward him.

Caroline looked pale, exhausted and out of breath.

"Go!" Caroline said, panting. "We're the last! Butler's down." She sagged forward.

Razor caught her. "Niall, get out onto the roof and into the copter!"

"But . . . Mrs. Wagner!"

"We'll be right behind you. Run! Don't stop for anything!"

Niall darted away.

A man screamed on the floor below.

"Razor . . . Go," Caroline said. "Leave me."

"As Colin might say, not bloody likely." He scooped Caroline up in his arms and began to run toward the entrance. "You've got the baby to think about."

He charged up the stairs, out onto the roof.

Façade stood in the copter's hatchway, Niall standing next to him. "Give her to me."

Razor passed Caroline up to Façade's waiting arms, then grabbed the handhold next to the hatchway and began to pull himself up.

Something slammed into his back, sending him sprawling.

He lifted his head to look around just as Mina's foot caught him in the throat.

He tried to make a grab for her but she somersaulted backward out of reach, dropped to the ground and spun on her hands, again clipping him in the face with her feet.

Razor spat out a mouthful of blood and tried to roll underneath the helicopter; a powerful hand grabbed his ankle and dragged him out, his fingernails splintering painfully on the concrete as he desperately tried to find a handhold.

"Get out of here, Façade!" Razor yelled, his voice cracked and wheezing. "Now!"

"No! We're not leaving you!"

"Just go!"

They locked eyes for a second, then Façade nodded, and saluted. He stepped back and the hatch began to close.

As the helicopter soared into the air, Mina lifted Razor up with her left hand and stared at him.

Through his bloodshot eyes, Razor stared back. "Stop! Please!"

She pulled back her right fist and punched.

The blow sent Razor sliding across the roof.

That should have killed me . . . Then he spotted Butler Redmond—his face covered in cuts and bruises—slowly making his way up the stairs. *He used his force-field to cushion the punch.*

As he watched, Mina was knocked backward as though hit by a sudden wall of invisible water. She tumbled once, landing on her feet, but the force-field hit her again and again. Then she was picked up, lifted into the air as though gripped by a giant unseen hand.

Then she disappeared.

Butler staggered backward. "What? How did she . . . ?"

Razor screamed, "Behind you!"

Butler whirled around to see that Mina was lunging at him. She collided with the invisible force-field and dropped to the ground, landing on her hands and feet, crouched, ready to pounce.

As Razor watched, Butler concentrated on the force-field, strengthening it, so that it became almost solid, visible only by the light it refracted.

Razor looked around to see that he too was now safe inside the force-field.

"How did she *do* that?" Butler asked.

"She must be a short-range teleporter," Razor said, his voice still croaking. "Watch her. . . . She could—"

Mina vanished.

And reappeared inside the force-field, directly behind Butler. She locked her hands around his throat, and began to squeeze.

Butler struggled to break free and dropped to his knees, his force-field disappearing.

Razor shouted, "Mina! No! You'll kill him!"

There was a blur and a burst of wind, and suddenly Mina was gone and Butler crashed facedown on the roof.

Ignoring the pain in his back and arms, Razor staggered over. "Butler! Talk to me! You OK?"

He checked Butler's pulse—it was racing, but strong. He moved Butler into the recovery position, then painfully stood up. *That wasn't the same as before. . . . She didn't teleport away. Where is she? What just happened?*

30

DANNY COOPER CARRIED MINA DOWN THE
stairs and through the doorway to the top floor of Sakkara as he
looked for somewhere to lock her up.

He passed a couple of guards lying on the floor, but couldn't
tell whether they were alive or dead, and didn't have time to
check. He turned left at the end of the corridor, heading for the
machine room.

Then Mina's elbow lashed out, catching him in the face.
Danny stumbled, spilling Mina to the floor.

She rolled, then flipped on to her feet.

Danny shifted to normal-time. "Mina! What are you doing?
It's me! Danny Cooper!"

Mina lunged forward, landing in front of him before he had
a chance to move back into slow-time.

She moved almost faster than even he could see. He tried to
duck aside, but her fist still connected, clipping his jaw. Danny
was slammed back against the wall.

Mina grabbed his mechanical arm and threw him over her
shoulder.

He landed heavily, dazed. He pushed himself to his feet and
saw that Mina was already at the end of the corridor.

He darted after her and jumped, twisting in the air so that his
heavy mechanical arm hit Mina square in the small of her back.

Mina was knocked forward, but tumbled over and sprang to
her feet, spinning around to face him.

She swung a punch and Danny raised his arm to block it, then hit her in the face with the mechanical arm.

How can she be reacting so fast? Danny wondered. *She's even faster than Colin is!*

Mina swung another punch, and again Danny ducked.

Her fist plowed straight through one of the steel safety doors. As she struggled to get free, Danny saw his chance: He whipped around behind her, and planted a powerful kick in the back of her knees.

Mina collapsed, her arm still stuck in the door.

Danny shifted back to normal-time. "Mina! Please! You've got to stop this!"

There was a scream of tearing metal: Mina ripped the door from its hinges and swung it at Danny.

He leaped backward, the edge of the door barely missing the top of his head. The door slammed into the wall, and was wedged tight.

She's stuck! I can—

Mina vanished and reappeared a few feet away, free of the door.

I did not *just see that!* Keeping his distance, walking backward as Mina approached, Danny said, "Don't you know who I am? It's me. Danny Cooper."

She hesitated for a second, then continued, glaring at him.

"Mina, you've been in a coma for the past four months. It was your sister. It was Yvonne. She did that to you!"

Mina stopped and stared at him, frowning.

"Mina . . . Do you remember me?"

"Danny?"

"Yes! Yes, it's me!"

Mina's shoulders sagged. "What's going on? Why am I . . . My God! Did I attack you?"

He approached her cautiously. "You've been under Yvonne's mind-control, Mina." He reached out his hand. "Just come with me. . . . They'll check you out, make sure you're OK."

Then Mina stared at his mechanical arm. "Danny, what happened to your real arm?"

Danny realized: *She never knew me before I lost my arm. It's a trick!*

He was too slow.

Mina's fist collided with his jaw. Danny sailed through the air and crashed into the wall at the far end of the corridor. As he lost consciousness, the last thing he saw was Mina blinking out of existence once again.

Renata had watched, unmoving, as Colin approached the StratoTruck and detonated the mines. She saw the massive explosion rip the StratoTruck apart and tear into the surrounding buildings.

She knew that it was time to turn back, to track down Yvonne and force her to put an end to the war.

But she was scared.

In this form, having only changed herself, there was no pain.

The pain is still there, she said to herself, *waiting for me to change back.*

But I can deal with the pain. That's not the problem.

The problem is that pain doesn't happen for no reason. Pain is the body's equivalent of a fire alarm, and you don't deal with a fire by just turning off the alarm.

Something's wrong inside me. Something bad.

Clutching his swollen jaw, Danny slowly made his way to the roof of Sakkara.

Razor was slumped against the low wall that went around the edge. His face was covered in blood, and his left arm was limp by his side. "Danny? What happened?"

"She . . . she got past me. Didn't know she could teleport."

"No one did," Razor said.

"How's Butler?"

"He's coming around, I think."

"Who else do we have?"

"Just the three of us. The rest of them evacuated. I kinda got left behind." Razor jerked his thumb over his shoulder, toward the ground far below. "We lost."

Danny peered over the edge.

The Trutopian soldiers had completely overwhelmed the army base. The ground was strewn with the bodies of the dead and injured. Vehicles and gun emplacements were destroyed, some burning furiously.

"They didn't stand a chance," Razor said. "The Trutopians have weapons like I've never seen. Big things, no recoil, no sound. They just pull the triggers and people die. Either they don't know we're up here, or they don't care. They already took Brawn and Dioxin. A few of the others."

"They're starting to pull out," Danny said. "They . . . The kids from the mine! The Trutopians are loading them into a truck!"

"You're going to have to stop them," Razor said.

"No kidding."

"Well? Go!" Razor said.

"Just . . . give me a couple of minutes, will you? I just beat up on my best friend, ran nearly a thousand kilometers and got beaten up by a girl who can move almost as fast as me and disappear at will. I'm not exactly having the best day ever. And on top of that . . ."

"Renata?"

"Yeah. She's sick, Razor. She can use her power to change other people and things, but it's doing something to her."

"She'll be OK, Dan."

"I wish I could believe that."

A voice came over Danny's radio. "Danny? This is Impervia."

"Great. What do *you* want?"

"This is not the time for attitude. I've been trying to get through to Razor."

"Yeah, he's here with me. His radio's gone."

"Tell him that the countdown has begun."

Brandishing the Trutopian soldier's handgun, Stephanie Cord broke cover and darted down to the ground, next to the huge crater in the middle of the town's square.

She'd spent the past few minutes staring at Colin's unmoving body before finally deciding it was safe to check him out. Her infrared display showed that he was still alive, but she wanted to be sure. She had to see with her own eyes.

She touched down next to him and shut off the jetpack. "Colin?"

His face was a red mass of cuts and bruises. His nose was swollen and looked like it had been broken. His left eye was caked in blood, and a razor-sharp piece of shrapnel had embedded itself in his cheek. His breathing was shallow, but regular.

That's good enough. Stephanie said to herself.

She ran to the edge of the crater and half jumped, half slid down to where Renata was lying on her side, in the same sitting position she'd been in when she'd turned solid.

Stephanie moved herself into Renata's line of sight. "Can you hear me? Come on, Renata! Move! Change back! Do whatever it is that you do!"

Then Renata's body shimmered, the crystalline substance rippling as she turned back to her human form.

She immediately rolled into a ball, clutching her head and moaning.

For a moment, Stephanie just stood there, not knowing what she should do, then Renata uncurled herself, and opened her eyes. "Steph . . ."

"I'm here. What do you want me to do?"

"We need . . . to get to Yvonne. Have to find her."

"I think I know where she is, but I can't get close."

Renata raised her hand. "Help me up."

Stephanie grabbed Renata's arm, and pulled her to her feet. "Show me."

"It's that way, a couple of blocks. Big apartment building. But it's defended. Anything that gets near it is shot down."

"Where's Danny?" Renata asked.

"I don't know. Colin's up there, unconscious, but I don't know what happened to him."

"He was caught in the explosion. The Trutopians planted motion-sensitive mines all over the StratoTruck, probably hoping to kill me if I ever woke up." She began to climb up the sides of the crater. "We need to get inside their HQ and sort out that psycho once and for all."

Stephanie activated her jetpack and flew up to the edge. "Yeah, but how?"

"We'll think of something."

"Stephanie? You there?" Danny's voice said over the radio.

"I'm here, Danny. And so's Renata. She's . . . She's OK."

"Good—you can carry her. The two of you need to get out of there. The army is pulling out. You've got less than twenty minutes to get at least five miles away. I'm not going to be able to get to you in time."

"Danny, what is it? What's going to happen?"

"Impervia's just told me: They've got a missile ready to disperse a payload of VX nerve gas directly over the town. Steph, she told me what it does. . . . Exposure to just a fifth of a milligram is fatal. That's smaller than you can even see!"

Stephanie shook her head. "No way. I cannot believe that someone authorized the use of chemical weapons against U.S. citizens."

"But that's just it, Steph. The Trutopians are *not* U.S. citizens anymore. They declared independence."

31

DANNY HAD REACHED SAKKARA'S ROOF by running so fast he was able to charge straight up the building's sloping walls. After the last of the Trutopian soldiers had departed, he left the roof by the same method.

He raced along the deserted highway, following the path of the truck that was carrying the children and teenagers from the Lieberstanian platinum mine.

The speeding truck was guarded by two soldiers on the rear running board, and one hanging out of each door.

They might as well not be there for all the good they're going to do.

Danny ran up to the truck, grabbed hold of the nearest guard's gun and snatched it from his hand. The man didn't even have time to register what had happened before Danny swung the gun by the barrel and clubbed him in the stomach with it.

He had disabled the second and third guards and was racing for the fourth before the first one even hit the ground.

The guard hanging out of the passenger-side door was facing the driver. Danny grabbed hold of the man's belt and pulled him backward, leaving him skidding and rolling on the road.

Danny tore open the driver's door and pulled the man out of the truck, then climbed into the driver's seat and shifted back to real-time. "Razor! I've got the truck but . . . how in the world do I stop this thing?"

Razor's voice said, "OK, calm down."

"Calm down? Razor, I can't drive!"

"First things first, Dan. Hold the steering wheel steady. . . . As long as the truck is going in a straight line, and so is the road, you won't need to turn the wheel. Now, prepare yourself for the complicated bit."

Danny took a deep breath. "I'm ready."

"Take the keys out of the ignition."

"Oh."

He reached down and removed the keys. The truck's engine cut out, and the enormous vehicle began to slow down.

"Thanks, Raze!"

"Get the kids back here as quick as you can. If I can wake Butler, then he'll be able to shield them."

The copter roared through the sky, heading south, away from the worst of the fighting. Caroline Wagner sat clutching her unconscious husband's hand. "We shouldn't have left them behind."

"We didn't have any choice," Façade replied.

Niall said, "Why won't anyone tell me what's going on?"

"It's a war," his mother said. "And we're going somewhere safe until it's over."

Niall turned his head to look at the others. "But . . . Everyone here is a superhero! Why aren't they fighting?"

"We . . . We're not superhuman anymore, Niall," Caroline said.

"I know that," Niall said. "But Paragon wasn't a superhuman, and he was still a super*hero*."

"Yes. He was."

"I heard some of the soldiers talking about what Colin did to his dad and Danny and Renata and Butler. Is he one of the bad guys now?"

Caroline said, "It's not that simple. He's—"

The helicopter suddenly shuddered, lurched and began losing altitude.

"What the . . . ?" Façade unclipped his seat belt and scrambled to his feet. "Something *hit* us! The pilot . . ."

Caroline and Façade reached the bullet-ridden cockpit at the same time. The pilot was slumped sideways in his seat, a trickle of blood running down the side of his face.

"He's alive. Barely. Can you fly this thing?" Caroline asked.

"Yeah, I can fly her. I can fly anything. Just sit back down and strap in." Façade hauled the unconscious pilot out of his seat and climbed in. He grabbed the joystick and eased back, settling the copter's path. "I can't tell how much damage she's received, so I'm going to have to set her down."

"Just take it as far away from Sakkara as you can." Then she heard Rose Cooper's voice saying, "Oh my God!"

Caroline turned to see Mina standing in the copter, next to the passengers.

The blond girl smiled at her, then reached out her hand and placed it on Niall's head.

The two of them disappeared, leaving Niall's seat belt to drop back to the seat.

His mother screamed.

Colin Wagner opened his eyes. *What happened to me . . . ? Oh. Right. The explosion.*

He floated up into the air, pivoted about and landed on his feet.

He looked around, and could see nothing but devastation.

Yvonne's voice came over the radio. "So you *are* alive. We weren't sure."

Furious, Colin reached up to pull the radio headset from his head, but stopped. *She ordered me not to do that, so I can't.* "What do you want now, you psycho?"

"Danny went back to Sakkara. Go after him and stop him. And this time, kill him."

"No."

"At least rip that damned mechanical arm off him, then!"

Colin didn't want to fight Danny, but he knew that he had no choice. *I have to obey her commands. But unless she's specific, I can take my time about it, give Danny a chance to stop all this.*

He began to walk.

"Fly there, Colin. As fast as you can," Yvonne added.

Danny led the freed children and teenagers across the rough ground and over a low hill. "Come on, for crying out loud! Move! They're going to be coming for us!"

Don't be so hard on them, he said to himself. *Most of them can barely walk. They've spent their entire lives in the platinum mine. They've absolutely no idea what's going on.*

"Please!" he shouted. "You have to trust me!"

One of the children nearby said, "Sir?"

He turned to look at her, and realized that this was the same little girl he'd met in Lieberstan. "Estelle? Is that you?"

She nodded.

He did his best to give her an encouraging smile. "Well, look at you. All cleaned up and out of those rags."

"Mr. Danny, the bad people are coming. A lot of them."

Danny paused. "Why do you think that, Estelle?"

She pointed back the way they had come, toward the trucks. "They're coming from over there. Cassandra told me."

"Cassandra?"

One of the older girls moved closer to him.

"Are you Cassandra?"

The girl nodded, and inside Danny's head her voice said, *I am.*

Got to be telepathy, Danny thought. *She's about my age, so she's old enough to have powers.*

Cassandra nodded again.

"All right, everyone. Run! If you're strong enough, carry the smaller ones!" Danny scooped up Estelle in his arms.

He desperately wanted to go into slow-time, and carry the little girl to the relative safety of Sakkara, but that would mean leaving the others behind.

One of the smaller boys stumbled. He was grabbed by two others, not much bigger than he was, and hoisted back on to his feet.

They must have learned how to look after each other in the mine.

That's right, Cassandra's voice said inside his head. *It was the only way to survive.*

God, I wish she wouldn't do that!

"Sorry," the girl said. She moved closer to Danny. "Let me take her. You have work to do."

Danny pointed east, toward Sakkara. "Lead them that way."

He watched as the children and teenagers streamed past.

A line of Trutopian soldiers appeared over the crest of the hill, carrying large, powerful-looking weapons. *What are those things? Something familiar about them . . .*

Cassandra's voice said, *They think of them as rail-guns. I don't know what that means.*

I do, Danny thought, *and it's not good.* He remembered the power of the rail-guns protecting Victor Cross's power-damping machine back in California. He prayed that these handheld versions weren't anywhere near as dangerous.

He looked back toward the others. *Cassandra, the kids are all grouped too close together. Get them to spread out.*

Why? she asked.

Because then they'll be harder to hit. The way they are now, they could all be wiped out with a single burst from one of those guns.

Danny looked around. *We are not going to make it.*

Then he felt something wash over him, like a cool breeze.

Oh God, the Trutopians aren't even bothering to run! They know they can stop us with those things. I could run now, but the longer I stay here, the better chance the kids will have to get away. In slow-time I might be able to disarm some of them . . . but I can't take the risk that one of the others would have a chance to fire at the kids.

He glanced around, and for a moment he thought he saw one of the teenagers standing right behind him. He shuddered.

One of the soldiers shouted, "Shoot him!"

Danny instinctively raised his arm to protect himself, though he knew that it wouldn't do any good. He slipped into slow-time, and everything fell silent.

I hope Renata can get away from the town before the VX gas hits—

I hope she comes back here and beats the living snot out of these guys!

I hope she can stop Colin.

I hope she doesn't miss me too much.

I hope she lives a good life, a long and happy one.

The soldiers fired.

And I really *hope this won't hurt.*

Danny Cooper closed his eyes.

32

"ANYTHING THAT GETS ANYWHERE NEAR that building will be ripped apart by the guns," Stephanie said.

She and Renata were standing on the roof of a tall building a block away from the Trutopian headquarters. "The army launched rockets right at it, and they were shot down before they got close to it. How much time do we have left?"

"That depends on how long it would take you to fly me out to the five-mile limit."

"About three or four minutes, but—"

"Then we have about twelve minutes to get in and stop Yvonne."

"The nerve gas will stop her."

"We can't be certain of that. But even if it does, then how are we going to reverse the brainwashing she did on all the Trutopians? They'll just keep on fighting. Are you *sure* there's no way past their guns?"

"I really can't see it. I don't think they'd be able to damage you when you're completely solid, but then you can't move."

Danny opened his eyes.

In a perfect semicircle around him, the ground was littered with thousands of small silver pellets.

The Trutopian soldiers were still shooting at him, the pellets from their rail-guns bouncing harmlessly off an invisible shield.

Thank you Butler Redmond! Danny said to himself. *I'll never call you Bubbles again.*

Over the radio, Butler's voice said, "Good thing I followed you. You OK, Dan?"

"Yeah. Thanks." He looked around: In the distance, the teenagers and children were huddled on the ground, with Butler standing in the middle of them. "You've got the force-field around the kids too?"

"Yeah, but if I release it to let you out, then they could be hit."

"Extend it outward, push the Trutopians back. You just need to knock them off balance for a second, then I can take them out."

"You're sure?" Butler asked.

"I'm sure. As soon as you see me disappear, put the force-field back around the kids."

"All right . . . *Now!*"

The Trutopian soldiers were suddenly knocked back, some of them losing their grip on their weapons.

Danny shifted into slow-time, darted toward the nearest Trutopian, grabbed the barrel of the rail-gun with his mechanical hand and crushed it, then punched the man in the face.

He moved on to the next one, and did the same thing, and the next.

From Danny's perspective it seemed to take forever to defeat them all, but he knew that less than a second had passed.

He moved back to real-time and watched with satisfaction as each of the Trutopians crumpled to the ground.

Then something slammed hard into his legs, grabbing them at the same time, pulling him high into the air.

Panicking, Danny looked up to see Colin holding on to his feet at the ankles. The ground raced away from them.

Six hundred miles to the northwest, Renata Soliz was also being carried through the air.

"Anyone tries to get out of that building—" Renata shouted to Stephanie.

"I'll stop them. You ready?"

"Do it!"

Stephanie let go of Renata's wrists.

Renata curled herself into a ball and turned solid, praying that Stephanie's judgment was accurate. *This is the only chance we're going to get. If I miss . . .*

Arcing through the air, Renata couldn't feel anything, but she could see from the muzzle flashes on the automated weapons on the building's corners that she was being shot at.

As she crashed down on to the HQ's roof, the firing stopped, just as Stephanie had predicted. The automated guns were still tracking her, but not firing. This low, they couldn't shoot at her without damaging each other.

Renata turned to flesh again. "I'm down!" she called over the radio.

"I see you. Good luck!"

One of Impervia's lessons was that on any mission it was vital to secure an escape route. Renata ran to the nearest of the automated guns and tore it apart. She picked up the gun's barrel and used it to smash the remaining weapons.

She looked around. A pair of large steel doors was set into the roof at the far end. *Some sort of hangar. If there's a craft in there I might be able to use it to get out.*

The hangar doors looked too strong for her to break through, but then she spotted a smaller metal hatch close to the edge. She ran toward it, punched her powerful fingers through the metal, tore the hatch off and dropped down.

Trutopian guards were already streaming toward her position.

Renata locked her fingers together and cracked her knuckles. She smiled at them. "All right. Let's do this."

Got to put him where he can't do any harm, Colin thought.

He didn't know how his powers enabled him to fly, and he didn't want too think to much about it. He remembered learning to ride a bike—for the first few months he'd had no problems unless he thought about exactly what he was doing, at which point the wheels would wobble and he'd topple over.

But falling off a bike was one thing; losing the power of flight at the height of half a mile would be a lot messier. Colin knew that he would survive the fall, but wasn't sure about Danny.

He'd found Danny several miles west of Sakkara, surrounded by a ragged line of unconscious Trutopian soldiers.

Colin had dropped to ground level, flipped over so that he was flying upside down, grabbed hold of Danny's ankles and soared into the air.

After the initial shock, Danny had begun to struggle, to try to pull himself free of Colin's grip.

Colin held on as tight as he could without breaking Danny's

ankles—though a part of him knew that a broken ankle would definitely slow Danny down—and whipped through the sky on as erratic and unpredictable a course as he could manage.

He looked down and saw Danny's body blur as he shifted into and out of his high-speed mode.

Colin desperately wanted to set his friend down and let him go, but the feeling was overwhelmed by Yvonne's orders, which seemed to be burned into his brain.

He realized that this was more than just an inability to resist her commands; there was something about her that made him *want* to do what she told him.

Is that how her power works? Not so much by controlling us, but by making us want to please her?

Again, he considered letting Danny go free, and again that thought was drowned out by the need to obey Yvonne.

But I won't kill for her, Colin thought.

No matter how strong the need to obey was, it was nothing compared to his inherent revulsion at the thought of killing someone.

Renata tore her way through the last set of doors leading to the Trutopian control center. The men and women working at their computer stations didn't even look up.

She moved to the nearest computer and punched her fist right through it.

A voice from above said, "I wouldn't bother if I was you. Everything is protected with a triple backup system."

She looked up to see Yvonne on the gantry, smiling down at her.

"Your armies have retreated, Renata. You've lost."

Renata glanced at the clock on the wall. Eight minutes until the countdown expired. "No, *you've* lost, Yvonne. You know why they've retreated?"

"They've realized they can't win."

"They've been prepared for a superhuman threat ever since your father's last battle. In less than eight minutes a missile will detonate over this town, showering it with VX gas. I'm sure you know what that is."

Yvonne hesitated. "I do. But this building is completely self-contained and sealed off from the outside world. Our air and water can be recycled for years. We can just wait it out."

Renata began to climb the steps to the gantry. "You mean, the building *was* sealed off from the outside world. Until I tore my way in."

Yvonne backed away.

"I'm one of the lucky ones," Renata said. "You can't control me. And I know I'm stronger than you are. So surrender now. This doesn't have to go any further. You're already responsible for the deaths of thousands of people. But if you give yourself up then maybe you won't be executed."

The girls were now almost face-to-face.

Yvonne said, "I may not be stronger than you, Soliz, but I am smarter. I don't do *anything* without having a backup plan." She smiled. "You remember my sister, don't you?"

Behind her, Mina stepped out of the shadows, her hands locked around Niall Cooper's neck.

"One word from me, and Mina will kill him."

Yvonne started to descend the stairs. Renata reached out to

grab her, but Yvonne stepped aside. "One word, remember? And just in case you're thinking of using your power to solidify me, Mina's also been instructed to kill him if that happens. So whatever way you look at it, *you* lose."

She turned to one of the engineers. "Prepare the escape pod." To Renata, she said, "I have to give you people credit, Renata. I really didn't think you'd ever get this far. Mina? *If she tries to follow me, kill the boy, then do whatever it takes to stop her.*"

Yvonne raced down the metal stairway, and darted from the room.

Renata turned back to Mina. "Can you hear me?"

Mina nodded.

"You do know that she's controlling you, don't you?"

"Yes."

"Still as talkative as ever, I see. Can you find a way to resist her control?"

"No. I . . . We're clones. We're closer than sisters. She can control me more efficiently than anyone else. I'm sorry, Renata. I can't help myself."

Renata looked down at Niall. "I'm sorry too, Niall. I did my best."

"I don't want to die, Renata!"

"I know," she said. She glanced at the clock: *Only six minutes to go before the nerve gas hits.* To Mina, she said, "You won't do it."

"I don't have a choice."

Renata concentrated. She staggered against the wave of agony that surged through her brain, and when she could open her eyes again, Mina was staring at her in shock.

Niall Cooper was now a crystal statue.

Renata forced a smile. "See, I couldn't change *you,* because then I'd never be able to break your grip on his neck. So now what are you going to do? Yvonne ordered you to kill him, and *then* stop me. But you can't kill Niall now, so that means . . ."

Mina nodded. "I can't carry out her order. Renata, I . . . I can't stop her. She's too powerful. You might have a chance, but . . . I can read your aura."

"What about it?"

"Every time you use your powers, you're making your condition worse."

"I know."

Renata pulled Niall's crystalline body away from Mina, threw him over her shoulder and leaped over the gantry's railing.

She darted from the room, not caring that she was stepping on the unconscious bodies of the guards who had tried to stop her on the way in.

She reached the hatchway and scrambled up the ladder. The huge hangar doors were open, and in the distant sky Renata could see a small, powerful-looking craft rocketing away.

Colin set Danny down on the edge of a rocky plateau.

Danny wasn't sure where they were, but it looked like the Grand Canyon. He immediately zipped away from Colin, and stood on the opposite edge of the plateau. "So what are you going to do? Kill me?"

"No. I only have to defeat you. And I can do that by leaving you here. There's no easy way off this rock for someone who can't fly."

Even as Colin rose into the air, Danny shifted into slow-time and raced forward, slamming his mechanical arm into Colin's stomach.

As Danny watched, Colin slowly doubled over, collapsed to the ground.

He darted back to the edge of the plateau and looked down. The walls of the plateau sloped almost vertically. There was no way down, not even for someone with his great speed.

The hot air rising up from the canyon floor caused a slow, lazy shimmer, and it triggered a memory of the last time Danny was in a desert.

It came true.

The vision I had in the California desert. I saw myself leading a group of teenagers and kids away from an army. I saw the mechanical arm.

The Trutopians are the army, and the other kids with me are the prisoners from Lieberstan.

God . . . I thought I could prevent the vision coming true by never accepting the arm. But then I had to take it because it was the only thing that would give me an advantage over Colin.

When he'd returned to Sakkara from Lieberstan, the government agent had instructed him to say that the Trutopians had been behind the prison camp.

I couldn't do that, Danny thought. *Whatever the Trutopians have done, I couldn't lie about something like that.*

And the woman from the government had said, "Then you have condemned us to war."

Is that how it's going to be? They're going to blame me for the war.

Maybe that's what Quantum picked up in his vision. He was certain that the war would be my fault. That's what this whole thing is about. He wanted to prevent the war from happening by stripping my powers.

It didn't work, and—from some people's points of view—I'm now responsible for this war with the Trutopians.

Danny remembered meeting with his father, learning the truth behind Ragnarök's final attack and his power-stripping machine.

Quantum said that billions of people will die in the war.

Billions.

Everyone thought I was going to be a villain. But they didn't understand. I'm not a bad guy. I just have to do what I know is right.

A sudden thought jumped into his head, and caused him to shudder.

But if I do what I'm sure is right, and everyone else thinks I'm wrong, doesn't that make me just as bad as Ragnarök or Victor Cross?

33

YVONNE CURSED HERSELF FOR NOT
having been better prepared. *Next time, I'll set up my base somewhere
they can't find me.*

She frantically worked at the controls of the escape craft. *God,
I don't even have another hideout! Why did I believe that I was going to
be able to just walk all over them? They're superhumans too.*

*At least the war is still going strong. All I have to do is find some-
where to lie low for a few months, and then I can start again.*

The radar screen blipped, showing an incoming object.

Some kind of missile. Yvonne stared at the screen. *But the army
retreated, and there're still a couple of minutes to go before the nerve gas
canister gets here.*

The missile zoomed closer.

Yvonne banked the craft to the left; the missile adjusted
its course to match. *Should have spent more time practicing the
controls. . . . All those times I had a chance to fly the StratoTruck and I
didn't bother . . .*

The craft rocked slightly as the missile struck.

No explosion. It wasn't a missile. Yvonne looked around frantically. *But the only superhuman who can fly is Colin, and he's under
orders not to harm me!*

Unless he finally found a way to resist my control.

Then she spotted a figure crawling toward the cockpit, a pistol
in its hand.

Stephanie Cord tapped on the cockpit's glass with the muzzle of the gun, then aimed it at Yvonne's head. Her amplified voice came through the helmet's built-in loudspeaker. "Set this thing down. Now."

Yvonne slammed the craft's joystick back, flipping it over. Upside-down, she watched as Stephanie lost her grip and slipped away.

On the top of the plateau, Danny and Colin had been fighting for several minutes, but still neither of them had managed to land a punch strong enough to disable the other.

In slow-time Danny ducked and weaved, then lashed out with his mechanical fist and struck Colin square in the face.

As his friend staggered back, Danny zipped away.

He knew that he couldn't risk returning to normal speed; if he did, Colin would either blast him with a fireball or simply fly away and leave him stranded.

He raced around behind Colin and slammed into him shoulder-first. It was like hitting a stone wall.

At a speed far greater than any normal human could manage, Colin jabbed back with his right elbow.

Danny saw it coming and ducked down to the left—

—and Colin's left elbow clipped his jaw, sent him spinning into the air.

Danny recovered quickly, shook his head to clear it and realized that he was still in slow-time, and still hadn't hit the ground.

Too late, he tried to twist around to see where he was going.

His head slammed into a beach-ball-sized rock.

A blinding pain shot through his entire body, and he collapsed face-first onto the uneven ground.

Got to move, got to get up—

He was vaguely aware of someone grabbing his shoulder, rolling him onto his side, then he heard Colin say, "You're going to be OK."

Danny opened his eyes; Colin was silhouetted against the sun, floating three meters off the ground, looking down at him.

Danny tried to speak, but the only sound he could make was a weak groan.

"You're bleeding, but it's not bad. It'll stop soon. I'm going to leave you here, Dan. I'll tell someone to pick you up. It won't be more than a few hours."

Danny shifted his left leg, and groaned again. He gritted his teeth and said, "Then tell them to send a paramedic—I think my leg is broken." He looked up at Colin again. "Col . . . The vision I had in the desert in California . . . It came true."

Colin stared down at him. "What? Seriously?"

Danny nodded, then winced at the sudden burst of pain from the wound in his forehead.

"A few minutes before you found me. The Trutopians, the kids from Lieberstan. Everything happened just as I saw it last year."

"But . . . But that means that—"

Danny finished the sentence. "That maybe my father's prophecy will come true as well."

Colin swallowed. "But he said that billions of people are going to die."

"They're *already* dying, Col. And you're helping the Trutopians make that happen."

"I can't resist Yvonne's orders."

"How hard are you trying?"

They stared at each other for a moment.

Danny said, "If you have to leave me here, then at least move me into the shade. I can't do it myself." He raised his left arm.

Colin drifted lower and grabbed hold of Danny's arm.

Danny shifted into slow-time and swung his mechanical arm toward Colin's face.

Colin caught the arm at its wrist, and before Danny could break free, he placed his other arm on Danny's shoulder and pulled.

Danny staggered back as his artificial arm was torn apart. He moved back to real-time, as Colin casually tossed the ruined hunk of metal to the ground.

Danny stared at it. "Damn. I was getting used to having that."

"It was your only advantage against me," Colin said. "Sure, you're a lot faster than I am, but I'm stronger and much more powerful. Without your weapon, you might as well be an ordinary person. You know you can't beat me, Danny. So you can just stay here, where you can't do any damage."

Colin turned his back and began to rise into the air.

Danny switched to slow-time, snatched up the ruined mechanical arm and charged at Colin, slamming him across the back of the head with as much strength as he could muster.

Colin was knocked to the ground. He instantly spun about and crashed his fist into Danny's stomach.

Renata activated her radio. "Razor! It's me! You have to get Impervia to stop the nerve gas!"

"I've already asked her. She won't do it."

"But there's no point now—Yvonne's already escaped!"

"I—"

Impervia's voice cut across Razor's. "We've been monitoring your communications. Renata, I'm sorry, but the plan goes ahead. If Yvonne's gone, then we're not going to be able to stop the war anyway."

"These people here can't help what they've done. They're innocent!"

"They're still controlling the Trutopian forces. Turn yourself solid. The nerve agent will strike in two minutes. Once it's been deployed we're going to napalm the entire area to destroy the gas. Assuming you survive, we should be able to pick you up in a week or so."

Stephanie Cord recovered quickly, activated her jetpack and righted herself. Yvonne's escape craft was streaking toward the west.

She raced after it, her jetpack set to full power. She aimed the handgun, steadied herself and fired, over and over, into the craft's engine.

It shuddered and began to spin out of control, dropping out of the sky.

Stephanie caught up with the craft, adjusted her trajectory to match. Inside, Yvonne was desperately trying to get the controls to respond.

Stephanie shot through the cockpit's canopy, shattering the glass. "Give me your hands!" She yelled. "Now!"

She let go of the gun and grabbed Yvonne's hands, pulling her free from the craft.

As they slowly began to descend, the escape craft clipped the edge of a concrete water tower and spun into the side of an abandoned truck. It bounced once to the grating sound of tearing metal, then tumbled to a stop upside down, its flattened cockpit now consumed by fire.

Yvonne struggled against Stephanie's grip. "You set me down or I'll tear your head off!"

Stephanie lashed out and hit Yvonne in the face with her knee, stunning her. "I blamed Colin for what happened to my father. But it wasn't his fault. He made the only choice he could. Victor Cross planned it. And *you* . . . you're the one who captured him." She grinned. "Remember how *your* father died?"

Stephanie opened her hands.

Yvonne screamed as she plummeted to the ground.

And landed on her feet, to find that they had only been a few meters up.

On the roof of the Trutopian headquarters, Renata Soliz sat cross-legged next to Niall Cooper's crystalline body. There was no way to get clear in time. She was going to have to solidify herself and wait out the nerve gas.

"Renata!" Stephanie said over the radio. "I've got her! She's on the ground and I'm flying out of reach."

Renata jumped to her feet. "Where are you?"

"We're about four miles southwest of the town. Near a big

water tower. Look, I need help here. The Trutopians are advancing on this position, and if I leave, Yvonne will escape."

"Get out of there, Steph! You need to be farther away. The nerve gas is going to hit any second now."

"Can you do it from a distance? Can you turn Yvonne solid from where you are?"

Renata frowned. *Can I?*

If I can solidify someone across the room, then I should be able to do it from miles away. But if I don't know exactly where she is . . .

"I'm sorry, Steph. Just . . . Get to safety. If Yvonne survives we'll track her down somehow." *And until we do, the war will continue and millions more people will die.*

This has to end. And it has to end now.

She looked up. A black dot was racing across the sky.

The missile.

I could solidify it, but that won't help Steph.

And then Renata knew what she had to do to.

She swallowed. "Oh God . . . This is *really* going to hurt."

She began to concentrate.

Pain tore through Renata's entire body, every nerve burning. She collapsed to the roof, blood streaming from her nose, ears and eyes.

A wave of energy rippled out from Renata's body.

The building itself turned solid and transparent, the people inside becoming crystal statues.

The wave continued to spread. Everything it touched was solidified.

Above the Trutopian town, the VX missile turned to crystal and plummeted, untriggered, to the ground.

On a rocky plateau in Arizona, Danny Cooper and Colin Wagner stopped and stared as a curtain of energy zoomed toward them from the north.

"My God . . . Danny! Take my hand! We have to—"

They were too late. The energy wave was on them.

Three miles west of Sakkara, Butler Redmond and the children from the platinum mine were motionless inside Butler's now-solid force-field.

The helicopters carrying the refugees from Sakkara turned to glass and dropped out of the sky, tumbling end-over-end.

In Indiana, Alia Cord and Grant Paramjeet watched the TV news with growing horror as the screen showed the spreading crystalline transformation of a battlefield. Then the picture was replaced with static. Alia reached out and took hold of Grant's hand, and then they too were suddenly solid and unmoving.

The energy wave continued.

Everything it touched was turned to crystal.

Everything.

The people. The animals. The land. The sea.

The entire planet.

34

RENATA SOLIZ SAT UP AND WIPED THE
blood from her face.

She looked around, squinting against the sunlight that was
reflected from every surface.

She pushed herself to her feet, swaying a little. She didn't
know how much time had passed, but the pain had eased a little,
and she no longer felt like she was going to throw up.

Everything, as far as she could see in all directions, appeared
to be made of glass.

The silence was almost overwhelming.

Then, from far away, there came the sound of something
crashing to the ground, then another, and another. For almost a
minute the same sound seemed to be coming from everywhere.

What is *that?* "Hello?" Renata called. The echo of her voice
seemed to go on forever.

Something landed on the roof, and Renata saw that it was a
bird. She picked it up. It appeared to be completely intact. She
set it down again. *So that's what all the noise was.*

*Now . . . Where did Steph say she was? Four miles southwest, near
the water tower.*

Renata looked over the edge of the building. It was a long
way to climb, but she didn't have a choice: The building's doors
would be completely sealed.

She picked up Niall and threw him over the edge, then started to climb down. After a few meters, she thought, *Why am I doing this the hard way?*

She let go, turned herself solid and crashed to the ground.

With Niall Cooper now returned to his human form, and holding her hand, Renata made her way across the crystalline landscape. It took them almost two hours to find Yvonne and Stephanie, close to the crashed escape craft.

"Wow! It's on fire, but the flames are frozen," Niall said, looking at the pod. "That's the coolest thing I've ever seen!"

"I turned the whole world into crystal and *that's* what you find cool? You are one weird little kid, Niall."

"And you're not?"

Stephanie Cord was lying faceup on the ground.

"You should stand her up," Niall said, "because when you change her back her jetpack will start working again."

"No, it won't," Renata said. "The StratoTruck's engines were shut down after I changed *it* back." She walked toward Yvonne. "So what do you think, Niall? Should I change her back first, or everything together?"

"Just her," Niall said. "That'll scare the pants off her."

"You think so?"

"It bloody scared *me*."

Renata laughed. She focused on Yvonne and turned her back to human.

Yvonne screamed. She backed away from Renata and started to run.

"Where are you going to go?" Renata called. "It's hard to find a hiding place in a glass world."

Yvonne skidded to a stop and looked around. "Oh my God, Renata! What have you done?"

"I did the only thing I could do to stop the fighting. I froze the world."

"Everything?"

Renata nodded.

"How long . . . ?"

"A couple of hours, I think."

"But that's . . . This could cause irrevocable damage to the ecosystem!"

"What, more damage than your war has caused? I don't think so." She walked over to Yvonne. "I'm going to change it all back, and *you* are going to order your people to stop fighting. Understand me?"

"What if I don't?"

"Then I will solidify you and leave you. You will be a crystal statue, aware of everything around you but unable to eat, or sleep or move. The war will come to an end one way or the other. In about five billion years, the sun will burn itself out, and turn into a red giant, forcing the Earth out of its orbit. You'll remain on this spot, drifting through space on a dark, dead planet, until the universe itself comes to an end." Renata shrugged. "After that . . . who knows?"

Yvonne sank to her knees. "All right. I'll do it. I'll end the war."

On the plateau in Arizona, Danny and Colin collapsed into a heap.

"What the hell just happened?" Colin said, rolling aside.

Danny zipped away. "Renata—she must have changed us."

"Not just us," Colin said. "Everything."

They looked at each other for a moment.

"Wow."

"My thoughts exactly," Colin said. He started to move toward Danny, then frowned and raised his hand to his communicator. "Getting a message." He grinned. "Yes!"

"Yes what? Should I be worried?"

"Yvonne's just canceled her orders." Colin ripped the communicator from his head and crushed it in his hands.

Danny realized he'd been holding his breath, and let it out suddenly. "Oh thank God!"

Danny's own radio came to life. "Danny? Can you hear me?"

"I hear you, Steph. What's the situation?"

"We've got Yvonne. It's over."

In Sakkara's half-destroyed infirmary, the New Heroes were crowded around Renata's bed.

Colin Wagner asked, "And you're *sure* you're all right now?"

"Yes." Renata said. "I wish people would stop asking me that!" She glanced at Mina, who was staring at her. "What?"

"Your aura . . ."

"What about it?"

"It looks normal," Mina told her.

"Well, that's good to know," Renata said.

Mina frowned. "No, I mean—"

They looked up as Colin's father entered the room. Warren was leaning heavily on his crutch. His right leg was encased in a tight plastic frame that held it immobile. The base of the frame was fitted with a small wheel that allowed him to move around using only one crutch: His broken left hand prevented him from using two.

Warren limped over to the chair. "Up, Danny. I've got a broken arm *and* a broken leg, you know."

"Sorry, Mr. Wagner."

Warren carefully lowered himself into the chair and turned to Renata. "We got the results of the scans back. Apart from being exhausted, you're in perfect health. We didn't see anything that indicated the source of the pain. A couple more days in bed and you'll be fine."

Renata said, "There was no pain when I changed everything back. Maybe I just needed to get used to using the power that way. But I tried to turn myself solid this morning and it didn't work. And I don't seem to be strong anymore."

"You probably just overloaded something in your brain," Danny said. "Like blowing a fuse."

Colin said, "Yeah, it's just temporary. Your powers will come back, like Danny's did."

Then Mina said, "It's *not* temporary." She looked at Renata. "When we were in the Trutopian headquarters I told you I could see your aura, and that every time you changed something you were making your condition worse. And now your aura is normal."

"That means I'm not dying or anything," Renata said.

"No, it means your powers are not coming back. Ever. You're no longer a superhuman, Renata. You're normal."

The silence that followed was finally broken by Renata. "I see." She glanced at Mina. "You're certain?"

Mina nodded. "Every superhuman—even former ones like Mister Wagner—have an extra twist to their aura. You used to have one, but not anymore. You're just like everyone else now."

After a moment, Warren reached out his good hand to Colin and pulled himself up. "She needs rest, and a lot of it. Everyone out. Now. You too, Danny."

"No," Renata said. "He can stay."

"All right. But everyone else, get out. Move!"

Colin followed Mina, Razor and Butler from the room, then stopped at the door and looked back. "If you need anything . . ."

Renata smiled at him. "I know. Thanks."

Colin closed the door and turned to see that his father was standing a few meters away.

"You'd better get that broken nose seen to, Colin."

"Yeah, I . . ." He looked away. "Dad, I'm sorry. I couldn't help myself."

Warren nodded. "Come on, I've got something to tell you." He turned and began to slowly make his way down the corridor.

They reached Sakkara's dining hall, where Colin's mother was talking to Vienna Cord.

Caroline jumped to her feet and ran to Colin, throwing her arms around him. "Do you have *any* idea what you put us through?"

Colin stepped back. "I'm sorry. It wasn't me! Yvonne was controlling me."

"*Before* that. No one's blaming you for what she made you do. But she didn't make you run away, Colin. You did that by yourself. God only knows what could have happened."

"I'm able to look after myself. I'm more powerful than you

and Dad ever were. There's no one else who has *two* superhumans for parents."

"That's only going to be true for the next few months."

He frowned. "What?"

"Sometime around the start of October, you're going to have a little brother or sister."

Colin stared at his mother's stomach. "Seriously?"

She nodded. "Yes."

Warren said, "So no running away again, got that? We're going to need you to help out." He raised his plaster-covered left hand. "In fact, if this hasn't healed by the time the baby comes you're going to be doing *everything* around the apartment."

"OK," Colin said, then froze. He could hear a familiar sound approaching the building's roof. "I've got to . . . I'll be back in a few minutes."

Colin left the dining hall and made his way to the stairs. He didn't bother walking up them: Stairs seemed kind of pointless now that he could fly.

He emerged onto the roof and looked toward the west, where a figure was zipping through the sky.

Stephanie Cord switched her jetpack to hover mode as Colin approached. She removed her helmet and held it by her side. "Hey."

Colin floated in place a couple of meters away from her. "You OK?"

She nodded. "Yeah. I . . . Colin, I'm sorry about everything I said to you after my dad died. I shouldn't have blamed you. Cross didn't give you any choice."

"I don't blame *you* for being angry with me. I shouldn't have promised you that I'd get him back. Sol was . . . He was a great man. He was the only one of the old heroes who didn't have any powers, but he never let that stop him. I've only met one other person with as much courage as he had."

"Who?"

He smiled. "You."

Stephanie returned the smile. "What do we do now?"

Colin looked around. On the horizon, fires were still burning. On the ground below, in front of Sakkara, some of the younger children from the platinum mine were using Brawn as a jungle gym. The giant seemed to be having the time of his life.

"Now we have to clean up this mess," Colin said. "Put everything right."

"I mean, what do *we* do now? What happens to you and me?"

"Let's just see what the future brings us."

Danny sat by Renata's bed until he was sure she was asleep, then he gently pulled his hand free from hers and walked over to the window. Night was creeping over the horizon, the clouds orange-tinted from the fires in Topeka.

He knew he should be out there with Colin and the others, helping to restore some semblance of normality to the world, but they hadn't asked him and he hadn't felt inclined to offer.

The vision came true.

A sudden violent shudder rippled through him.

Oh God, it came true.

He realized now that he'd been scared ever since he'd seen the vision of his future self in the California desert.

Quantum had foreseen the deaths of billions of people, and had known—somehow—that Danny would be responsible.

That didn't happen, Danny thought. *Thousands died—maybe even hundreds of thousands—but not billions. So either we changed the future Quantum saw or his vision wasn't about the Trutopian war.*

What scared him most was that Quantum's visions had driven him almost insane.

Is that what's going to happen to me?

How long do I have before I can't take it anymore?

He checked once more that Renata was sleeping comfortably, then silently left the infirmary and made his way to his own room.

As his bedroom door hissed open, the door to the next room did the same. Niall leaned out, grinned and padded barefoot toward him. "Is she gonna be all right?"

Danny nodded. "Yeah. I think so."

Niall followed his brother into his room. "Can't you, like, see into the future and tell for sure?"

"Doesn't work like that," Danny said. "I can't control it."

"Dad said that the visions are like watching a tiny bit of a movie you've never seen before. You can see what's happening but you don't know exactly what it means. Is that right?"

"That's it exactly."

Niall climbed onto the bed and sat cross-legged, absently picking at his toenails as he looked at Danny. "They keep talking about how it's all your fault."

Danny stopped in the middle of pulling on his jacket. "They?"

"The news. They're saying that you forced everyone into going to Lieberstan, and if you hadn't done that then there wouldn't have been a war."

"The war has nothing to do with Lieberstan, Niall."

"Yeah, but they keep saying—"

"I know. They do that because if you tell the same lie over and over and don't give anyone a chance to hear the truth, then eventually you'll get enough people believing your story that the lie becomes the truth. Give me a hand with this, would you?"

Niall jumped off the bed and zipped up Danny's jacket. "Are you gonna get another robot arm?"

"Yeah. If they'll make me one. Thanks."

"But—"

"Sorry, Niall. But I don't want to talk about that now. OK?"

"Sure. But . . ."

"What?"

Niall looked away. "What about me, Danny? What powers am I going to get?"

"You might get the same powers Façade had. You know, being able to change your appearance." He smiled. "Be pretty cool, wouldn't it?"

"I guess. But Dad was a bad guy. For a while."

"I know, but he did the right thing in the end. He's not a bad guy now. You just make sure you always do the right thing, and you'll be OK."

Niall looked up at him, unblinking. "*You* did the right thing, and look what they're saying about you."

Danny gave his brother another smile, showing a confidence he didn't feel. "Things'll work out all right in the end. Now go on back to your room. I've got to go out there and help Colin and the others."

He winked, then slipped into slow-time and left the room.

Seconds later Danny stood on the roof of Sakkara and looked out toward the city.

Quantum said that I would be responsible for a war in which billions of people are going to die. Well, I know I'm not responsible, but everyone is blaming me anyway. Is that what he was sensing?

The visions come without context.

I saw myself leading a group of kids away from an army, and that's what happened. But in the vision, when they fired at me, I raised my mechanical arm and the bullets bounced off an invisible shield.

I figured that was something built into the arm, but it was Butler's force-field.

And I wasn't leading the kids, I was rescuing them.

He stepped up onto the low wall that skirted the edge of the roof, paused for a moment, then ran down the building's sloping side and through the now-deserted army base.

Despite everything that had happened, Danny was a little cheered up by this.

I can move so fast that gravity doesn't have enough time to take hold of me. It reminded him of a cartoon character running off the edge of a cliff. As long as the character doesn't look down, he's safe.

In slow-time I can do almost anything. I could—

He stopped himself in midspeculation.

Slow-time. Why do I call it that? If anything it should be fast-*time.*

He couldn't remember when he'd first started to use the phrase, but it felt right.

He remembered his old teacher, Mr. Stone, telling them that speed was "distance over time." "Thirty miles per hour," Mr. Stone had said. "That means that in an hour the car would cover thirty miles. Obviously."

Danny skidded to a stop. He was now in the heart of Topeka, at the northeast corner of Gage Park.

Time.

My powers are connected to time, *not speed. That's why I get visions of the future.*

He thought back to Max Dalton's power-damping machine in California. Colin had been trying to break through the machine's armor plating, and Danny had placed his arm on Colin's shoulder in the hope of somehow imparting some of his speed to Colin, but it hadn't worked.

Why did I even think that was possible?

He shifted back into normal-time, and looked around. This part of the city had been relatively untouched by the war, but a few hours earlier it—like the rest of the world—had been completely crystalline.

Renata was able to extend her powers beyond herself, so maybe I can too.

Maybe I can alter everyone's *perception of time.*

He closed his eyes and tried to concentrate on his own future, tried to see what was coming.

There was nothing.

After the vision in California, all he'd had since were vague feelings.

But if it happened once, then it can happen again. Everything I saw came true. Does that mean that the future can't be changed?

Something moving through the night sky caught his attention. Danny looked up to see Colin drifting down toward him.

Colin was grinning, but looked exhausted. "Thought that was you! It's crazy out there, Dan. I saw a man stuck on the roof of his house and when I went to help him he threw a brick at me. Then he panicked and fell off and I almost didn't catch him. So, how's Renata?"

"She was asleep when I left her. I think she's going to be OK. Apart from losing her powers."

Colin nodded. "Well, I'm glad you're with us now. Steph and Mina and Butler are out on the west side trying to persuade a bunch of Trutopians to give up. They didn't hear Yvonne's message. There're probably a lot of them out there still fighting. Come on, I'll fly you over that way." He was already rising into the air, his hand outstretched to Danny.

Danny reached out and grabbed hold of Colin's hand . . .

. . . and suddenly he was in a different place. A huge crater. Colin was at the center, lying on the ground, his entire body blackened and burned. He wasn't moving. He wasn't breathing.

Another flash, and Danny was looking at himself, about the same age as he was now, but with both arms intact. And there was another difference: This two-armed Danny had a look in his eyes that chilled him; a glare of pure hatred and ruthlessness.

Then a third flash. Danny was crouched on the ground, looking down at the dead body of a man he didn't recognize. But now, for the first time, the vision came with sound: A voice behind him said, "You didn't have to kill him."

Danny jerked his hand back.

"What? What is it?" Colin said.

"Nothing, I just . . . Maybe I'd better go back and get some armor."

"'Kay. I'll wait here."

Danny shifted into slow-time, and ran back toward Sakkara.

He couldn't let himself think about the visions now. *There's work to be done. People to be saved. That's what the good guys do, after all. And I'm one of the good guys.*

But he couldn't help asking himself, *Are you sure about that?*

EPILOGUE

Evan Laurie stood on the gantry, looking down into the cavernous room. He was wrapped in a thick coat and gloves. That was one problem with living inside a hollowed-out glacier—it wasn't easy to keep the place warm.

Almost five months had passed since the war had broken out, and it still wasn't really over.

Every day for the first month, every television and radio channel in the world broadcast a live message from Yvonne, ordering the Trutopians to stop fighting.

Then, somehow, an unknown assassin had managed to get close enough to Yvonne to put a bullet in her throat.

Yvonne survived the attack, but she would never be able to speak again.

Laurie made his way along the gantry, down the treacherously slippery metal stairs and into the huge room.

Some days he wished that the superheroes would just find this place and arrest everyone. A warm prison cell seemed like a very attractive alternative.

He walked up to the nearest steel pod. It was three meters tall, almost two meters in diameter. He checked the pod's readout.

Victor Cross strolled over to him. "Have you picked one out yet, Mr. Laurie?"

"What difference does it make?" Laurie asked. "They're all identical." He tapped the pod beside him. "This one."

Victor attached a small keypad to the pod's control panel and entered a sequence of codes. There was a sharp hiss as the metal casing split open.

Inside the pod, suspended in an artificial amniotic fluid, was a fully formed baby.

Victor said, "The data on Ragnarök's technology, which Dioxin's men stole from Sakkara, was a good starting point, but we've surpassed it in every way."

"He's perfect," Laurie said.

"And he's ready to be taken out. The accelerated growth means that he's now the equivalent of a three-week-old baby."

"How long can he stay in there, Victor?"

"Until he gets too big for the pod. Which won't be for quite some time yet. All right. Good job. Seal it up." Victor turned his back on Laurie and walked away.

Evan Laurie climbed back up the staircase and stopped again on the gantry.

He looked down at the pods.

All twenty-four of them.

Each one containing a rapidly growing clone of Colin Wagner.

Turn the page for a preview of

PROLOGUE

4,493 years ago . . .

The afternoon air was thick with dust and screams, blood and war cries, flashing blades and piercing arrows. So much blood had already been spilled that in places the desert sand had turned to red mud.

Krodin had long since abandoned his shield and was now swinging a sword in each hand, the weapons almost too heavy for the average man to lift, let alone wield.

He was of average height, though well-muscled. His bronzed skin was flawless, completely lacking the battle scars and tattoos of his comrades. He kept his dark beard close-cropped, and his long, sweat-drenched hair hung loose, free to whip around his head as he fought.

He was the greatest warrior the Assyrian empire had ever seen, and today's battle was only serving to strengthen his reputation.

A desperate Egyptian lunged at Krodin with his spear, but Krodin simply spun: The blade in his left hand severed the spear's shaft, the tip of his right blade passed through the Egyptian's torso.

Krodin had already sent another Egyptian to the next world before the spearman's body had collapsed to the ground.

A quartet of swordsmen surrounded him, rushed at him with their shields raised, their weapons flailing. Krodin leaped at one of the men, ducked under his swinging sword, crashed into the man's shield. Behind him, the Egyptian's colleagues slammed into each other, stumbled.

It was a moment's work to cut them down: He sliced at the knees of the first, punctured the stomachs of the second and third with a double-thrust of his swords, and slashed at the fourth with such force that the man's feet left the ground.

Krodin's hands and arms were thick with his enemies' blood. He dropped both swords and took a moment to flex his fists—the knuckles cracking loud enough to be heard over the roar of the battle—and wipe his hands on a dead man's tunic.

There was a wound on his upper right arm, a deep cut that seeped his own blood. He didn't recall receiving it and didn't care. It was already healing, and within the hour his skin would be as flawless as ever.

From the west came a low rumbling. Krodin didn't waste time looking to see what had caused the sound—it was all too familiar. He snatched up two of the dead Egyptians' shields and ducked down behind them.

Moments later the sky darkened. Like rain from Hell, ten thousand arrows fell on the battlefield, piercing friend and foe alike.

Protected behind the shields, Krodin grinned. Only a truly foolish or desperate leader would order his archers to take such action at this stage in the battle.

As the last arrows thudded into the shields, Krodin grabbed his swords and began to run.

For as far as he could see, the bodies of the dead and dying littered the sand. The air was laced with the metallic tang of blood, and filled with screams and moans and panic-filled prayers.

He leaped over bodies, skirted around shattered and burning siege vehicles, and—without slowing—slaughtered every Egyptian in his path, regardless of whether the man was fit enough to hold a weapon.

He knew that somewhere to the west the Egyptian general was watching. And he was sure that the general was praying to the war god Onuris that Krodin would be struck down before he got too close.

Another rumble, another barrage of arrows was loosed.

Krodin took shelter in the lee of a half-dead rhinoceros, tucked himself inside its bronze armor-plating. The stench of the animal was almost strong enough to block out the smell of blood, and the ground shook from its desperate, pain-filled roars.

Then the arrows fell, and the rhinoceros shuddered, bellowed one last time, and was still.

The Egyptian general would be already planning his retreat, Krodin knew. The coward would disappear across the desert and lie to his king about the success of this attack.

In terms of numbers, the Egyptians had already won. They were remarkable warriors, highly trained and well-equipped. Krodin's own men were also excellent warriors, but the Assyrian empire had been greatly outnumbered and was unprepared for this attack—though Krodin knew that it was hardly unprovoked. It was retaliation for an earlier incursion into Egypt by the Assyrians, which in turn had been sparked by a previous event.

Krodin didn't know for certain how many of his men had fallen, but he strongly suspected that by now almost all six thousand of them had been guided toward the short, agonizing path to the afterlife.

But Those Who Dwell Above—the gods of the other world, if they existed—would have to wait a long time before they greeted Krodin at their gates. He would not die this day.

And the Assyrian empire would not fall this day, not to the Egyptians.

He broke cover and raced for the enemy's encampment.

A frenzied cry rose from their ranks, and their archers began to shoot at will, no longer waiting for orders.

Again, this was a good sign. Krodin grinned, and—still running—he closed his eyes.

An arrow whipped toward his face. Krodin knocked it aside with the sword in his right hand, and with his left sword he split the shaft of a thrown spear.

Less than a minute later he was too close to the Egyptian pikemen for their archers to fire.

A dozen or more pikemen rushed at him at once. Krodin ran, tensed his muscles, leaped over their heads. He spun and twisted in the air, slashing out with his swords, taking down four of the pikemen before he touched the ground.

The Egyptians came at him with swords, and he hacked at them with a speed and fury like they had never imagined.

Now desperate and mindless of their own men, the archers unleashed a thick cloud of arrows, and Krodin dodged or shattered every one.

They launched spears and tridents and nets. His flashing swords moved so fast that nothing could touch him.

An enormous, enraged, armored rhinoceros was set loose. Krodin stood his ground, waited until the beast was almost on him, then dodged to the right. His swords pierced its armor-plated headgear and the rhinoceros crashed roaring to the ground. Krodin, still holding on to the swords' hilts, vaulted onto the beast's back and jerked the swords free.

The Egyptian slaves—promised freedom if they could stop the Assyrian—launched themselves at him with daggers and clubs. Krodin knew that they were not warriors, neither bred nor trained to fight. They were weak, terrified, and clumsy. Even a moderately experienced fighter would be able to disarm them without issuing a single fatal wound. They did not deserve death, certainly not like this.

Still Krodin killed them all.

Then a deep, powerful voice bellowed, "Enough!"

Krodin stopped. His breathing was heavy now, his body drenched in sweat and spattered with blood.

The voice boomed out once more. "We yield, Assyrian! Enough!"

Krodin finally opened his eyes, and turned in a slow circle. The scene was much as he had pictured it in his mind. So much destruction and death that the desert floor looked like a dense field of scarlet flowers.

The remaining Egyptians encircled him, their weapons at the ready. They were out of reach of his swords, four or five men deep.

But Krodin knew that they would not attack.

Then a parting appeared in the crowd, and a tall, thin man

strode through. He had coal-black hair and bronzed skin, and wore a long, spotless white tunic. There was a simple gold loop around his forehead.

"I am Imkhamun, first general of the royal guard of the palace of his sacred majesty—"

"Kneel," Krodin said, his teeth bared. "Kneel before the might of the Assyrian empire."

Without hesitation the Egyptian dropped to his knees, lowered his head. Then Krodin looked around at Imkhamun's men. "Drop your weapons."

The sound of spears and swords hitting the ground was almost deafening. Krodin pointed to one man at random, an archer. "You. Water. Now."

The archer stumbled backward into his colleagues, then pushed through them and ran.

"Raise your right hand, Egyptian," Krodin said to Imkhamun. "Spread your fingers."

Trembling, the thin man did as he was told. Krodin's sword flashed, and Imkhamun's right thumb dropped to the ground. The Egyptian screamed and doubled over, cradling his wounded hand to his chest. A crimson blossom appeared on his tunic and grew rapidly.

The archer pushed his way through his fellows, carrying a skin of water. He slowed almost to a crawl as he approached Krodin.

Krodin snatched the skin from his hands, passed it to Imkhamun. "Drink, so that I know it is not poisoned."

Fumbling, hindered by the loss of his right thumb and his shaking, blood-slicked hands, the Egyptian pulled the stopper from the skin, took a long drink, thin streams of water spilling from the corners of his mouth.

Krodin watched him for a moment, then, satisfied, took back the skin and sipped from it.

"You are mine," Krodin said. "All of you. Every man in your army now belongs to Assyria. You will move through the battlefield. Scavenge the dead for weapons and supplies. Any Assyrian you find who still lives, tend his wounds. Any Egyptian too badly wounded to march, you will kill."

Half-whimpering, Imkhamun asked, "You . . . you would take us to Assyria?"

"No. We will march on Memphis. Your king will be put to the sword, your vaults plundered." Krodin leaned closer. "And you will burn your crops, salt the land so that nothing will ever grow again. Before the week is out, Egypt's lush fields will be a desert. Your kingdom will fall. This is the price you pay for attacking Assyria."

Slowly, awkwardly, Imkhamun climbed to his feet. "This will not happen."

Krodin grinned. "Earlier I thought you a coward, for only a coward attacks without reason or warning. But . . . you are not a coward, Egyptian. You stand up to me even though you have seen me devastate your army. There are many humans I would call brave, but surely you are among the bravest." He raised his left sword, pressed its point against Imkhamun's throat. "Or the most stupid."

"Then strike me down, Assyrian. I have lived well and served King Sahure with unwavering loyalty, and I am ready to walk the fields of Aaru. But before you extinguish my light, tell me your name that I might warn Osiris and Ammit of your eventual coming."

"Oh, I have had many names, Egyptian. I have called myself Krodin these past two centuries."

Despite his fear, despite the sword at his throat, Imkhamun frowned. "Two centuries? Impossible. No man can live so long."

"I have lived that, and longer. And I will live longer still. The gods of your afterlife have no need to fear me, Egyptian, for I cannot die. I am immortal, ageless, indestructible. Already I have walked this Earth for more than five hundred years. I have seen many empires rise and fall, and I have no doubt that I will see many more. I ally myself with Assyria simply because it suits me to do so. But make no mistake: I am not Assyrian."

"You . . . you are a god?"

"No. I am not a god. Nor am I human."